THE
BOOMERANG
GANG

The Feathered Adventures
of Harold and Friends

Written and Illustrated by

DIANE BEDFORD

◆ FriesenPress

One Printers Way
Altona, MB R0G 0B0
Canada

www.friesenpress.com

Thank you to the W. D. Berry Family for permission to take my inspiration for Madleine's sketch from their father's artwork.

ISBN
978-1-03-919889-0 (Hardcover)
978-1-03-919888-3 (Paperback)
978-1-03-919890-6 (eBook)

1. Juvenile Fiction, Animals, Ducks, Geese, Etc.
2. Juvenile Fiction, Readers, Chapter Books
3. Juvenile Fiction, Action & Adventure

Distributed to the trade by The Ingram Book Company

Dedicated in loving memory
of my amazing father,
LLOYD,
who lived life to the fullest.
From building bird houses together with
a rusty old hand saw, to our many
Father/Daughter Globetrotting Adventures,
I cherish the times we shared.

And Dedicated to
MARK
You are always there for me.
I love *you*. I love *us*.
You bring joy to my life every day.

LYNN
My loving, kind-hearted cousin.
My confidant, my muse.

FRIENDLY DISCLAIMER

While extensively researching for my story, I always tried to ensure accuracy to the best of my ability. Any errors were unintentional and may I suggest remain as creative license.

CONTENTS

REVIEWS

"Anthropomorphic animals exhibit lots of personality
in this entertaining and enlightening tale."
"There's plenty of humor throughout . . . ."
"The cast is all-around solid, including foxes, hares, owls, ..."
"Bedford's mostly lighthearted story is chock-full
of educational bits for readers."
"Darker moments hit home as well . . . ."
"Bedford's detailed black-and-white sketches
enhance memorable descriptions . . . ."

— *Kirkus Reviews*

"Charming and educational, *The Boomerang Gang* takes young
readers on an exciting journey across North America. Kids and adults
will enjoy this fun and suspenseful story that educates while it entertains."
"Bedford's illustrations are a specially-added charm that will tickle readers'
hearts. *The Boomerang Gang* is a perfect read — summer or winter."

— Kathryne Cardwell, writer

"A cute, heartwarming love story, showing kindness,
compassion, and friendships of all different kinds while
educating on the migration of the Mallard Duck."

— Corinn L.

"Bedford is a natural storyteller."

—Janine

"The unique animal characters were all very relatable.
You could empathize, laugh, and cry with them
with the ordeals they went through."

—T. Di Carlo, retired teacher

"Humorous, fun, packed with interesting educational information,
well-developed characters, wonderful visual descriptions of events and
places, plus cool integrated 'human' activities for the ducks. Sequel, please!"

— L. Marshall, retired teacher

WELCOME!

You're about to join the Boomerang Gang flock of Mallard ducks on their migration adventure and Harold and his friends are thrilled you're here to share in the fun!

As you take flight on this journey, you'll meet lots of different characters along the way. If you ever forget anyone, there's an appendix at the end of the book where you can find everybody's names and a little about them.

Are you ready to turn the page and see what Harold's up to?

Let's go!

DIANE

CHAPTER 1

"Harold, what are you doing? Playing *Twister* by yourself?" Markie asks his best friend as he tucks in his wings to help keep himself warm. Squatting on a patch of gravelly sand, Markie, a conservative Mallard duck, watches Harold twisting and turning his body into odd positions, which is both puzzling and worrisome. Harold points his right wing straight out to the side, displaying its shimmery blue wing patch, then slicks his left wing back to tightly hug his body. He carefully spreads his orange webbed feet as far apart as possible without doing the splits, then raises his glossy green head stretching his neck, proudly showing off his decorative white-collar ring. Feeling bold, Harold positions his rump high in the air, flaunting his two curled black tail feathers while puffing up his reddish-brown chest.

Markie stares, in awe that Harold hasn't toppled over.

"Are you trying to become a 'new and improved' Mallard Duck, Harold?"

"Nope. Well, kind of. I'm tweaking my new marsh landing. Unlike you,

I don't have a lot of flying experience and I've never done a migration so I thought I would add in some fancy moves to look impressive. What do you think?" Harold asks, desperately trying to hold his pose but feeling himself starting to sway.

Markie is just about to ask why Harold cares so much when he glances across the marsh. Safely tucked away and paddling among the withered yellow grasses and shrivelled-up cattails are two lovely hen Mallards named Beverly and Lynn. "Oh, now I see who he wants to impress," Markie mumbles.

Markie stands up, looks up to the sky, then rotates his head to take in the view of the surroundings. Now with the necessary information, he squats and begins writing an equation in the sand with his bill. With speed and a serious look on his face, he calculates many numbers to get the perfect formula.

"I have it, Harold! Fly to the tallest tamarack tree, then turn right, follow the beaver dam to its end, then turn yourself around to fly back to me. You should pick up a gentle breeze. Steady yourself, hold your head high and lower your back just a little. Extend your wings straight out, slightly tilt them forward. Angle your feet up and spread your toes wide. You should gracefully descend flying over Beverly and Lynn right before you do your stylish landing on the marsh."

Excited to begin, Harold calls out, "Thanks, Markie!"

Together, they waddle from the base of the sparsely-grassed hill through a thicket of low-growing prickly shrubs, being careful not to rough up their feathers. With their heads facing down, they carefully plan each step over the beachy area that's littered with pebbles.

"Slow down, Harold! You don't want to stub a toe."

Wading into the marsh, they swim around in the frigid water strategically discussing where Harold's perfect takeoff and landing location should be.

"Right here is good. The beaver dam and lodge are far enough away.

There are no aquatic plants to get caught up in, and the surrounding forest shouldn't affect you," Markie tells Harold.

"It IS a great day for my debut performance, isn't it? It's sunny, and the fluffy clouds are high enough in the sky that everyone should be able to see me. It's a little chilly, but that's okay—it will keep me alert."

"You've got this, buddy," Markie says excitedly.

As Harold gets himself into position, he takes a minute to review the plan in his head. Then with two beats of his wings, he springs out of the water. Flapping with gusto, he calls out low-pitched, raspy *kreep*s to get everyone's attention for his upcoming unique marsh landing. Following his flight path, he swiftly banks to the right.

"Okay, here he comes, just as planned. His wings are out and tilted, and his feet are perfectly placed. He's making all of us drakes look good right now. Any hen would be impressed with the flying skills that Harold's showing off," Markie mumbles.

WHAT DO MALLARD DUCKS SOUND LIKE?

Male and female Mallards each make distinct sounds. The most familiar duck call, the quack, is only made by the females, often in a series of two to ten quacks that begin loudly and then get softer. The male does not quack; instead, he produces a quieter, rasping, wheezing noise that sounds like "kreep," usually in a one-or two-noted call.

Just as he flies over Beverly and Lynn and right before his fancy landing an unexpected strong northerly wind catches Harold under his wings. Panicking, he loudly lets out rapid-fire *kreep*s as he somersaults head over tail. Everything he sees is a blur: ducks, water, trees, ducks, water, trees. Harold desperately tries to regain his composure, but it's too late. His feet are dangling behind him, his head is lower than his chest, and his tail feathers are all willy-nilly. His landing gear isn't in position, he's got one nasty faceplant in his future as he's unable to stabilize himself. Harold tumbles.

"This is not good," Markie utters.

SMACK. Landing headfirst, Harold comes to a sudden stop in the chilly water. Dazed and embarrassed he raises his head and shakes the water off as a neon-yellow aspen leaf gently flutters down to rest like a beanie on Harold's head.

"Oh no," grumbles Harold as Beverly and Lynn swim towards him.

"Are you alright, Harold?" they ask, slowly paddling their bright orange webbed feet back and forth to keep themselves in place.

"Yes," Harold mutters, lowering his head. Slowly the yellow leaf slides down his olive-yellow-coloured bill, pausing briefly at the small black nail at the tip before tumbling into the water. Harold mindlessly watches it drift away on the rippled surface.

"I think your routine was unique and daring," Beverly says sweetly.

Harold slowly raises his head and looks into her large brown eyes. "You do?" he says, noticing how Beverly's dull, mottled brown and tan coloured feathers glow in the sunlight. Her bright orange bill, smudged with black and gray, is moving, but he isn't focusing on a single word she's saying. His mind is racing and his thoughts are jumbled.

"Absolutely," Beverly reassures him.

"What's with you drakes always trying to show off?" Lynn asks as she and Beverly turn to swim back to their secretive hiding and dining area.

Lynn looks over her shoulder and quacks, "See you later!"

Markie splashes down right beside Harold.

"Are you okay, buddy?"

"I guess so. Some impressive show I put on," Harold says as he stares at the churned-up water.

Markie paddles around Harold. "Just checking for damage. Looking good. No bump on your head. No feathers missing. How many wings am I holding up?" he asks, extending his left wing into the air.

Harold pauses before he quietly answers, "One."

"Good. Although you might get a goose egg on your crown later," Markie warns.

"Do you know what this means, Markie?"

"That you need more practice."

"NO!" Harold blurts. "That strong northern breeze means that autumn has arrived, and it's getting close to migration time."

"Ahhhhhh. Yes! So it is, Harold. So it is."

Wanting to leave the marsh and the memory of his unsuccessful fancy landing behind, Harold says, "Let's get out of here." Turning to his right, he realizes he and Markie must swim by some of their waterfowl friends to get to the shore.

"Hey, Harold! Are you okay?" shouts Jayson and some of the other Mallards.

"All good," Harold says sheepishly, giving them a little nod as he quickly paddles by.

"I wanted an audience—I just didn't expect it to turn out like this," Harold whispers to Markie.

"Don't worry, buddy. They'll soon forget about it. Remember when Susie did a faceplant on a ground landing? Ouch! It soon became old news, but everyone still appreciates how she showed us why we prefer to land on water."

"Oh, right," Harold replies, remembering how Susie's faceplant was actually the talk around the marsh for at least a month.

Reaching the shore, Harold and Markie waddle carefully over gravelly sand and then through a clump of small prickly bushes to reach the perfect spot at the base of the hill. As they squat on a pillow of lichen, they agree to relax in the sunshine and not discuss the landing. Harold immediately starts preening his dishevelled feathers.

After a while, Markie notices Harold's gone from aggressive feather maintenance to being unusually quiet, slouched over, and just staring at a pebble.

WHAT IS PREENING?

Constant daily preening (feather maintenance) is vital for every duck to help keep the whole flock healthy. Twisting their necks to reach their preen gland at the base of their tails, they use the gland's waxy, oily secretion to evenly coat each feather. This helps keep their feathers strong and flexible (not brittle and breakable) to withstand the stresses of flight and swimming. It also improves their waterproofing, insulates their bodies against cold and hot weather, and protects them against diseases, illness, and feather damage caused by lice, dust, dirt, insects, and parasites. They also preen to look their best, to attract a suitable mate.

"What's up, Harold? You look like you're deep in thought."

"Hmm. I guess I am."

"What are you thinking about?" asks Markie.

"Beverly."

Harold raises his head, stretches his neck from side to side—and freezes. From across the clearing, his eyes lock with Beverly's.

"I see her! She's near the jack pine trees. Gotta go," Harold says as he stands up, kicks the pebble out of his way, and waddles off.

"Good luck, buddy!" shouts Markie, but Harold's not listening.

Trekking across the gravelly soil, unaware that clusters of prickly low-growing bushes are scratching his feet and feathers, Harold's heart is racing.

"Hi, Harold!" Beverly calls out, watching as he tries to catch his breath. "How are you feeling after your special landing?"

Harold takes a deep breath, puffs up his chest, and raises his head high. "Oh, I'm good. There are always going to be little mishaps when you try something new and adventurous," he explains.

"For sure," Beverly says, giving Harold a wink.

Rusty III, a native red fox, scurries by and shouts, "Harold! I heard about your landing. You okay?"

"All good, thanks," Harold replies with a stutter. *Really? Does everyone know?*

"You're a star!" Beverly brags.

"Oh, is that what you are now?" Lynn teases.

Harold shuffles his feet from side to side, bashfully looking at Beverly. His voice cracking, he says, "We'll be migrating south pretty soon. Tomorrow is the migration meeting; will you be there?"

Beverly gazes into Harold's big brown eyes and replies, "Yes. Will you?"

"Yup!" Harold blurts a little too loudly. "See you there!" Without even a goodbye, Harold rushes away. With his eyes focusing on every step, he kicks up little puffs of dust as he hurries along.

Puzzled, Beverly looks at Lynn and asks, "Why did he leave so fast?"

"Who knows? Drakes can be such weird ducks."

Needing to give Markie an update, Harold waddles as quickly and safely as his clumsy, webbed feet will carry him. After all, two faceplants in one day would not be good.

"Markie! Markie!" Harold wheezes as he squats beside him.

"What?" Markie replies, annoyed at having his sunbathing time disturbed.

"Beverly's going to the migration meeting, and I want to impress her. I need to come up with a plan," Harold says, pumping his head up and down.

With his eyes half closed, Markie asks, "What are you thinking?"

Harold stands up and begins to pace back and forth. "I want to be Lead Duck of our V formation. I know I haven't done a migration before, and I know that my fancy landing didn't go exactly as planned, but I really think I can do it," Harold says as he stops pacing and leans over Markie's face.

"Back up, buddy," says Markie, raising his head. "All the strong hens and drakes take a turn as Lead Duck of our V. It gives each one of us a chance to rest."

V FORMATION

A V formation is the symmetric V-shaped flight pattern of migratory birds, including ducks, geese, and swans. The birds alternate the leader of the V to help their flock's energy efficiency for long flights.

"Right. I kind of remember hearing about that," Harold says, shaking his head. He returns to pacing while muttering, "Think, Harold, think."

"I've got it! Plan B," he says eagerly, squatting beside Markie. "I'm going to... "

"That sounds like the beginning of a good plan, buddy."

Harold leans into Markie and clacks his bill repeatedly. "Will you help me?"

"Be happy to. Anything for love."

Harold can barely contain his excitement. His head repeatedly bobs up and down as he lets out raspy-sounding *kreep*s: some loud, some soft, some long, some short.

As darkness sets in, Harold sees Beverly, Lynn, and some of their hen friends waddle to the marsh and wade in. As they cluster together for the night, Harold decides he shouldn't crash their slumber party.

"Let's sleep on land tonight," Harold reluctantly tells Markie.

"Sounds good to me. Hopefully, it's not my night to be on duty," Markie groans.

They waddle over to a group of their Mallard friends that are organizing tonight's sleeping lineup.

Harold looks at Jayson and asks, "Mind if we join your group?"

"Sure! There's safety in numbers."

"Okay, whose turn is it to be on watch?" Jayson asks.

"I'll take the far end," Michael answers.

"And I'll be on the other end," Davor says.

"Great!" Markie whispers to Harold. "I'm too tired to keep one eye open and have half my brain on predator alert all night. I'm exhausted."

"Me too. I need to sleep so I'm well rested to work on Plan B," Harold says.

Tucked under a tamarack tree by the water's edge, the Mallards squat together close enough to share body heat while allowing everyone enough space to spread their wings for a quick escape. Side-by-side in the middle of the lineup, Markie and Harold wish each other a good night, then prepare to get comfy, resting their heads on their backs to relax their neck muscles while nuzzling their bills into their back feathers for maximum warmth.

And with that, they close their weary eyes and settle in, as the moon rises coyotes begin to howl.

CHAPTER 2

Harold wakes at the crack of dawn to a chilly morning.

"Markie! Wake up!" Harold says, poking Markie's chest feathers with his bill.

"What's up? Did you hear the coyotes howling during the night? Was it a full moon? I should have been on guard duty; I was half awake anyway. Did they keep you awake, too?"

"No, and I don't want to talk about coyotes. Today's the migration meeting, and we need to work on perfecting Plan B," Harold says, his bill chattering and his wings flapping—partly because he's cold, but mostly from excitement.

"Let's eat before we go to the meeting," Markie suggests.

"Yes, let's!" Harold nods enthusiastically. He's fully awake, wired,

and anxious to go. Markie, on the other hand, is still groggy. With a yawn, he slowly rises to his feet and joins Harold, and they head to the marsh to fill their growling stomachs.

Standing at the water's edge, they are surprised to see what they see.

"I think we are the last to arrive," Harold says.

Clusters of their Mallard friends are dining in their dabbling duck style, dunking their heads under the water in what's known as "tipping up." The surface of the marsh is dotted with the tightly curled black tail feathers of the drakes' black rumps and the tan brown-speckled rumps of the hens, all pointing up to the sky as they search for scrumptious eats. Just below the surface of the water, Harold and Markie see that everyone's bright orange legs and webbed feet are spread apart and paddling back and forth to help them stabilize while they forage for plants, insects, and larvae on the marsh bottom.

WHAT ARE DABBLING DUCKS?

Dabbling ducks (also known as puddle ducks) are a group of 50–60 shallow-water birds, including Mallards, Teals, Northern Pintails, and American Wigeons. Dabbling ducks tip headfirst into the water to search the muddy bottom for plants and insects, which is known as "tipping up." They are also surface feeders, using their bills to skim along the top of the water for food, and on land, they feed on seeds, grains, nuts, and insects. Dabbling ducks rarely dive under the water and are usually found in small ponds, rivers, and other shallow bodies of water.

As he wades in to join the others, Markie turns toward Harold and says, "I'm hungry. Are you coming?"

"I'll be right there," Harold replies, scanning the bobbing hens and watching for Beverly to raise her head between tipping up.

Excited to finally spot her, he immediately swims next to her, tips up, and playfully tugs on the plant she is grazing on. Annoyed and protective of her meal, Beverly firmly yanks the plant back and devours it. Madder than the time she stubbed her toe on a log, she surfaces to scold the wannabe thief.

Harold quickly raises his head and looks at her.

"Harold!" she quacks. "What were you thinking? You're lucky I didn't nip you to teach you a lesson."

"Aww, c'mon, I was just fooling around," Harold says.

"Humph. See how you'd like it if I messed with your food!" But there's a sparkle in her eye. She's annoyed, but not upset with him.

Thinking about how cute and spunky she was, protecting her aquatic morsel, Harold says, "I'm sorry, Beverly. Let's start over. Good morning!"

"Morning, Harold," Beverly giggles, unaware that a limp piece of slimy green plant is dangling from her bill.

"The marsh is really crowded. Would you like to check out the shore for something to eat?" Harold asks.

"Good idea. Race you!" Beverly says as she starts paddling as fast as she can.

"Hey, you started before me!"

"I win!" Beverly boasts.

"You are the cutest little cheater," Harold teases.

Beverly lets out a sweet little quack.

With their heads facing down, they eagerly use their long flat bills to hoover the shore, digging up tasty treats.

"Harold, watch this!"

Using her nail—a bump at the tip of her upper bill—Beverly hooks and then positions a medium-sized snail in her mouth. She gets a mouthful of shoreline, too, but the mud, debris, and water filter back out through the soft, comb-like fringe on the front edge of her bill. That fringe is called her lamellae, and it helps Beverly swallow her food and not the dirt.

With a loud crunch and a big gulp, Beverly swallows the snail. Her eyes light up, obviously quite proud of herself.

"That snail didn't have a chance," Harold says, giving her a tap on her head with his wing.

Together, they feverishly return to foraging for tasty morsels on the shore.

After some time, Beverly raises her head to see Harold standing still and looking at her, a wiggly earthworm dangling from his bill. He slowly waddles over to her and lays it at her feet.

Beverly gives Harold a quick look of appreciation, then glances down and says, "You're not going to get away from me," quickly gobbling up the worm. "Yum. Thanks."

Harold puffs up his chest.

With their stomachs full of aquatic plants, a few insects and snails, and a big juicy earthworm for Beverly, they shuffle to a comfortable place to squat, preen, chat, and relax.

Markie and Lynn leave the marsh in search of Harold and Beverly. Waddling across the shore, their oily, waterproof feathers leave a drip line of their path.

Spying Harold and Beverly, Lynn calls out, "Hey, you two! Do you want to join us at the meeting?"

"Sounds good," Beverly replies.

The four feathered friends waddle from the marsh area on a short narrow pathway that leads to a small clearing. Regularly stomped on by ducks, the pathway is level and safe for awkward, webbed feet of all sizes.

Harold stops, bends over, and says, "How dare you grow on this path," as he latches his bill onto a small plant to pull it out.

"Come on, Harold! I want to get to our spot," Markie shouts. Swallowing the last of his green snack, Harold hurries to catch up with the group. "Wait for me!" he calls after them, excited about what might happen at the meeting.

CHAPTER 3

There's a buzz of activity as the wildlife of Havenwood Cove begin to gather at a small clearing. Circular in shape, the soil is muddy when wet, but today it's dusty and dry. Clumps of ground-hugging shrubs and patches of colourful lichen are scattered throughout. Tall green conifers and deciduous trees stretch toward the sky, some bare and others lightly leafed in their bright yellow autumn colours, bordering half of the clearing. The rest of the border is made up of a small, sparsely grassed hill and the ducks pathway, which is nestled in between trees and bushes.

The Annual Winter Preparation Meeting is about to begin, and the host is Sir Lloyd, the well-respected Great Horned Owl. Tardiness is not acceptable, so everyone rushes to arrive on time.

"Follow me," Markie says as he waddles a few feet, then squats under the drooping branches of a large white spruce tree.

"This is my spot, and everyone knows it. I claimed it last year."

"Thanks for looking after us newbies, Markie," Harold says, letting Beverly squat first. Just as Lynn tries to sit next to her, Harold forcefully wiggles his body into the tight space, pressuring Lynn to scoot over or get her feathers ruffled. Annoyed, Lynn moves over, and Harold happily squats beside Beverly.

"Comfy?" she asks him.

"I sure am."

Moving his head from side to side, Harold scans the crowd. He's focused on seeing which of his friends are attending and whether there might be any possible new friends in the group.

"Look, Beverly! There's Ella," Harold says, pointing his wing toward the frisky, white-tailed deer coming out of the forest. Together, they watch to see where she chooses as her perfect spot for the meeting.

"That's nice—she's chatting with Ginger. Ginger's a friendly enough native red fox, but sometimes I think she has a hoity-toity attitude—maybe because she's so beautiful. Rusty III must be close by," Harold tells Beverly.

"It's no secret that Ginger's the vixen he likes," Beverly says.

Harold and Beverly watch the Benjamin beaver family waddle in and take the ground floor center stage. Wanda, a shy grizzly bear, saunters in from the forest, chooses a secluded spot under a jack pine, and curls up.

"Oh, there's Miss Marie," Harold notices, pointing to a slow-moving porcupine.

"She always looks mean," Beverly comments.

"I don't think she's mean, but you don't want to get too close to her because of her quills," Harold explains.

"She looks armed and dangerous," Lynn laughs.

A beautiful Canada lynx wanders in, draped in luxurious thick silvery-gray and mottled brown fur. She's smaller than a cougar but bigger than a bobcat.

"Who's that?" Harold asks Markie.

"That's Harlow."

Harold leans into Markie and says quietly, "The long black tufts at the tips of her ears and the tip of her tail are super cool. Is she friendly?"

"Harlow loves attending these meetings. She's probably lonely being a solitary nighttime stalker, but don't mistake her adorable face with its finely black-outlined cute pink nose and stunning caramel-coloured eyes for her being a playful feline. She's a wildcat that pounces!" Markie warns.

"Got it. Did you see the size of her paws?" Harold asks.

"When she spreads her furry toes it's like she silently floats over the snow," Markie responds. "Glad there is a 'safe rule' for all of us at our meetings. I bet the snowshoe hares are still a little nervous about attending."

The four feathered friends eagerly watch the excitement build as the guests continue to gather. Friends passing by join in a bit of conversation while others share a quick hello as they zoom by.

Harold's ears can't help but follow the harsh sounding: tschick-a-dee-dee, tschick-a-dee dee calls of a flock of small, fluffy, round bodied, brown-capped Boreal Chickadees. With their comedic acrobatic moves, they dash between conifer limbs, occasionally stopping to hang upside down, to eat an insect or seed, then go back to playing a game of *Catch Me If You Can.*

The air is full of exhilaration with chirps, chatter, honking, *hrink*ing, quacks, *kreeps*, flapping, and conversations as Harrison, the Hairy Woodpecker, and his family and friends add to the sounds by *tap, tap, tap*ping on tree trunks, looking for insect snacks before the meeting.

"Markie!" Harold says, nudging him to get his attention.

"The Gray Jays (Canada's National Bird. Nicknames: camp robber and whiskey jack) usually are super fun, real tricksters imitating other birds, but today they're looking sad," Harold comments.

"I guarantee they're not happy because winter's coming, and that's when they build their nest. In the bitter cold with howling winds she lays her eggs and sits on them day and night for weeks to keep them warm and safe, while waiting for her mate to bring her bits of food from their larder," Markie explains.

"Too bad they can't migrate south with us," Harold comments.

Bouncing out of the woods into the gathering area comes a band of snowshoe hares. Named for the size of their large, furry, snowshoe-shaped feet, the big-eared masters of disguise are still wearing their thin, gray-brown fur coats from the warm summer months.

"Hey, Markie," the leader says.

"Hi, Poppy."

"Who are your friends?" she asks.

"Poppy, this is my buddy Harold, and our friends Beverly and Lynn."

"Nice to meet you," Poppy says in a perky, bouncy voice.

Harold, Beverly, and Lynn each greet Poppy with a friendly hello.

"This springy bunch is my family and some friends. Pixie, Penelope, Peter, Paxton and …. wait a minute. Where's Prudence?" Poppy asks.

"Ugh. From the moment she came into the world fully furred and with her eyes and ears wide open, she's been a carefree and curious doe. Most leverets are happy taking a couple of days before wandering around the nest, but not Prudence. She was born with a sense of adventure. It's like a full-time job trying to keep her safe," Poppy says, standing on her hind legs and looking around.

The worried hares start thumping their hind feet and making loud snorting sounds, trying to get Prudence's attention. They certainly have everyone else's, including Harlow's.

Using her large furry feet and her powerful hind legs, Prudence jumps (3m) nine feet in a single hop to join her band.

"Sorry I'm late, but I found a small clump of green grass, and I just couldn't resist a little nibble. Yummy! Our winter dining selection is so boring: twigs, buds, bark, and needles. I mean, what am I? A moose?" Prudence says with a whimsical snort.

"Are you and your friends ready for your migration, Markie?" Poppy asks.

"I think so. We'll get last-minute instructions soon, and then we'll be off," Markie explains.

"Lucky you get to leave the cold."

Harold, Beverly, and Lynn each give Poppy a friendly nod of excitement.

"What about you? Do you hibernate?" Markie asks Poppy.

"No cozy warm winter rest for us. Soon everything but the black tips of our ears will turn into thick white fur to match the snow and we'll try our best to stay away from predators. Sadly, we seem to be a favourite meal for many. Our fate is death by tooth or talon," Poppy says.

"Speaking of predators, where is Harlow?" Poppy asks.

Markie stretches his wing and points to the left, "Over there."

"Thanks. Safe meeting zone or not, we aren't going to take any chances. Travel safely, and we'll see you in the spring, hopefully," Poppy says.

"See you when the weather warms up," Markie replies.

Poppy and her band of bouncy snowshoe hares hop away in the opposite direction of Harlow.

CHAPTER 4

Harold puffs up his chest, elongates his neck, and looks around. Suddenly the crowd starts chanting, "Here he comes! Here he comes!"

Harold looks up to see a robust, thick, barrel-shaped raptor silently approaching and recognizes that it's Sir Lloyd. With one deep beat of his broad, rounded wings, the owl silently glides in and skillfully pilots himself among the trees.

Everyone watches Sir Lloyd use his large and powerful feathered legs, feet, and lethal talons to grip and steady himself onto a sturdy branch of a tamarack tree. Soon the tamarack will drop its autumn-coloured, bright-yellow, feathery needles but today it's the perfect contrast to highlight Sir Lloyd's heavily patterned gray-brown feathers.

Markie leans close to Harold and says, "He's nicknamed the tiger owl because his plumage has mottled and barred markings. Perfect camouflage for blending in with tree bark."

"Have you ever seen a tiger?" Harold asks Markie.

"Don't think so."

Sir Lloyd's tall, feathery ear tufts pop straight up on the top of his head.

"Oh, now I see why he's named a Great Horned Owl! His ear tufts look like horns," Harold tells Markie.

"I know Sir Lloyd looks threatening. But wait till you see a female Great Horned Owl, Harold. She's even larger."

"Really?"

"Really."

Sir Lloyd slowly rotates his neck from side to side, exposing his white chin and white throat patch. Intensely, he gazes over the gathering with his intimidating, large, round, yellow eyes and piercing black pupils.

Everyone quietly waits for Sir Lloyd's words of wisdom.

"Welcome! Please listen," Sir Lloyd's deep voice echoes throughout the forest.

"It is my honour to conduct this meeting. As family, friends, and neighbours of Havenwood Cove, there is a rule that everyone is safe here. No seeking out your next meal. Understand?"

The crowd becomes quiet. A pinecone hitting the ground breaks the silence. Everyone knows and respects the unspoken rule, but to have it said out loud is awkward. Some slyly look around with their heads slightly tilting down, others shuffle their feet, and a few become still. Harlow sits quietly, scanning the gathering while the hares avoid making eye contact with her. Sir Lloyd notices heads bobbing one by one in agreement, so he continues.

"Do you feel the crispness in the air?" Sir Lloyd asks while stifling a yawn.

Harold looks around. Many birds have puffed up their breast feathers, tucked in their wings, and are perched on one leg or squatting to keep warm. Ginger is cozy with her thick, bushy tail wrapped around her. The snowshoe hares are huddled together to share body warmth. Even little

Ruby, a red-sided garter snake, only has her head poking out from under a rock. Most are doing their best to keep warm.

"We are blessed to be living in Havenwood Cove with its wetlands and boreal forest. Autumn is here. Our forest is bursting with colour, neon yellows, vibrant oranges and brilliant red leaves. Even the spiders delicate webs glisten in the morning frost. Look around you!" Sir Lloyd asks, swiveling his head to fully appreciate a panoramic view."

Everyone takes a moment and looks around as oohs and ahhs fill the air.

"With winter fast approaching our marsh will soon freeze, and the ground will be covered in snow. There'll be fewer food sources for some and none for others, so we need to prepare. There will be fewer sunshine hours, and the nighttime darkness will be longer. Personally, we owls like that," Sir Lloyd says as he puffs up his white throat patch and lets out a *hoo-hoo hooooo hoo-hoo* in his deep voice.

"Today is bittersweet. Soon our waterfowl friends will migrate south following the traditions and routes of their ancestors, and we will miss them. But don't worry, come spring, they will return home to us where they will mate, nest, and start a family."

Harold gives Beverly a little nudge, she bashfully looks away.

"Others of you will be hibernating or enjoying a restful torpor in your cozy homes, while some of you, like me, will brave the bitterness of the winter. It is around this time every year that our lively community becomes quiet and still," Sir Lloyd recalls, with a quiver in his voice. He looks down and pauses.

After a moment of reflection, Sir Lloyd raises his head, regains his composure, and says, "I will be thankful to hear the snores coming from the dens to break the silence. Especially Winston's den," Sir Lloyd *hoo-hoo hooooo hoo-hoo*'s.

All who know Winston agree he's a loveable grizzly bear. But he is perhaps more well known for his thunderous baritone snores when napping in the afternoon sunshine. Winston is a deep sleeper.

"Wait! Wait for me!" comes an out-of-breath voice from beyond a nearby clump of aspen trees. The crowd turns to see who the latecomer is. Walking slowly but deliberately comes a short-legged, stout body with thick black glossy fur and bold white stripes. Its bushy, black, white-tipped tail is pointing up and aggressively swishing back and forth.

It's Squire, a striped skunk, crawling over the dense debris of fallen leaves and broken twigs.

Squire flashes a big smile to the patiently waiting crowd as he shuffles under the branches of the last tree before reaching the clearing. Suddenly, something enormous, strong, and muscular pounces on him. The weight of the furry mass lying on top of him chokes his airflow. Squire fights to keep breathing. He squirms, trying to get free from his attacker.

Sir Lloyd lets out a high-pitched, chilling shriek. Outraged, and in shock, the onlookers chant, "Leave him alone! Leave him alone!"

Laying on his belly with his paws flailing about, Squire tries to calm himself. He doesn't think he's wounded; nothing hurts, he doesn't feel like he's bleeding, and he realizes he's just being held captive. Out of the corner of his right eye, he sees his attacker's long, lethal claws. He's stunned that they're not doing the damage they're capable of. With his heart racing, he starts sniffing and picks up some familiar scents—smelly fur and ghastly breath that makes him gag.

Squire now realizes who his attacker is, and he is mad.

"Get off me, you two-toned, striped beast! You nasty cat! You skunk bear!" growls Squire as his attacker rolls off him, gently lifting him up and placing Squire, ever so carefully, back on his feet.

Squire looks up and gives a disgusted look to Baxter, the wolverine. "What were you thinking slamming me like that? You scared me. Now I'm probably going to be covered in bruises!" Squire stands on his hind legs and stomps his feet. Getting a quick glimpse of the crowd, Squire notices that they're feeling sorry for him, so he stomps his feet faster and harder and growls louder before he returns to standing on all fours.

Shifting his weight from side to side, a bashful Baxter looks towards Squire's face, but not directly at it.

"Geez, just having some fun. I wanted to surprise you. Can't a friend say hello?" Baxter mumbles while gently brushing some twigs off Squire.

"You're a bully. Typical wolverine …" Squire puffs up his fur and hisses.

"We've been given a bad rap," Baxter says, mindful that wolverines are also fun and playful.

"You make me so mad. I should spray you to teach you a lesson." Squire arches his back, raises his tail high in the air, turns his back towards Baxter, and stomps his front feet.

The crowd gasps.

Harold, Beverly, Markie, and Lynn watch in shock at what might happen.

"Now, now. I wouldn't try that if I were you," Baxter says to Squire as he lifts his tail even higher.

Squire thinks about it, understanding that in a battle of the stinks, he would probably lose.

"Fellas, please hurry up and join our meeting," Sir Lloyd calls to Squire and Baxter.

Best friends again, they scurry to go join the others.

Roxy raccoon leans into Squire. "That will teach you for playing tricks on us by threatening stink bombs," she says.

Squire gives her a little nod, then looks away.

Remembering his duty, Sir Lloyd clears his throat and says, "For your safety and as the keeper of the records for Havenwood Cove community, I need to know who will be wintering here and who will be migrating south to warmer weather."

Sir Lloyd takes a moment to recall what's next on his agenda.

"First, let's give a big thank you to, Benjamin beaver and his family: natures engineers. They work tirelessly day and night, building dams and canals, so we have a beautiful home. Please join me in a big cheer of appreciation!" Sir Lloyd says, flapping his wings and letting out a deep, low booming hoo-hoo hooooo hoo-hoo.

The crowd goes wild in celebration. The shy Boreal Chickadees leave the conifers and swoop among the gathering. Oliver, a booted Golden Eagle, soars and glides overhead. Ruby nervously slithers around, trying not to be trampled. Ella romps through the crowd and Harlow sleeks around. Harold and his friends waddle about, flapping their wings while the hens quack with delight and the drakes *kreep* loudly. Sadly, quill-covered Miss Marie wanders around trying to be social, but everyone darts away when she comes close. Squire and Baxter hang out as besties do. Sebastian, a feisty red squirrel, scurries around like a red flash, not wanting to take any time away from collecting white spruce pinecones and seeds. Rusty III hovers around Ginger. The snowshoe hares are bouncing everywhere except near Harlow. The Gray Jays whisper quiet *click*s from their perch. Roxy raccoon chitters with her family and friends.

Harold looks around with some concern. Despite all the activity, someone is obviously missing. Where is Winston?

Feeling appreciated Benjamin, Betty, and their kits turn to face the crowd. Standing upright on their hind legs, propping their weight on their flat, wide, scaled, fleshy, very sturdy tail, they take a bow which they follow up with an enormous smile showing off their four enormous iron-stained, orange-coloured, front incisors. Everyone gasps at such a spectacle.

Harold turns to Markie, "Lucky us; no teeth, so no orange ones."

CHAPTER 5

arkie, have you seen Winston?" Harold asks.

"Nope. Sure haven't."

"Hey, Beverly! Do you want to help me find Winston to see if he wants to join in the fun?"

"Let's go!"

Together, they waddle around the outskirts of the gathering, searching for Winston.

"There he is," Harold says as he eagerly shuffles up to him.

Feeling anxious, Beverly stays a few steps behind.

"It's okay. Winston's really nice," Harold assures her.

The big brown grizzly bear is in a stupor. His large, muscular shoulder hump is slumped up against a huge boulder, and his enormous two

front paws are hanging on either side of his roly-poly belly. His hind legs are stretched straight out in front of him, with his ten toes and dagger-sharp, (10 cm) four-inch long, light-coloured claws facing up. Basking in the warmth of the sun, his large, round, dished (concave)-shaped face and snout (nose) are resting on top of his tummy. His small round ears are not listening to anything or anyone.

"Winston! Wake up!" Harold says loudly, poking Winston's belly with his bill.

"Should you be doing that? He's a bear—a big bear—and he probably doesn't want to be disturbed," Beverly says, slowly backing up while not taking her eyes off Winston as she tries to maneuver her awkward, webbed feet.

Winston doesn't move. He doesn't open an eye. He doesn't even grunt.

Markie waddles as fast as he can to get to Harold. "Buddy, what are you doing?"

"Winston's missing all the fun."

"I wouldn't wake him if I were you. Winston's a happy, friendly bear, but he's probably exhausted. Can you imagine how many months he spent foraging for berries, fruits, and roots to fill a belly this big?" Markie tells Harold.

"You're right. He's too tired to have fun," Harold reluctantly agrees.

"The good thing is it looks like he won't be hungry over the winter. I think Winston just wants to have a little nap before wandering off to his den for a few months of torpor. We'll see him in the spring when we come back home and he wakes up," Markie says.

"Sure," Harold says, his head hanging low.

"Let's go back to the gathering," Beverly tells Harold.

Just as the three feathered friends are waddling away, Winston lets out a short, loud, thunderous groan. Harold picks up his feet and speedily rushes right past Markie and Beverly. Realizing he might have overreacted, he stops and looks away from Beverly and Markie.

"Were you frightened?" Beverly asks.

"No, I just was startled. That's all. No big deal," Harold explains in a crackling voice.

"Winston's groan was really loud. He sure shocked me," Beverly says.

"He took me by surprise too, buddy."

Markie, Harold, and Beverly casually waddle back to find Lynn, enjoying little chit-chats with friends along the way.

Sir Lloyd lets out a short but alarming screech to get everyone's attention, and it works.

"We are family, friends, and neighbours, and we need to look after each other."

Becoming impatient, he directs whoever is wintering at home to please line up and register with Miss Marie.

"For our migrating friends, Instructor Riley will be here shortly to update you on your trip south," Sir Lloyd announces.

"How about visiting and catching up with our other Mallard friends until Instructor Riley shows up?" Markie asks.

"Sounds good to me," Harold says as Beverly and Lynn nod in agreement.

Miss Marie is known as a no-nonsense, take-charge porcupine with a prickly personality and the quills to make a point. Clenching her bright orange teeth and with a steady grip of her claw, she forcefully plucks a quill from her side to scratch letters into a remnant piece of tree bark, much like a pen. After releasing a sharp, heroic "ouch," she flips the bark over to the smooth side, ready to engrave her notes on her new tablet.

Somewhat of a stampede is taking place, with many rushing to line up to register.

Hyper and overzealous, Rusty III, with his small dog-like frame, light body build, and being quick on his feet, scurries to be first in line.

"Ladies first, my dear Rusty III," Ginger says in a hushed voice as she positions herself to be first in line ahead of the handsome Rusty III. From the corner of her eye, she shyly gazes at his long snout, black nose, large, pointy, black-tipped ears, black paws, grayish-white throat, chin, and belly, noticing that he's only slightly larger than she is.

"Most certainly," Rusty III says, politely moving aside.

Swirling her long, silky red, white-tipped bushy tail around her curvy body, Ginger responds coyly, "I see chivalry is not lost," before turning her attention to Miss Marie.

"I will not be hibernating, Miss Marie. I'm nocturnal, although I occasionally like to wander around during the day, adding a little class and colour to our charming community. I sleep in the open, curled up with my luxurious tail to keep me warm."

"I haven't chosen my perfect mate yet." Ginger lets it be known as she gracefully turns to face Rusty III. Daydreaming, she thinks about how once she has mated, she'll make her den in a lovely, abandoned woodchuck burrow she's found nearby. Her litter of one to ten darling little kits will be born between March and May. She's snapped out of her dreamy thoughts by a loud voice.

"Noted. NEXT!" Miss Marie bellows in a low, irritated tone as she glances at her short, thick, non-luxurious tail.

Recognizing Ginger's possible flirtatious invitation, Rusty III is beyond excited, racing around to share his good news.

"Harold! Harold!"

"What's up, Rusty III?"

"Ginger, my dream vixen, just told Miss Marie that she is looking for a mate—and she looked right at me when she said it! She's letting me know she likes me, right?"

"It sure sounds like it, you lucky dog," Harold says, hoping he's right because the screaming sound of an unhappy red fox is extremely horrible to listen to.

"What about you? Have you told Beverly how you feel about her?" Rusty III asks.

"Shhh, not so loud. She's right over there. But um, no. I haven't told her. Not in so many words, " Harold says, shuffling his triangular-shaped feet in the dirt, making fan shapes.

"What are you waiting for?" Rusty III whispers.

"I'm waiting for just the right time."

"Don't wait too long, or some other drake will win her over," Rusty III says as he scurries back to the lineup, hoping to sneak back to the front of it. "See you before you fly away!" he calls over his shoulder.

"NEXT!" orders Miss Marie.

"I'm next!" Squire says, threatening Rusty III with a stink bomb if he tries to cut in line.

"Hey there, Squire! I have a question I want to ask you. Do you ever feel that nobody really wants to be our friend—you with your smelly musk spray and me with my sharp quills?" Miss Marie asks.

"Sure do! Especially since sometimes I tease by raising my tail. All in good fun, I say, but others see it differently. I guess I should try to be more understanding," Squire confesses.

"Me too. Everyone thinks I can 'shoot' my sharp-tipped barbed quills, but that's not true. They do, however, detach easily from me when touched," Miss Marie explains while Squire strategically backs away from her.

"No, no, no, you silly striped skunk," Miss Marie giggles. Giggling is something no one has ever seen her do before.

"I'm the prickliest of all rodents, so everyone keeps their distance from me," Miss Marie says with sadness in her eyes.

"Look! I'm also a little bit of a softie. I have some hair on my sides, back, and tail. Yes, my quills are mixed in with the hair, but it's only when I'm threatened that they stand up. That's when you know I am serious."

Squire thinks about it for a minute, but he's still not sure he can be comfortable with Miss Marie and her quill situation.

"Go ahead, ask me," Miss Marie says.

Squire wrinkles his snout, "Ask you what?"

"Many are curious but too scared to ask how I can give birth to such prickly babies. The answer is that my little porcupettes are born with soft quills that harden within a few days," Miss Marie whispers as if she's divulging a secret.

Squire nods. And yes, he was always curious about that.

Miss Marie grins ear to ear, "Let's try and make some friends."

Squire agrees, wondering if they just shared a friendship bonding experience.

"Okay, Squire. Back to the task at hand. Where will you be this winter?"

"Well, Miss Marie, striped skunks are kind of lazy, and we're opportunists. Right now, I'm deciding between a sweet little abandoned fox den and a cozy spot in a rock pile for my new home. Between lining my new den with leaves and having put on extra winter weight, I should have a comfy, cozy, warm torpor," he boasts. "This buck plans to sleep till February, wake up with a sleek physique, and then trek around during the night till I locate a desirable doe for a mate. If all goes as per my plan, our litter of four to six kits will be born in May."

"And a thorough plan it is, Squire. Thank you," Miss Marie says, scratching her notes into the bark with her quill stylus and playfully giving him a wink.

That lighthearted feeling changes when a gentle breeze suddenly glides in with a subtle feeling of peril, that noticeable and unexplainable eeriness that shocks their sixth sense into fight or flight mode. It pings their intuition, that gut feeling that speaks louder than words, and their internal survival instincts warn them of possible danger and to be on high alert. Harold, Beverly, Markie, and Lynn huddle close, each of them thinking about taking flight. Like all their wildlife friends, their hearts are thumping. Every little sound intensifies and is scrutinized. It's a feeling of the calm before the storm. Heads whiplash at the crunching sound of fallen dry and brittle leaves. Then there's silence. The gentle breeze changes direction, and with it, the possible threat vanishes. Or so they think.

Many relax and go back to enjoying time with their friends, while others remain cautious.

"That was scary," Beverly says to Harold, Lynn, and Markie.

"It sure was. You can't see it; you just feel it," Harold says as everyone nods in agreement.

The four feathered friends waddle to meet up with their other duck friends. Miss Marie returns to her task at hand.

"NEXT!" Miss Marie bellows.

"Sebastian, get over here!" Miss Marie shouts in a tone that Sebastian knows is serious this time. He immediately scurries over to see her, with his bushy tail—two-toned with a red top and gray underneath—waving about wildly.

"What's up?" he asks.

"Sebastian, stop fidgeting!"

"Can't. I've got too much to do. I've got to protect my middens, gather spruce pinecones…"

WHAT IS A MIDDEN?

A midden is a burrow that some animals, including red squirrels, dig into the ground to use for food storage.

"Housekeeping, my dear Sebastian," Miss Marie interrupts.

"Our lovely community is starting to look like a slum with you wedging mushrooms between branches, hanging them to dry. And your dug burrows—your middens—are growing into unsightly pyramids with years of hoarding green pinecones, stripping the seeds, and letting the scales pile up when they drop. Your constant noisy and aggressive behaviour of hunting for insects and eggs, along with your loud chatter, squeaks, barks, and thumping of your feet, is disrupting the community. No one dares go near your middens," she concludes before taking a deep, long breath.

With his prominent black eyes outlined in white, Sebastian boldly looks at Miss Marie and bravely begins negotiations, keeping in mind not to get too close to her.

"Miss Marie, you see me as a bit of an annoyance, but I consider myself an overachiever just being prepared for tomorrow. Isn't that a good way to be?" Sebastian asks.

"Yes, but . . . "

"But what?"

"Sebastian, perhaps you can relax a little. Do you think you can do that?"

He pauses to consider her request. "I'll have to think about it."

"Fine," replies Miss Marie, annoyed. She was hoping for a quieter, calmer squirrel and less tension in the community.

She eyes Sebastian, observing things about the little red squirrel she hadn't really noticed before. From the tip of his nose to the tip of his bushy tail, he's only about (30 cm) twelve inches long, and his brownish-red furry body has a white underside with a thin black strip separating the two colours.

"I find it amazing how this little body can create so much havoc and be so frustrating yet be so adorable. Ugh. I haven't quite decided if I actually admire his spunkiness or not," Miss Marie grumbles to herself.

"Sebastian!" Miss Marie says impatiently, trying to get him to focus. "What are your plans for winter?"

"I don't hibernate. I've hidden my food supply in tree hollows and some small burrows. I've put my special scent on my underground stash so I can sniff them out when the snow comes. Smart, right?" Sebastian stands up on his hind legs and points to a ball constructed of twigs, bark, grass, lichen, and leaves. "I'm moving from my bolus nest; do you see it?"

Miss Marie twists her body out of alignment to look up, up, up to where Sebastian is pointing and spies a large clump nestled between branches of a bare deciduous tree. Feeling the effects of her now-sore neck, she says, "Yes, I see it."

She quickly realizes that with her stalky, short-legged body, she might have been better to have laid on her back to look up that far.

Miss Marie snaps back from thinking about her sore neck when she hears Sebastian's voice, continuing the story about his bolus nest. "That was my summer home. Now I'm moving to my new winter home for this year, one that's still close to my stash. I'm redesigning a rotted tree root system to be cozy, safe, and warm. Come early spring, March to May, this buck is excited to meet a doe during her one day of mating. I will charm her with my personality. Of course, I will scare off all other bushy-tailed bucks," Sebastian says.

"Yes, I am very much aware of the red squirrel speed-dating frenzy that happens in the spring and then again between August and early

September," Miss Marie says, knowing full well to try and stay clear of the growling red flashes twice a year.

Miss Marie keeps writing her notes as she says, "Thank you, Sebastian," giving him a wave with her other claw to let him know that he's free to leave, but he's already gone.

Just as Miss Marie gets ready to bellow, "NEXT!", a streak of grayish-brown mangy fur bolts past her with such momentum that it spins her around. Heads turn, noticing the intrusion. DANGER! Shrieks of terror fill the air. It's a chaotic scene of panic-stricken animals bumping into each other in search of safety.

Markie's voice rises above the commotion as he shouts to Harold, Beverly, and Lynn, "Quick! Get up in the air, NOW!"

All four instantly bolt into the air. Safely out of predator danger, they're now contending with a sky of frenzied waterfowl and raptors jostling around, trying to get airborne and oriented. Distressed, they head to the marsh, where they see Benjamin beaver and his family giving forceful warning slaps of predator alert.

The lethal predator, an unknown lone coyote, is moving swiftly and silently. Ravenous and laser-focused on its next meal, the coyote is heading for sweet little Prudence. Unaware of the terrible danger she's in, she continues happily munching on a single blade of luscious grass. "An especially lucky find," she thinks. Or is it? Hearing sounds of a ruckus—sharp shrills, shrieks, hissing, and the sounds of flapping wings—Prudence looks up to see chilling golden-brown eyes looking back at her. Terrified with fear, she freezes.

The coyote rushes towards her. Just as it gets ready to pounce, it yelps in pain from talons piercing deeply into its neck and shoulder.

Blood trickles and sprays as the coyote violently shakes its head, trying to release its assailant. Hungry and desperate, it remains focused on its prey and lunges at Prudence, who lets out gruesome, high-pitched squeals. She struggles to breathe and frantically fights for her life, but her attacker's sharp teeth and strong jaws hold her tight. Her weakened fluffy body can barely squirm. Her once-powerful long legs and large furry back paws quiver. Her head, with its adorable, pink-veined ears, charming twitchy nose, and whiskers, is now still. Her once delightful enormous chestnut brown eyes stare, lifeless. Her legs dangle from the clutch of her attacker. Oliver, the booted Golden Eagle, pushes his lethal talons deeper into the coyote's muscular body. Realizing that he's too late to save his friend, he releases his hold and flies to the nearest tree branch.

From a safe distance, everyone watches in horror and sadness as the coyote turns and runs away with Prudence's breathless body dangling from its mouth.

A stunned silence hangs in the air for a few moments before the snowshoe hares begin to re-emerge from their hiding places. They meet under the bough of a pine tree to comfort each other and share their sorrow and heartbreak over what just happened. Tearful woodland friends gather around to offer support, and all the animals reluctantly discuss continuing without her.

Eventually, they all begin to return to the gathering. Living in danger every day is just part of their life. And they know they must carry on.

CHAPTER 6

"**I** think I'm going to stay on the marsh for a little while and maybe have a nibble," Beverly says quietly to no one in particular, seemingly lost in thought.

Harold watches her drift around aimlessly, her legs dragging behind her as she looks down at her rippled reflection in the water.

"I think that's a great idea. I'll join you."

"Make that three for lunch," Lynn says.

"How about you, Markie?" Lynn asks.

"Sure. Reservation for four. I'm always hungry."

"How would you like to forage today, Beverly? Dabbling or skimming?" Harold gently asks.

"I don't feel much like tipping up. I think I'd just like to relax, float around and let my bill catch whatever is sitting on the water," Beverly tells Harold in a listless, soft voice.

"That's exactly what I want to do," Harold says. "Mind if I join you?" He doesn't wait for an answer before he begins swimming alongside her.

The four feathered friends quietly float around with their necks stretched out as they move their heads slowly from side to side, letting their bills filter the water's surface for eats. After filling up on water insects, floating algae, and plants, Beverly, Harold, and Lynn relax and spend quality time fussing with their feathers. In the meantime, Markie just can't resist doing a few dabbling duck tip-ups to dig through the marsh bottom mud to dine on delectable aquatic plant roots.

Back in the clearing with the dust now settling, Miss Marie gathers her confidence and gets back to business.

"Next!" she says, but not so loud this time.

Wanda, a shy grizzly bear meanders up to Miss Marie and quietly explains that she's dug out a den and lined it with branches and leaves.

"Miss Marie, I'm expecting my very first litter in January, February or March. I'm excited to be a mother of one or two, or maybe even three cubs but I'm also a little nervous because I might not wake up while I am giving birth. What if I roll on them?" Wanda asks.

"Everything will be fine," Miss Marie assures her.

"Thank you. Hopefully, when I have my next litter in three or four years, I will feel more confident."

"You will. Have a lovely, restful torpor," Miss Marie says as she adds Wanda's details to her list before motioning goodbye.

WHAT'S THE DIFFERENCE BETWEEN TORPOR AND HIBERNATION?

Bears spend the winter in a state of torpor which is different than hibernation. During **torpor**, the animal's breathing rate and heart rate decrease slightly, allowing them to wake easily from sleep if they are hurt or in danger. They do not eat, drink, or release bodily waste during torpor; a bear's body can recycle its urine into protein.

Hibernation is when animals are in a deep "sleep" through the winter. Their body temperature, heart rate, and breathing rate drop drastically so they can survive for a long period of time without food. True hibernators (woodchucks, ground squirrels, and bats) don't sleep the winter away; they fully awaken every few weeks to eat small amounts of stored food and pass waste, then go back to sleep.

"Hello, Miss Marie," Betty beaver says, flashing a friendly, toothy orange smile.

"Hello, Betty! It's always nice to see you. How's the family?"

"Well, after twelve years, my Benny and I are still blissfully happy. Tired but happy. Like clockwork, we'll have somewhere between one to six adorable kits between April and June," Betty says.

Miss Marie writes her notes; it's the same as every year before.

Betty sighs. Sounding downtrodden, she adds, "I can hardly wait for winter and for the marsh to freeze over. I just want to relax, enjoy being with my family, and eat in our lodge without having to work all day and all night, building this, fixing that, and collecting food for our larder. I've stored enough fat in my tail for me to survive two winters. It's stressful having most of Havenwood Cove's community depend on us for their habitat."

"Yes, you deserve a long break. I look forward to seeing you when the ice thaws and meeting your adorable new kits," Miss Marie says in a soothing, appreciative tone.

Back on the water, Harold, Markie, and Lynn are concerned about Beverly's stress level as they watch her aggressively pull on her feathers rather than delicately preen them.

"I'm ready to go back and see our friends," Harold says. Lynn and Markie agree, hopeful that Beverly will join them before she causes herself harm or major bald spots.

"How do I look, Harold? I used my bill and feet and nibbled and stroked every feather with lots of my oil."

"You certainly did. Your slicked-back feathers are aerodynamically aligned, so you'll be able to fly barely using any energy. Imagine all the fancy acrobatic moves you'll be able to perform! You look beautiful," Harold praises.

"Awesome!" Beverly says, quite proud of herself.

"Can't see any bald spots," Markie teases.

Lynn gives Markie a scolding look.

"Good job. You will definitely be warmer and waterproofed now," Lynn tells her.

The four feathered friends waddle back to the meeting area.

"Where did you go?" Rusty III asks Harold.

"We flew to the marsh. I'm thinking the intruder is no longer hungry," Harold whispers.

"Yup, he's gone."

"Glad you're all right. I see most of my friends, so who is no longer with us?" Harold asks.

"Prudence. Sad, but we all have to eat," Rusty III says.

"Don't tell Beverly and Lynn what happened. They're still shaken up. And don't comment on how glossy Beverly looks."

"Sure thing, Harold," Rusty III says before he leaves to continue looking for Ginger.

"Hi, Sebastian," Harold says to the red flash whizzing by.

Stopping almost in mid-motion, Sebastian turns around and dashes back to visit Harold.

"Hey, Harold! Are you excited about your first migration?" Sebastian asks, his tail flicking back and forth.

"I think I am. I've heard some great stories from some of the well-travelled Mallards. I'm looking forward to warmth and sunshine, but I'll miss my friends," Harold says, watching Sebastian's tail with fascination, noticing that it's half as long as the squirrel's body and imagining how this flimsy, out-of-control mass of bushy hair gives him balance when he flies from tree limb to tree limb.

"Don't worry about me. I'll be here when you come back in the spring. You know me, I'm too speedy for danger, and I'm prepared for the winter," Sebastian boasts.

"Speaking of you and danger, I saw you having a long chat with Miss Marie. Are you in trouble again?"

"I'm always in trouble."

"Yes, you are. Why are there leaves and little twigs stuck to your fur?"

Sebastian pauses for a moment, then grins before answering, "I mostly do this in the spring, but yesterday I just couldn't resist biting some bark off a white spruce tree to get to the tasty sugary sap. The problem is it's kind of messy and a little sticky. For a couple of days, I'm like a magnet. I attract everything! But don't you worry about me; all this stuff wears off eventually."

"Good to know. You be safe and try to stay out of trouble. I'll see you in the spring," Harold says.

"Have fun, Harold! I hope you get around to telling Beverly how you feel about her," Sebastian says as he scampers away to check on his middens.

In a daze, Harold stands motionless. *Does everyone know that I'm crushing on Beverly?*

Tired and a bit grumpy, Miss Marie carefully looks over her list. "Yes, I've got, hmm, and yes…."

"I'm finally done!" Miss Marie announces, feeling pleased with completing her task.

"Miss Marie, you missed my cousin, Madleine moose!" Ella shouts.

"I affectionally call her 'my little swamp donkey' even though she's pretty big. I don't see her often, but I still worry about her."

"How could I have missed that lovely, long-legged cow?" Miss Marie says. "We need to find her, make sure she's okay, and ask her what her plans are for winter. She's an elusive, almost mystical ungulate. How will we find her?"

WHAT'S AN UNGULATE?

Ungulates are primarily large mammals with hooves. They include odd-toed ungulates such as mule deer, donkeys, horses, rhinoceroses, and zebras, and even-toed ungulates such as many species of deer, moose, bison, elk, reindeer, hippopotamuses, antelopes, giraffes, camels, llamas, alpacas, cows, sheep, goats, pigs, and cattle.

"I can search for her!" Harold says.

"Is that such a good idea, Harold? You need to save your strength for migration," Beverly chimes in.

"I agree with Beverly. Migrations are exhausting. You'll soon find out," Markie says.

Sir Lloyd flies from his tamarack perch to walk among the crowd. "That's kind of you, Harold, but your friends are right," he says.

Beverly gives Harold a wink.

Harold puffs up his chest and stands tall.

I couldn't save Prudence, but I'll find Madleine," Oliver boasts as he repeatedly flaps his wings and spreads out his long black talons. He struts among the crowd before stopping and standing in front of Sir Lloyd.

"Wonderful!" Sir Lloyd *hoo-hoo hooooo hoo-hoo*'s in support of the plan.

"Our Madleine has a huge appetite. Aquatic plants are a favorite of hers, so check out the lily pond first. Between her poor eyesight and your near-silent flying, she might not notice you," Sir Lloyd tells Oliver.

"Another thing, Oliver. It's moose rut season. If you hear sounds of moans, lonely wails, some moo's, or the clacking of antlers, she might be close by. After all, our loveable Madleine would be a desirable mate for any superior bull moose. Good luck in finding her."

"I'll find her!" Oliver boasts with the confidence of a mature raptor, and cheers erupt from the crowd.

With his feathered legs that go down to his toes, Oliver is large, fast, and nimble—the perfect choice to find Madleine. His (2 m) seven-foot wingspan casts a shadow on the crowd as he gains altitude. Harold looks up and watches in amazement, noticing how one minute he can see Oliver's golden feathers on the back of his head glow in the sunlight, and then the next minute, he looks like a dark brown dot in the sky.

With Oliver gone on his assignment, Sir Lloyd flies back to his tamarack tree perch, gazes down at the crowd, and says, "Miss Marie, thank you for handling the long and daunting task of registration. It's far beyond my capabilities and patience. Well done!" Sir Lloyd *hoo-hoo hooooo hoo-hoo*'s.

Cheers of thanks for Miss Marie fill the air.

Miss Marie bows her head and shuffles her feet. In a moment of excitement, her quills stand up, and everyone gasps—but then they lay back down. Slowly she raises her head, looks at the appreciative crowd, and grins. Harold observes that Miss Marie suddenly doesn't look so tired and grumpy.

Maybe she realizes that she really does have some friends after all.

CHAPTER 7

"**L**isten up, everyone! If I can get all the Mallards to please gather around the old stump near the entrance to the marsh pathway, your migration meeting instructor will be with you shortly." Sir Lloyd is in the middle of his announcement when he's suddenly interrupted by the wheezing whistle sounds of *jeeeb, jeeeb, jeeeb*. The sounds are coming from the north, behind him, beyond the jack pines, and they're rising in pitch. Is it a bush plane? A threat of some sort? All eyes look up, intensely focusing on the direction of the droning noise. Fight or flight is once again on their minds as their ears perk up and their heartbeats race. The unique noise is becoming clearer, harsher, and louder.

"Stay put! Do not panic!" Sir Lloyd shouts.

Harold notices Beverly's trembling. "We'll be okay," he says as he gives her a peck on her cheek, trying to calm her while he's resisting his sudden urge to suggest they fly away for safety. Since the possible threat is in the air, he agrees with Sir Lloyd to stay put till the danger presents itself.

But watching the others around him, Harold starts to doubt his decision. He hears beaver tail warning slaps coming from the marsh. He watches squealing snowshoe hares hop to safety under the branches of a nearby tamarack, and he spots Ella 'flagging' to signal possible danger by raising her tail showing the large white patch on the underside. In a blink of an eye, she's disappeared into the woods. As usual, Sebastian is a blur of red as he quickly scurries up an aspen tree.

"Let's stay here like Sir Lloyd said to do," Markie says.

Harold and his Mallard friends cluster together, staying alert while watching and waiting to see what happens next.

Finally, the perceived danger presents itself. Barely clearing the treetops, a pair of Wood Ducks come into focus. Their rising and falling, wheezing and whistling *jeeeb* calls announce their arrival.

Harold and Markie's bills drop open. Their eyes double in size at the sight of the two handsome examples of feathered perfection coming in for a landing.

Markie turns to Harold and whispers, "Don't worry buddy, Beverly probably isn't paying attention to those featherheads." Harold and Markie

glance over to see Beverly, Lynn, and their hen friends waddling from their safe place to the open area to get a better look at the gorgeous Wood Ducks as they fly over. Harold's heart sinks into his stomach as he watches Beverly and the other hens fluffing their feathers and grooming themselves in preparation to meet the exciting waterfowl guests.

Harold catches the eyes of one of the Wood Ducks as it flies overhead, only to be given a brazen look and brash-sounding whistle. Harold responds by standing tall, puffing up his chest, stretching his neck, and letting out a defiant, boisterous *KREEP*. After a perfect landing on the marsh, barely making a splash, the Wood Ducks march to the gathering place.

Sir Lloyd flies from his tamarack perch to ground level. With open wings, he graciously welcomes the newcomers. "What brings you flyboys this way? Haven't seen your kind this far north before," he tells them.

"We decided to expand our adventures this year and travel north to Yellowknife. Now we're flying our way down south. We need rest and some food," one Wood Duck explains. Harold watches the other Wood Duck checking out the hens, particularly Beverly.

In his friendliest tone, Sir Lloyd says, "Well, drakes, rest and eat up. Enjoy your stay at Havenwood Cove."

Sir Lloyd flies back to his tamarack perch, where he looks over the gathering before announcing, "Attention, please! I'd like to invite you to take a minute to say hello to our guests, Dirk and Dylan, then carry on with your day. Mallards, please make your way to your migration meeting. Your instructor will be there momentarily. That's all for now."

"I wonder which one is Dirk and which one is Dylan?" Harold says to Markie.

"Don't know. They look identical. They're not like drake Mallards, with each one of us being unique," Markie brags.

Harold gives him a puzzled look. "I know our hens are known to be friendly and flirty but look at them. Beverly and Lynn are waddling so fast that they're practically tripping over their feet to get to the Wood Ducks.

Taleena, Susie, and Anne are neck-in-neck right behind. And poor Janis; with her injured wing, she doesn't have much chance of keeping up," he says, shaking his head.

"Our hens are certainly making fools of themselves. What's so great about Dirk and Dylan, anyway? Sure, the Wood Ducks are dramatic looking and colourful, but I've heard that their Mandarin drake cousins have even more elaborate plumage: orange plumes on their cheeks, orange sails on their back, and pale orange sides," Markie adds.

While the hens are quacking and bobbing their heads, each trying to impress the Wood Ducks, the Mallard drakes cluster together. Clacking and *kreep*ing, each voices his opinion.

"Look at Taleena over there. She's as happy as if she's just found a puddle full of juicy worms," Davor grumbles.

"What do our hens see in those duckwads?" Jayson hisses.

Harold tunes out all the clacking and *kreeping* around him as he stands still and watches Beverly happily quacking with one of the Wood Ducks.

Oliver quietly returns from his search for Madeleine moose, seemingly unnoticed by the group as he glides in on a glorious zephyr breeze and lands beside the team of upset drakes.

Noticing the hens are gathered across the clearing, he asks, "What's going on, fellas?"

Harold speaks up. "Do you see the Wood Ducks over there? They just flew in, and now all our hens are starry-eyed over them. I can hardly blame them. With their brilliant, iridescent colours, they look like rock stars."

"Yeah. They look like designer waterfowl, with their bizarre, shiny rainbow face-patterns and swept-back crests," Easton says.

Their chestnut brown chests have a pattern of little white feathers that makes them look like they're wearing a quilted armour breastplate," Markie says.

"And what about their aggressive-looking, fiery red eyes?" Davor adds.

"Even their white neck looks like it has a protective chin strap," Michael comments, thinking that Janis is most likely weak in her knees for Dirk and Dylan.

"Did you see the huge, hooked, can-opener-shaped nail at the tip of their bill? It looks like a heavy-duty excavator! I bet they can dig through debris and mud and uncover small roots, seeds, and worms super easily. Our nail is just a little bump," Jayson hisses.

"You hit the 'nail' on the head," Michael snickers as he shuffles his feet and flaps his wings. No one appreciates his humour.

"Now, look at us! Our shiny green heads have no dramatic markings, no crest, and our white neck rings are 'cute' not bold looking. Our brown chests look cuddly—nothing like a warrior's armoured plate," Harold mutters defeatedly, his bill pressed into his chest.

Oliver looks at the upset drakes and says, "Hey, greenies. The Wood Ducks don't have your bright orange legs and feet. They're real showstoppers!"

"They sure are!" Markie says enthusiastically. One by one, the drakes hesitantly agree. With sad-looking head bobs, each acknowledges that they have at least one impressive feature that the Wood Ducks don't have, and their moods begin to lighten.

Putting his bruised ego aside, Harold asks, "Hey Oliver, any luck finding Madleine?"

"I tried, but who knows where she could be by now? With those broad, even-toed hooves of hers, she can travel anywhere," Oliver answers.

Dirk and Dylan break away from their hen admirers in search of their favourite meal of acorns and nuts. The hens shuffle back to meet up with the drakes.

"So, did you have a nice visit with the flyboys?" Harold asks Beverly and Lynn, looking away and up to the sky while he nervously waits for their answer.

"Sorry Harold. Did you say something?" Lynn asks, distracted by her search for Dirk and Dylan.

Beverly notices Harold's twitching feathers and that he's not making eye contact with her. "Oh, they seem friendly enough, but they're not as charming as you drakes," she says, casually waving her wing at Harold.

Harold's racing heart relaxes, but he realizes his Plan B must be organized right away—to help eliminate the possible romantic competition of Dirk and Dylan.

Harold whispers, "Markie, I need to talk with you."

"Sure thing, buddy. Right after the meeting."

CHAPTER 8

The four feathered friends and their Mallard comrades waddle to their migration meeting area. They watch their instructor fly over the gathering, skillfully land on the ground, then jump up onto the pine tree stump located near the edge of the marsh. Positioning her webbed feet to balance herself, she looks around at her audience of anxious, hopeful, and eager faces.

Standing tall on her podium, she clears her throat and spreads her wings to welcome everyone. "Hello, all! I'm Instructor Riley. As a senior member of this flock, I'll be your commander for this year's migration south. I've done many migrations, and I'm excited to educate you on what's involved in this journey."

Enthusiastic head bobbing and bill clacking welcomes their leader. Harold, Beverly, Lynn, and Markie huddle close in the front row. With a round trip migration under his wings, Markie is not as intensely focused on what Instructor Riley is going to say. While everyone waits for Jayson to waddle from the marsh to the meeting, Harold looks around. He sees newbie migrator Susie standing and nervously fidgeting, making weird shapes in the gravel with her webbed feet. Anne, who's already flown three migrations, is sitting and looking eager to learn more. Experienced migrator Davor stands close to Taleena, his right wing draped over her to warm and relax her; it's her first migration, and she's feeling a bit nervous. Michael, another experienced migrator, scans the crowd with a look of "new year, same old meeting" on his face, obviously somewhat bored. And Janis, who has flown a few migrations, is flexing her sore wing in preparation for the flights ahead. Harold's not sure whether Easton is a newbie, but notices he's preoccupied with moving a pebble back and forth with his bill. He appears to not really be concerned when the meeting begins.

Once Jayson finally arrives, Harold turns his attention back to Instructor Riley.

"Like you, I'm anxious to leave the cold for the warmth down south. This meeting is happening none too soon. Snow should be here in a few days," Instructor Riley says, rapidly flapping her wings, trying to stay warm.

"Markie, do you think she'll be able to lead us? She looks frail and worn out, like she's been through a couple of tornados. She's missing a few feathers, and her right wing is a little bent," Harold observes as he watches Instructor Riley shiver, her knees knocking together.

"Don't fret, Harold. She's spindly but muscular. She was born with that bent wing, but that hasn't slowed her down. She might fly a little wonky with a bit of a constant tilt, but she's an ace flyer and an inspiration to us all. From what I've heard, she has bravely and successfully led a few migrations through some brutal weather and has the reputation of having the spirit, humility, and courage of a born leader. You're right, though; I don't know how many more migrations she's physically capable of."

"For some of you, this will be your first migration," Instructor Riley continues. "Yes, it will be physically and emotionally exhausting, but this is what we must do to survive. There's no food here for us in winter. We're like family, and we look after each other to keep us all safe. I'm encouraged to see that many of you have been preparing for our long journey. Davor and Taleena, I saw you doing circuits over the marsh to strengthen your wings."

"We are going to do a few more circuits today," Davor says as Taleena nods her head in agreement.

"Excellent!" Instructor Riley replies.

"This morning, I noticed the marsh was crowded, with many of you wholeheartedly eating more than usual. Wonderful! The extra stored fat will give you the energy you need for endurance. You will lose up to half of your body weight during this migration but don't be worried; we stop to rest and eat for a few days after a few hours of a long flight. Once we arrive at our destination, you will have months of warm weather, relaxation, and lots of tasty new eats. Many species of birds from many other places will also fly in, so the newbies will make new friends, and the experienced migrators will meet up again with old friends."

"It will be fun to make new friends," Lynn whispers to Beverly.

"Jayson, Michael, and I will discuss your strengths, weaknesses, and flying abilities. We will place you in the best position in our V formation to give you the most enjoyable start to your migration experience. We will let you know your position in our V just before taking off. Any questions?" The commander looks around and sees boredom on some faces, serious expressions on others, and excitement on a few others.

"Janis, I'd like an update on your injured wing after this meeting," Instructor Riley tells her.

"I'm the only one with an injury," Janis whispers to Michael.

"Don't worry. We'll pace our flying so you will be able to keep up," Michael reassures her.

Instructor Riley returns to wrapping up the meeting. "If there are no questions, please go rest up, eat lots for energy reserve, and make sure your feathers are in excellent condition for peak performance. Be mindful not to overexert yourself if you're doing a few practice circuits; you don't want to be tired before the migration even starts. We'll meet back here early dawn tomorrow, for final instructions before takeoff." And with those closing remarks, Instructor Riley hops off her podium to meet the few Mallards waddling towards her.

"This is so exciting! My first migration!" Lynn says, spinning around and around till her eyes look loopy and she starts wobbling about. "Whoa, oh," she says as her rump hits the ground.

Harold notices that Beverly is standing still and being quiet. Her beautiful brown eyes look glazed over, like she's deep in thought. "How are you feeling?" he asks.

"My stomach feels like the time I ate a sour tadpole, and my legs feel shaky. I don't know if I can do this."

Harold drapes his wing over her back. "You're a strong flyer, right?"

"I guess so, but I haven't flown anywhere other than around the marsh," Beverly whispers.

"Many of us, including me, are newbie migrators, so you're in good company."

"Uh-huh," Beverly hesitantly agrees.

"Just think how exciting it will be to see new places, taste new foods, and make new friends," Harold says with a cuddle.

"But aren't you nervous?"

"A little, but that's normal. Doing something new is exciting, but it still can make you feel a little uneasy."

Feeling less woozy and no longer seeing in double vision, Lynn slowly waddles over to Beverly.

"Just think how exciting it will be to meet other ducks. Maybe I'll meet a dashing drake who'll find me adorable, even with my quirkiness and my waddle that sometimes lacks balance," Lynn says as she calmly and gracefully waves her wings like a fluttering butterfly.

"I was nervous my first time, but you'll soon get into the groove. You'll see new landscapes, and you are going to love the tasty feasts of new foods. Wait till we get to the prairie potholes. I'll leave them as a surprise," Markie says.

"Are you feeling better now?" Harold asks as he holds her under his wing.

"I guess so. We'll be like four feathered adventurers!" Beverly jests, with a nervous giggle.

"Don't look around, buddy. Duckwad incoming," Markie warns Harold.

Dylan bumps Harold to get to Beverly.

"Well, hello there!" Dylan says, flaring his brilliant plumage. "What's your name?"

Feeling flattered but very aware that Harold is standing right there, she softly answers, "Beverly."

Harold takes his wing off Beverly's back in preparation to defend her or himself. He spreads his webbed feet wide apart for visual effect and balance in case there's a rumble. Standing tall with his neck elongated, he moves his face close to Dylan's, looks into his fiery red eyes, and asks, "Are you and your brother flying south with us?"

"Nah, we're lone rogues," Dylan boasts, puffing up his armour-plated-looking chest.

Harold stands firm, expands his chest, and gives Dylan a hardy bump in an effort to cause him to step back or lose his footing. Dylan steps back.

"We reviewed your flight path schedule with the navigators, so I'll try to catch up with you en route south, little sweet feet," Dylan says flirtatiously, looking directly at Beverly. Defiantly, he gives Harold a "game on" threatening wink with one of his piercing red eyes before he turns around and waddles away—acting like a winner of a rumble, even though he chose to back down from one.

"Harold! Oh my gosh. Are you okay?" Beverly asks.

"Sure am," Harold replies as he feels his body tightening up and getting warm.

"Lynn and I are going to go to the marsh to eat. You coming?"

"Markie and I will join you hens in a few minutes," Harold replies.

Beverly and Lynn waddle off.

Markie notices Harold's heaving chest and clacking bill.

"That good-for-nothing scoundrel," Harold gripes.

"Don't let him intimidate you, Harold."

"We really need to work on Plan B. Any more ideas?" Harold asks as he starts pacing back and forth, kicking pebbles out of his way.

"Absolutely! Let's go talk with Instructor Riley and some of the navigators to ask permission to carry out Plan B," Markie says.

The two scheming drakes wander off to get answers. Markie waddles calmly while Harold stomps along, glaring at the Wood Ducks in the distance.

With the necessary approval and even more exciting ideas offered by a couple of well-travelled Mallards, Harold and Markie squat under the drooping limbs of a black spruce. Nestled among the short, stiff, blue-green needles and purplish-brown, egg shaped cones they breath in the balsamic-fresh scent, and begin to fine-tune Plan B.

The four feathered friends spend the remainder of the day eating, resting, preening, and saying their goodbyes to their non-migrating friends.

As night falls, all the Mallards huddle together under the bough of a tamarack tree to sleep. Tomorrow's the big day!

CHAPTER 9

The next morning before daybreak, the Mallards waddle to the marsh for their last big feast before their flight. As the sun begins to rise, puffs of each duck's warm breath linger in the crisp morning air. After filling their stomachs, they anxiously waddle to their gathering place to listen to Instructor Riley's final migration guidelines.

Standing on her tree stump podium, Instructor Riley is surprised to see that some of the young ducks are stressfully scurrying about searching for more food to help fuel their long journey while the older ducks are calm and chatting with each other. Harold snuggles next to Beverly to keep her warm while he looks around at the chaos.

Noticing she's getting caught up in the frenzy, Markie shouts, "Lynn, come sit with us!"

Instructor Riley decides that it's time for her to take control of the whirlwind of anxiety, excitement, and anticipation within the flock.

"Good morning! Please gather around and be still. We have an exciting yet intense journey ahead, and we need to be organized. First, let's briefly discuss our famous V. Who knows why we fly in a V formation?" Instructor Riley asks.

"Because it looks impressive!" quacks Susie, a sassy young hen, wiggling her tail feathers to indicate she's pleased with her answer.

"Yes, it does look impressive, but that's not why." Instructor Riley shakes her head, looking a little annoyed. After all, migration is a serious, life-threatening undertaking.

Hoping to get a more responsible answer, she scans the crowd, her eyes landing on Harold.

"How about you, Harold? Do you know why?"

Markie gives Harold a wink, knowing that he's got this. It's the perfect time to impress Beverly!

Harold slowly stands up. With his heart racing and his voice cracking, he says, "We fly in a V formation so that each strong Mallard takes his or her turn leading the flock and giving the others a chance to rest."

"That's right." Instructor Riley says, sounding relieved to receive a proper answer. She adds a small head bob and a flap of her bent wing to show her appreciation.

Harold's heartbeat returns to normal. Feeling proud of his accomplishment, he sits back down with his head held high.

Beverly fondly nudges Harold and whispers, "You're no featherbrain."

Markie gives Harold a "good job, buddy" nod.

"Great answer, Harold, but there is more to it. Listen carefully," Instructor Riley says.

Harold slouches as if he's lost the wind beneath his wings.

Instructor Riley continues, "We have to be organized and work together. The Lead Duck has the most difficult and strenuous position. Not only do they have to know the route, but they act like a windbreaker, giving the rest of us a smoother flight. It's a serious responsibility and exhausting task to be Lead Duck."

"How long do we stay Lead Duck?" Taleena asks.

"Good question. Stay in the lead until you get tired, but don't push yourself to exhaustion."

"Where do we go next after being the lead?" Susie asks.

"Another excellent question," Instructor Riley says, impressed that Susie just might be taking this adventure seriously.

"The Lead Duck will fall back to the end of the V line that they came from. That's where there is the least amount of wind drag and where they can regain their strength. A rested duck will then take the lead. This is extremely important. We fly for hours. You can fly twice as far and save your energy if each of you flies just a little higher than the duck in front of you. You'll be taking advantage of their wings' uplifting power, which is called 'tailgating.' Does everyone understand?" Instructor Riley asks.

The group's head bobbing and clacking tells her they do.

Beverly and Lynn look at each other.

"This sounds a lot more technical than just flying around the marsh," Beverly says to Lynn, who nods in agreement.

Harold extends his right wing and once again drapes it over Beverly's back. Looking deeply into her worried brown eyes, he says, "I'll look after you."

"You promise?"

"I do," he whispers, giving her a little squeeze.

"Focus!" Instructor Riley says in a serious tone.

Everyone directs all their attention back to listening to every word she has to say.

"As we fly along, we continuously communicate with each other with our voices. The hens will quack, and the drakes will *kreep*. This lets the Lead Duck know that they're flying at a good pace and that we are all safe."

Unexpectedly, the air is full of loud quacks and *kreep*s from the overly excited younger ducks.

"Not now! When we are in flight. Although, I appreciate your effort," Instructor Riley bellows, shaking her head.

Immediately, there's silence.

"Migration is in our DNA. You will be amazed how you will instinctively know the general direction of our route and how to read the sun's location in the day and the stars at night to keep us flying on course. Having experienced migrators in our flock is certainly beneficial, as they are well-acquainted with the route, our favourite resting spots, and where the dangers are," Instructor Riley says.

"Did she say danger?" Beverly shrieks.

Markie leans into Beverly. "It's going to be okay. Don't worry. After all, I've done a round-trip migration, and I'm still here."

Beverly gives Markie a befuddled look, trying to decide if that helps her feel safer.

"Before I give you your position in the V, Sir Lloyd would like to have a word with you."

Sir Lloyd takes the podium and says, "Good morning, magnificent migrating Mallards! Many of your friends are here with me to wish you a safe journey south and a safe migration back to us in the spring."

Harold looks around and sees most of Havenwood Cove's wildlife including: Sebastian, who's scurrying around; Squire, who's sitting close (but not too close) to Miss Marie; Benjamin and Betty beaver; and Rusty III, who gives him a nod.

Sir Lloyd continues, "For you that are staying here hibernating or enjoying torpor, I wish you a wonderful sleepy time. If you are staying and not being tucked away till spring, I look forward to seeing you around. Just remember, come April or May, our family and friends will reunite, and the sights and sounds of new little ones will be exciting for all of us," Sir Lloyd hoo's.

There's a thunderous joy in the air as everyone cheers. Even Winston showed up, and lets out a booming, happy growl.

Just as Sir Lloyd is about to turn the meeting back to Instructor Riley, rustling and heavy thumping sounds from the marsh pathway get everyone's attention. With his paddles crashing into tree branches, a water-soaked Murphy moose trudges slowly towards the gathering.

"Sorry, everyone," he says in a gravelly voice. "I didn't mean to disrupt your meeting."

Concern for their dear friend shows on everyone's face. Murphy looks weak. He's struggling to hold up his head and balance his gnarly-looking, (1.5 m) five-foot-wide, humongous rack of antlers. Thin hair covers his undernourished body, except where there are blotches of raw, exposed skin. Even though his eyes look dull, there's a glimmer of warmth. When he speaks, the drooping hairy dewlap (bell) of long sagging skin under his neck flops around like a fish out of water. His body is proof of his senior age and a life well lived.

Everyone gathers around him as Sir Lloyd respectfully asks, "Murphy, are you okay?"

"I'm an old bull. I've had a wonderful life, but it's my time to leave. The ticks are eating me raw, leaving me no protection from the cold. I'm too exhausted to continue. I've come back for three reasons—first, I want to thank everyone for the years of friendship. Second, for the last time, I want to drop off my antlers for my special rodent friends. I know how much these little 'shed hunters' love eating them—almost as much as I love losing them."

Sebastian, Miss Marie, and their other rodent friends reluctantly nod in agreement. Murphy's annual shedded antlers are a gourmet delight. The calcium and minerals are healthy for them, and gnawing on the antlers helps keep their teeth filed down. This time, though, they're a bittersweet parting gift and won't be devoured with the same joy. Murphy's glad he made the effort; he can see on their faces that they're appreciative of his kindness.

"Sebastian, my feisty little squirrel friend, you have to share!" Murphy says with a wink.

Sebastian agrees with an impish grin and a nod.

"The third thing is a request."

"Absolutely! Anything you want," Sir Lloyd says.

"Do you know Madleine?"

A chorus of "yes" rises from the group.

"I just left her. She's near the old trapper's shed. I'm proud to say that she'll be carrying on my bloodline, and should have one to three calves sometime around mid-May to early June. I didn't have the heart to tell her that I won't be seeing her again. This tough old bull just couldn't bring himself to say goodbye." Murphy lowers his head and stares blankly at the ground, silent and motionless. Everyone holds their breath in anticipation and with great concern. In a quivering, raspy voice, he slowly says, "I need to know that she'll be cared for. Will you keep an eye on her and my new little ones?"

"It will be our honour. We adore Madleine, and look forward to meeting your offspring," Sir Lloyd promises on behalf of everyone.

Benjamin beaver adds, "And we'll let your calves know you were a noble bull and that you are missed by all of us."

Stifled sniffles can be heard as the sadness of the situation unfolds.

"Thank you all. Promise me you'll tell Madleine that she was the love of my life."

"We will, yes," soft whimpering voices agree.

With bowed heads and gentle nods of hopelessness, their tears sprinkle to the ground.

Murphy ambles over to the nearest tree and steadies his footing. Using all of his strength, he forcefully knocks his immense right, wide, flat antler against the trunk. It drops off. He carefully repositions his long spindly legs to balance himself. As he turns his head his dewlap sways. With the last of his remaining energy, he forcefully knocks off his left antler. It falls to the ground. For the very last time and with an aching heart and tears blurring his vision, Murphy gives one last goodbye nod to his friends.

As he trudges away into the forest, head down, shoulders slouched, and with each step looking as if it's riddled with pain, he mutters, "I won't miss carrying those (23 kg) fifty pounds of bone."

In a brief minute, all that his friends of Havenwood Cove will be left with is the painful grief of knowing they'll never see their dear friend Murphy moose again. Fond memories of this gentle giant will one day fill their hearts with joy, but for now, heartbreak is all they feel.

The air is dense with sorrow; everyone can barely breathe.

With sadness in his big yellow eyes, Sir Lloyd looks at Instructor Riley and nods for her to carry on with the meeting.

Being a strong, adaptable leader, Instructor Riley says compassionately, "Apologies to all at this difficult time, but we need to move forward with our departure. We are losing precious daylight. Mallards, please follow me to the marsh where I will give you your position in our V." Hopping off the stump, Instructor Riley starts waddling down the well-beaten path, her eager entourage in tow.

To help guide a nervous Beverly, Harold gives her a soft raspy *kreep* and a gentle tap with his wing. Their wildlife friends follow behind, except for Sebastian, who darts to be in front.

Everyone gathers on the shore as Instructor Riley wades in, swims a short distance away, then turns to face the flock. "Listen up, everyone," she says firmly.

"Jayson is our first Lead Duck, and his navigational expertise is stellar. He's an expert flyer and an esteemed member of the Kitty Hawk Club. On the right leg of the V formation, in order, we'll start with Easton, then Taleena, Davor, Anne, Michael, and Janis, who is nursing a sore wing."

THE KITTY HAWK CLUB

In this fictional story, The Kitty Hawk Club (referred to as the KHC) is an elite global club for Mallards who have exhibited exceptional flying skills, excellent leadership, and bravery in assisting their fellow birds in need. Membership is by reputation. The club is named in honour of the real first successful flight by a human in a self-propelled, heavier-than-air aircraft near Kitty Hawk, North Carolina, in 1903, by Orville and Wilbur Wright.

"On the left line of the V, starting at the front will be me, then Susie, Beverly, Harold, Lynn, and Markie."

Harold and Beverly give each other a little nudge, thrilled that they're in the same line.

"Positions, please!" Instructor Riley commands.

The migrating Mallards wade into the marsh. The newbies frantically swim around, aimlessly bumping into others as they search for their position. The onlookers are shocked at the scene of what looks like ducks being tossed around in a gale.

Swimming up to Easton, Instructor Riley says, "Follow me," then leads him to the first position of the right leg of the V. "You stay here."

Instructor Riley observes Janis bobbing beside Michael. "You are to be behind, not beside each other!"

"Oops," Janis says as she swims to get behind Michael.

Harold notices the look of confusion on Beverly's face. "Beverly, I remember that you follow Susie, but where is she?" he asks as they both look around for her.

"I think you're in my spot," Harold hears Anne say to Susie.

"Sorry," Susie says as she swims around in a circle. "I'm not sure where to go!"

Using her bent wing, Instructor Riley lightly taps Susie on her bill and then points to where she should be.

"Got it. Thanks."

With Susie now in her spot, Harold guides Beverly to her position. "You stay here, and I will be right behind you," he tells her.

Markie, in his position at the end of Line B, says to Lynn, "You'll be behind Harold, and I'm behind you."

"Thanks, Markie," Lynn says, feeling calmer now that she's in her proper place.

Instructor Riley calls out, "Line B, move closer to Line A at the beginning, then flare out away from Line A till you get to the end of your line."

"We fly in a V, not a crooked H!" Instructor Riley shouts while shaking her head, knowing this always happens on the southern migration. Returning home is easy-peasy since everyone will be experienced. "Maybe I'm getting too old for this," Instructor Riley grumbles.

After a few minutes of stressed quacking, *kreep*ing, and disorganized bobbing around, all thirteen Mallards settle into their V position and float in place, not daring to move.

Instructor Riley gives Lead Duck Jayson a boisterous-sounding quack of approval to proceed with liftoff.

Jayson turns around to face the flock and asks, "How about we first fly over the old trapper's shed and say goodbye to Madleine?"

Feeling the heartbreak of never seeing Murphy again, everyone agrees.

Jayson shouts to the well-wishers on the shore and to the anxious lineup of Mallards who are quietly bobbing on the water. "We have never flown together as a team. We need to pace ourselves so we don't smash into each other. If our dear friends on the shore will count to five, the two first ducks, one from each line of the V, will then lift off. On the next count of five, the next two will liftoff. We'll repeat this system till we are all airborne. Are you ready?"

Resounding cheers and chatter from the shore and the migrating Mallards' quacks and *kreeps* reassure him that this plan is a go.

"Okay, let's do this!" Jayson shouts as he turns himself back around to face forward. With his wings spread wide and resting on the surface of the water, he calls out, "Start counting!" and then waits for the signal to liftoff.

Harold's mind races with details. 'I hope I hear when it's my turn. I must remember to tailgate. How much higher do I fly above Beverly? Can I keep up? Can Beverly keep up? How far over do I fly to flare out?'

The excitement is building as the crowd of well-wishers start counting, one, two, three, four, five! Benjamin beaver slaps his tail on the water, and Winston lets out a big roar. That's the signal! All systems go.

WHOOSH!

With one powerful downbeat of his wings on the water, Jayson bolts almost vertically into the air. Using his tail for balance and with powerful beats and sweeps of his wings, he gains altitude, levels off, and calls out with a steady stream of loud *kreeps* to encourage the others.

Harold notices that Beverly's locked into her liftoff position with her wings spread out, resting on the water. He hears her repeating aloud in a steady monotone voice: "One, two, three, four, five, one, two, three, four, five, one, two, three, four, five, one, two, three…"

"Beverly, how are you feeling?"

"Can't talk, Harold. One, two, three, four…"

Harold hears Squire, Sebastian, Ella, and Miss Marie cheering as his other friends continue counting to five, followed by Benjamin's thunderous tail slap on the water and Winston's bellowing roar.

Instructor Riley and Easton spring out of the water, quacking and *kreep*-ing loudly to let Jayson know they're up and following him.

At the next sound of five and Benjamin's tail slap and Winston's roar, Susie and Taleena bolt out of the water, quacking loudly as they gain altitude to join the others.

"You've got this, Beverly!" Harold calls out as he hears five, the slap, and the roar.

With unstoppable determination, Beverly jumps out of the water and lets out deafening, rapid-fire quacks as she gains altitude. Davor calmly keeps pace with her as he lets out dignified low, raspy *kreep*s.

Harold feels his heart race as he anxiously waits to hear five, the slap, and roar.

"Five!" *Slap! Roar!*

On cue, Harold nervously springs out of the water. In overdrive, and with the determination of an adventurer, he beats his wings and calls out to let Beverly know he's behind her. To the right of him is Anne, who calmly quacks and matches his flapping.

As Harold rapidly gains altitude, he feels the bumpy air turbulence from the ducks he's following. His heart rate gradually relaxes, knowing that he and Beverly are holding their own with the experienced migrators in their very first V formation. He's proud to be part of a team.

On cue, Lynn, Michael, Markie, and Janis follow.

With cool and clear skies, it's a perfect day for liftoff. All thirteen Mallard migrators are airborne.

CHAPTER 10

Harold listens to the fading cheers of "bon voyage" from his friends. His head spins with all the exciting fanfare, and then feelings of sadness creep in. His stomach starts to feel uneasy, achy, and topsy-turvy. For the first time, he realizes that he's going away for a long time and leaving behind friends like Benjamin and Sebastian. And he's leaving Havenwood Cove, the only home he has known. His eyes fill with tears as he takes one last look back at his friends and Havenwood Cove's marsh.

Self-doubt and fear start playing in his mind, his thoughts tumbling about. *Snap out of it*, he tells himself. *I'm going to warmer weather where there's a lot of food. Beverly, Markie, and Lynn are with me. Markie has already done a migration, and he's okay. We have experienced migrators with us. I will see my friends again. I can make myself sad and scared, or I can embrace this adventure.* Harold thinks about it further. *Attitude is everything. I choose to be an adventurer!*

Harold feels himself relax, and starts enjoying the benefits of tailgating. Flying above Beverly, he watches her gracefully flap her wings as she moves through the air like a flickering dragonfly on a gentle summer breeze. Mesmerized by her stunning violet speculum feathers as they shimmer in the sunlight, he hears, "Hey buddy, you're flying a little wonky. You daydreaming?" Markie asks.

"Sorry, I was lost in thought." *Focus. Yes, smooth flying from here on,* Harold tells himself.

WHAT ARE SPECULUM FEATHERS?

A speculum is a patch of brightly coloured feathers on the secondary (flight) wing feathers of Mallards and other duck species. They are mostly visible when the wing is extended and viewed from behind. Colours vary with each duck species; Mallards are iridescent blue or purple. It is thought that these feathers help ducks identify their own species when flying in a flock.

In awe of Jayson's aviation skills, Harold watches and learns how to lead the flock higher and higher into the sky. *I can do what Jayson's doing. I also can be a great aviator and impress Beverly,* Harold tells himself. Then, he notices Jayson aggressively tilt his body to be angled vertically with his right wingtip facing the ground. Slicing through the air, Jayson drastically banks to the right. Harold panics.

"I've never done a move like that!" Harold blurts.

Then he hears, "I'm right behind you, buddy. Just breathe; you've got this!"

Harold lets out an uncontrollable shrill *KREEP*—a combination of panic and thanks.

Harold concentrates on Jayson's impressive banking maneuver when he hears chilling quacks.

From his vantage point as the fourth tailgater in left Line B, he looks past Beverly to see that Susie is no longer following Instructor Riley. She's banked too far to the right and is within a wingtip's distance of Taleena. If they touch, feathers will fly, and they both could tailspin out of control.

Taleena frantically quacks and blasts Susie, "What are you doing? Don't come any closer! Don't touch me!"

"Sorry! I'm sorry!" Susie quacks hysterically as she beats her left wing faster than her right, trying to avoid smashing into Taleena.

To worsen the situation, Markie sees Beverly, Harold, and Lynn following Susie's lead.

Markie yells, "Don't follow Susie!"—but it's too late.

From the corner of her right eye, Instructor Riley sees the impending collision. She shouts, "B Line! Get back in position behind me and flare out to the left NOW! Both lines, slow your speed!"

Susie, Beverly, Harold, and Lynn instantly reduce their wing flapping and beat their left wings faster and harder to counteract going right. Panicked and embarrassed, Susie's eyes flood with tears. The flock is unnerved and in a state of shock. After some confusion, the B Line safely angles itself away from the A Line.

"Hey, Jayson!" Instructor Riley shouts.

Jayson looks back and asks, "What happened?"

"First-time migrators. We need to simplify our moves."

"Sure thing."

"Great!" Instructor Riley says.

Harold sees the anger in the eyes of the A Line ducks, and feels the embarrassment of the B Line ducks' actions, that created such a dangerous situation.

Upbeat, Instructor Riley jests, "That was some creative flying, B Line. You certainly bamboozled your A Line friends. Until we all feel more confident, we are going to make wider turns and fly slower. How does that sound?"

Quacks and *kreeps* of relief fill the air.

Instructor Riley lightheartedly says, "B Line, were you trying to imitate the Canadian Forces' Snowbirds? They've been practicing their fancy moves for decades. But don't worry; you were born with the right equipment, and in time, you'll learn the technique."

Harold notices that Beverly's shaking her head and not saying a word.

"Beverly, we certainly showed off some fancy moves, didn't we?"

"Not really."

Harold's thoughts start to spin again. *I can't believe I followed Susie. Why did I do that? Beverly probably thinks that I'm just a naïve drake and not a good protector. I bet Dylan the duckwad wouldn't have followed Susie.*

Feeling emotionally crushed by the possible collision, Harold realizes the seriousness of flying in formation. *Am I flying the right distance behind Beverly? Am I flying at the correct height? Am I flying too slow? Am I flying too fast? I have so much to learn.* His mind is filled with self-doubt and questions. *Best to just concentrate on flying,* he decides.

"Hey, buddy! One mishap is just one mishap. It's all a learning experience. You're a newbie; it's expected. Stay positive!" Markie shouts to Harold.

Harold responds with a non-convincing *kreep* of, "Don't be a worrier; be a warrior."

"We're almost to the lily pond," Jayson informs the flock.

Harold sees glimpses of shimmering water between the tall conifers and the sparsely yellow-leafed aspens.

"Look, Beverly! Do you see water?"

"Yes!"

Jayson slowly leads his flock to a lower altitude, staying close to the edge of the oval-shaped pond. "We'll do a wide sweep around the shoreline and then fly over the old trapper's shed to look for Madleine. Call loudly to get her attention. Let's go!" Jayson instructs.

Everyone enthusiastically starts calling out. Harold notices that their noisy voices are frightening the wildlife below. He sees a mother raccoon and her three kits stop washing their food at the water's edge then rush to safety in the brush. A pair of grazing deer leave a small clearing to scurry for cover.

All eyes actively search for Madleine, but to no avail.

Jayson asks Instructor Riley, "Do you want to do a third flyover?"

"No, we're going to have to abandon this mission. We're losing daylight. Best to lead us south."

"Sure," Jayson replies, then turns his attention to flying to a higher altitude.

"What's happening? Why are we leaving?" Beverly asks Harold.

"Sorry, friends, but we have to get back on schedule," Instructor Riley says.

Disappointed that they couldn't say goodbye to Madleine, the flock's departure is less enthusiastic and quieter than their arrival.

"Are you okay, Janis?" Michael asks, concerned that her sore wing is causing her to lag behind.

"Carry on, Michael. I'll catch up. I'm just pacing myself."

Michael slows to half speed so he's equally positioned between the flock and Janis.

Harold sees Janis struggling and asks, "Are you sure you're going to be okay?"

"I'm a tough old bird, Harold. Don't you worry about me."

"Harold! Harold!" Beverly shouts.

"What is it? Something wrong?"

"I think I hear mooing!"

"Where?"

In between wing flaps, Beverly points to the left. "Over there!"

Harold shouts to Jayson, "Beverly hears mooing off our left side!"

"Got it," Jayson responds and immediately banks to the left, making a big, loopy turn. No need to risk a smash-up.

"Listen up!" Instructor Riley commands. "Our first plan was flawed. Madleine would be able to hear us with all of our noise, but we wouldn't be able to hear her. This time, I will do the calling out, and all of you can listen to see if she tries to contact us. Hopefully, this plan works."

Instructor Riley begins calling out, "QUACK... QUACK... QUACK," while the flock quietly looks for Madleine.

"Listen; do you hear that?" Beverly asks Harold.

Flying dangerously close over the treetops and over the pond, the ducks diligently watch for any sign of their moose friend. Concentrating on every little sound, all they hear are faint chirps of songbirds and the crunching sound of fallen leaves being walked on by a woodland animal.

"Good try, Beverly. We gave it an admirable effort, but now we need to get back on schedule," Instructor Riley says. "Continue south, Captain Jayson!"

Jayson nods and starts preparing to lead the ducks to a higher height.

Beverly tells Harold, "I really thought I heard mooing."

Just then, a familiar sound unexpectedly catches everyone's attention. The flock instantly becomes quiet; they stop beating their wings and glide.

"I hear her! I hear her! There she is!" Lynn quacks, pointing her wing in Madleine's direction.

Coming out of the woods, Madleine romps to a small open clearing. Looking up, she lets out lively *MOOOOs*, bobbing her head up and down and swaying her body from side to side. She's excited to see her friends, and her long, gangly legs are flailing about like she's dancing the boogaloo. Her dewlap of skin hanging from her neck is swishing to its own beat. For a (544 kg) 1200-pound gal, she looks like she's light on her feet, and shockingly, she can really shake her booty. *Who knew a moose could have so much fun?* Harold thinks.

Full of excitement, the Mallards challenge themselves by breaking out of formation. Trying not to crash into each other, a tree, or Madleine, this spectacle stresses Instructor Riley. It's a quack and *kreep* fest of good wishes: hello, stay safe, see you in the spring. Harold's not sure if Madleine understands what each duck is saying since everyone's quacking or *kreeping* at the same time, but what he knows for sure is that she understands the feeling of friendship, loud and clear.

"Time to leave," Instructor Riley tells the feathered follies.

Jayson gets in position and hovers the best he can as each duck gives a farewell dip of a wing and one last call out before positioning themselves into a V.

"We're making a V, not a U. Not an X, either," shouts Instructor Riley.

Surrounded by confused ducks fluttering in circles, Instructor Riley sternly calls out, "Enough!" Taking a deep breath, she gathers her thoughts and points with her bent wing to each duck showing them where they should be.

"Sloppy as it looks, it's definitely a V. It takes practice, but you're improving," she tells the flock, noticing that a few actually look pleased with their performance.

"I think we did a great job of getting back into formation," Beverly says.

Harold and Lynn agree. Markie doesn't comment.

The flock soars as they follow Jayson southbound on their migration adventure.

Harold takes one last look back at Madleine, who's hobbling back to the woods. *Perhaps she danced a little too much,* he thinks.

As they continue on their way, the ducks happily call out to let Jayson know that everybody is safe.

Looking back at the flock, Instructor Riley says, "Great job, but we need a little tailgate tweaking. Anne, fly higher than you are now, and

Michael and Janis, adjust your heights accordingly. Markie, keep an eye on Lynn and make sure she stays in line with you but not too close. Harold, fly a little higher and closer to Beverly. Beverly, great tailgating height from Susie, but stay back just a little more. Davor and Taleena, great positioning."

"Janis, how's your wing feeling?" Instructor Riley asks.

"Pretty good so far," she answers, vigorously beating her wings to show she's okay, even though she's exhausted and hurting.

Harold's concerned that she's already looking so tired at the beginning of the journey.

Instructor Riley notices that everyone has made the necessary flying adjustments. "Great teamwork," she says, giving Susie a wink.

Full of pride that he and Beverly are getting into the groove of formation flying, Harold puffs up his chest and breathes deeply. Considering himself in training to be a future esteemed member of the KHC, he scrutinizes Jayson's every move and how he studies the sky and the ground terrain.

I can do that. I can become a great leader, Harold says to himself as he tries to match Jayson's wing beats.

Being a bit of a jokester, Jayson announces, "This is your Captain speaking. We're flying southeast at an altitude of (122 m) 400 feet above ground level and at a cruising speed of (69 kph) 43 miles per hour. We've departed Havenwood Cove just south of Great Slave Lake in the Northwest Territories, and we are expected to reach today's destination of Lake Claire in Northern Alberta early this evening. There are no meals on this no-frills flight, but it does offer in-flight cinematic entertainment with two features. The first is 'Spectacular Northwest Territories,' and the second feature is 'Alberta: Wild Rose Country.' Both are free and available in full 360 surround for your viewing pleasure. Each of you has your own personal washroom. Use as needed. Plop away!" he laughs. "We expect a smooth flight with clear visibility. I'll be giving you updates as we fly along. Get comfortable and enjoy the journey. Thank you for choosing Jayson Air."

The ducks giggle uncontrollably, losing their focus on flying. Their V formation now looks a little wonky, with ziggy lines that are farther apart than they should be. Easton's boisterous laugh is contagious and isn't helping the situation. He's bouncing around and struggling to keep himself flying level.

After a few minutes and a displeased look from Instructor Riley, everyone calms down and repositions themselves back into a presentable V formation.

Harold glances at Beverly, who is beating her wings with the determination of an adventurer. "Are you enjoying the view?" he asks her.

"Yes. It's beautiful! The fresh scent of the pine trees makes me think of Havenwood Cove."

"I really like it, too," Harold responds, a feeling of nostalgia washing over him. He starts thinking of his friends and the relaxing times on the marsh.

"Look down! A wolf pack!" Markie shouts.

"Great find!" Michael says.

"Glad we're up here and they're down there," Beverly comments.

The first-time migrators are excited to experience new views.

"This is your Captain speaking. My shift is over. Thank you for flying Jayson Air. Davor has offered to replace me, so you are under good wings."

Jayson drops back to the end of the A Line to rest.

Even though Easton is next in the A Line, Jayson and a couple of other experienced ducks decided that Easton is just a little too rambunctious to be Lead Duck. Who knows where he would lead the flock? His fascination with pretending to be the Canadian flying ace of the First World War, Billy Bishop, is just a little unsettling.

Davor, on the other hand, is a quiet, studious drake who's familiar with the route and is extremely capable of the task at wing.

Lynn looks over at Janis, who is now directly to her right. "Janis, why do you look so worried? The Lead Duck transition was flawless."

"I know, but Jayson's flying behind me now, and I'm struggling to keep up. My wing is sore, and now I can't be a slow poke," she answers, just loud enough for Lynn to hear her.

"He'll understand. Besides, he's probably happy to have a slower pace after being Lead Duck."

"I guess so," Janis says as she continues to beat her wings with all the energy she can muster.

Harold's relieved that it's not his turn to lead; he's not quite ready—*but soon*, he tells himself. He knows he'll keep watching and learning from the Lead Duck, but for right now, he's happy to keep up with the flock, *kreep* continuously, and admire the cerulean-blue sky dotted with a few fluffy clouds.

"Beverly, is the breeze giving you some pushback?" Harold asks.

"Uh-huh. I have to beat my wings harder and faster to keep myself flying straight and stay level. What about you?"

"Me too."

"Today is a perfect autumn day for day one of our migration south. I wonder how many days we'll be flying. Do you know?"

"Your violet speculum feathers look beautiful. They're glowing in the sunlight," Harold says, trying to distract her. He doesn't have the heart to tell her there are many more days.

"Thanks Harold! They're my fashion statement. I really think that their black border and white edges give me a flyway model look," Beverly giggles.

Instructor Riley breaks into the regularly scheduled program of everyone quacking and *kreep*ing for an important message.

"For a while now, we've been flying over Wood Buffalo National Park, and we just flew over the second bend of Buffalo River. This means that in just a few flaps of our wings, we'll be flying over the 60th parallel and saying goodbye to our beautiful home in the Northwest Territories—the 'Land of the Midnight Sun'—and we'll be saying hello to Alberta, Canada's Rocky Mountain province."

"Are we flying over the Rockies?" Susie asks nervously.

"Thankfully, no. The Rockies are gigantic and have strong winds, unpredictable weather, and extremely cold temperatures. We're heading southeast of them," Instructor Riley tells her.

Susie exhales a relaxed *quaaaaack*.

After a spurt of cheerful quacking and *kreep*ing, the first-time migrators are quiet in thought. It's all real now. They won't be returning home for six months. Harold's wondering if his friends will miss him.

Markie senses their sadness and speaks up. "Well, I won't miss the short daylight hours and long, dark, cold nights. Imagine yourself being in the sunny south, swimming in warm water and enjoying fine dining. I can hardly wait. Are you with me?"

"Well said, Markie," Instructor Riley acknowledges.

"Sometimes you surprise me—in a good way," Lynn tells Markie.

Harold thinks about it. "Markie's right. We'll return to Havenwood Cove and see our friends when the sun rises at the end of April and doesn't fully set again until the middle of August. Three and a half months in 'The Land of the Midnight Sun.' What's not to love about that?"

"Yes! Here's to leaving the cold and going home when it's warm. Our friends will be there when we return. Let's make the most of our migration," Lynn quacks.

Joyful, uplifting *kreep*s and quacks once again fill the air, but they are short-lived.

Susie notices Taleena's quieter than usual. "Taleena, what's the matter?"

"I'm bored. Aren't you bored? Here a quack, there a *kreep*. Same old sounds over and over. Our boisterous calls are giving me a headache. We have no musicality. We're out of tune, and we're all calling out over each other."

"You're right. We certainly don't sound like songbirds," Susie says.

Harold overhears Susie and Taleena's conversation and thinks, *I bet*

Beverly's also bored. What can I do about it? Digging deep into his mind, he finally comes up with an idea.

"Hey, everyone! Why don't we try to put some rhythm into our voices? It might be a fun way to occupy ourselves, and we might end up sounding good. We certainly can't sound worse, right? What do you think?"

"I love it!" Taleena says, already forgetting about her headache.

"I love it, too!" Beverly quacks. Everyone agrees.

"Markie, why don't you start us off with some New Orleans Dixieland Jazz and give the newbies a taste of what's to come?" quacks Anne.

"Happy to! Michael and Anne, follow my lead. Let's get our NOLA* on," Markie jokes.

The flock becomes silent. All they hear are their heartbeats and the sound of the breeze rustling through their feathers as the musical extravaganza begins and their faux sound of trumpets fills the air. The flock begins tapping their webbed feet to the opening notes of "When The Saints Go Marching In," and with joyous quacks and *kreep*s, they all sing along.

After the performance, the sky has newly energized, happy flyers, each trying to stay with the rhythm. Janis slips in quacks of pain disguised as poor musicality.

Instructor Riley laughs and says to Jayson, "All that's missing is a trumpet and Satchmo."**

"I suddenly have a craving for crawfish," Jayson jokes.

Sadly, it doesn't take long for the flock to be back to their mundane routine of endless flap, flap, flap, flapping, and quacks and *kreep*s.

"Listen! Do you hear that?" Beverly shouts.

Harold shouts, "I hear it!"

Janis calls out, "Me too!"

---

*NOLA is a nickname for New Orleans, Louisiana.

**Born and raised in New Orleans, Louis Daniel Armstrong (1901–1971), nicknamed "Satchmo," was an American trumpeter and vocalist, and one of the most influential figures in jazz. Armstrong earned the nickname "Satchmo," short for "satchel mouth," because of his large sized mouth.

Taleena quacks enthusiastically.

Lynn shouts, "Sounds like fun!"

In between their calls, the ducks hear exciting sounds of commotion—other bird voices, that are new to the newbies' ears. With each flap of their wings, the noises get louder and louder.

"CIVILIZATION! We're not alone!" Lynn quacks.

The ducks have had a long, exhausting day of nonstop flapping, listening to the rustling sound of their wings slicing through the air. It's been hours of swooshing vibrations in their ears, cold wind in their eyes, listening to the thumping of their heartbeats and hearing the same repetitive quacking and *kreep*ing calls over and over and over. Finally, they hear exciting new sounds.

"Look! Water for as far as I can see!" Harold shouts.

In the near distance, peeking through the treetops, the flock sees a large body of water. After a long day of looking down and seeing trees, trees, and more trees occasionally broken up by some small grassy areas with a few rivers and ponds sprinkled in, the newbie migrators feel a rush of excitement knowing they are about to experience new terrain.

"Okay, team! We're getting ready to descend onto Lake Claire. We don't want any mishaps, so keep calling out to let everyone know that the fabulous flock from Havenwood Cove is arriving," Instructor Riley tells the worn-out travellers.

"I couldn't be happier! I felt like this flight would never end. My wings are tired; I think they only have a few flaps left in them. I'm hungry, and I'm cold. How about you, Harold?" Beverly asks.

"Ditto. I have no energy, and all my muscles ache. I'll be ready for an early night of shuteye. I don't know how Janis is still flying!"

Upon clearing the treetops, the newbies are stunned to see an expanse of water that looks like it goes on forever. It's bustling with activity and the sounds of many species of migrating waterfowl.

"Have you ever seen so many birds in one spot?" Beverly asks Anne.

"It's like this every time we pass through. Everyone's friendly but tired," Anne tells her.

Instructor Riley informs the flock, "Michael's going to lead us once around the lake to make sure our location is safe before settling down for the night. Follow closely."

As they do a safety check over the lake, the newbies are starstruck by all the different types of birds they've never seen before. Following proper protocol, they announce their arrival.

"Looks good. Pace yourselves to avoid colliding with each other and be aware of the other birds on the water," Lead Duck Michael directs. "Here we go!"

"Flare out and lower your wings, and release your feet for drag," Instructor Riley shouts.

Some exhausted ducks have already been dragging their feet for a while.

Harold listens nervously to Instructor Riley. *No messing up. Sure, my fancy marsh landing was a bust, but I can do this,* he tells himself.

Instructor Riley announces, "We're reaching our final approach. Head up, chest out, wings back, and feet forward. Remember to use your tail feathers to help stabilize and control your flight. Good luck, pace yourselves, and remember—teamwork. We've got this!"

Harold watches Michael flawlessly touchdown and then glide onto the rosy, sunset-tinted lake.

As Beverly gets herself into the final approach position, Harold cheers her on with, "You've got this, Beverly!"

Her feet catch a small wake on the water, causing her to bounce a couple of times before she glides to a full stop.

"My turn," Harold says out loud to boost his confidence, but quickly realizes that he's travelling a little faster than planned.

"Coming through!" he yells, his webbed feet skimming the water. With fear in her eyes, Beverly watches Harold coming directly for her, then feels him graze her left wing as he passes by. Finally, Harold comes to a stop, turns around, and bashfully swims to Beverly.

"I guess I miscalculated. I spread my toes out, but I still had a little too much power. Even my winglets didn't slow me down enough. Did I hurt your wing?" Harold nervously asks.

WHAT ARE WINGLETS?

Winglets (alula) are a group of three to five feathers on the top of the wings that create a break on the wings' even surface and act as brakes to help slow down a landing.

"I'm okay. You?" she asks him.

"Yep! All good."

"I think I'm going to start calling you 'hot wings,'" Beverly giggles.

Together they wait and watch for the others to land. Not the most elegant landings for some, but no major mishaps. Overall, taxiing in was a success.

With some ducks feeling frazzled, and everyone tuckered out and hungry, they bob on the icy water, tipping up searching for eats. Barely able to keep their eyes open and without enough energy to tend to their roughed-up feathers, the flock huddles together on their frigid waterbed and calls it a day. A dreadfully long day.

As Jayson and Easton patrol for predators, the sounds of *hoo, hoo, hoo* waft through the night air. Hidden in the shadows of the surrounding forest, an owl that sounds different than Sir Lloyd serenades the weary travellers as they fall asleep under a blanket of stars.

"Sweet dreams, Beverly," Harold whispers.

"Sweet dreams, *hot wings*," Beverly giggles.

Cloaked in darkness, Harold looks up and makes a wish on the billion stars: *Just once, can I please do an impressive landing—or even just a good one?*

CHAPTER 11

Whoosh! Honk, whoosh, *rhink*, whoosh! Whoosh.

The flock is abruptly awakened from a deep sleep, gusts of air swirling above them.

"What's happening?" Lynn shouts. "I can barely hear myself think. It's so noisy! Can anyone hear me?"

"I hear you!" Markie shouts.

"Are you okay, Beverly?" Harold asks.

"Harold! What's happening?" Beverly shrieks. "I can barely see you in the dark and fog. It sounds like waterfowl rush hour."

Davor shouts, "It sounds like some Canada geese coming in for a landing. I don't think they can see us. Let's call out so they know we're here!"

Some of the flock let out confident calls, while others give out crackled, nervous ones.

"Everyone okay?" Michael asks as he cradles Janis.

"Nothing to worry about, folks. The Canada geese have landed, and the nearby squawks you hear sound like Whooping Cranes prepping for an early takeoff. Just stay close for a little while," Instructor Riley tells the flock.

"Brrrr," says Beverly, ruffling her feathers to shake off the ice crystals.

"Well, I'm awake now, so I might as well swim around and try to warm up. I think I'll check out what's on Lake Claire's early bird breakfast special," she giggles.

"Sounds like a plan. No sleeping in with all this commotion," Harold says.

The sun's rays slowly burn off the morning fog, giving warmth to their feathered bodies and exposing their new surroundings. For some, it's their very first time on new water.

"It's so beautiful here with the lake and forest. It kind of reminds me of home, but with a lot more water," Lynn says to Susie, in between tipping up and looking around.

"Look at the long legs on the birds over there! Did you ever imagine that there would be so many types of birds?" Beverly asks Lynn.

"Gather close, please! Markie, will you be our tour representative today and let everyone know where we are?" Instructor Riley asks.

"Sure," Markie responds, stretching his neck and letting out three deep, raspy sounds from the back of his throat. Paddling to stay in place, he addresses his fellow flock mates.

"We're in Wood Buffalo National Park, the largest national park in Canada and one of the largest in the world, second only to Northeast Greenland National Park. Lake Claire is the world's largest natural nesting area for the endangered Whooping Crane."

"Wow! Our migration is full of famous world spots. It's like we're booked on the Premium Tour Excursion," Taleena boasts.

"We only travel first class, sweetie," Davor tells her.

"That's all I have for now," Markie says.

"Thanks, Markie. Ok everyone, we're going to rest here for a couple of days. Over a million ducks, geese, swans, and Whooping Cranes rest and eat here on their way south. Have fun exploring Lake Claire and its marshes. Make friends, get some rest, and clean yourselves up. Make sure you eat lots to replenish your weight loss; you'll need the energy. Stay close and see me if you have any concerns. Janis, please let me know how you're managing with your hurt wing. That's all," Instructor Riley says.

"Whoa. It's like waterfowl central! This is my first time away from home, and it's all so exciting. Let's have a top-notch day! Who wants to explore?" Susie asks as she swims around, recruiting a posse.

The flock separates into groups. Some dine among the cattails in shallower water, while others choose to swim around, exploring the lake and meeting new birds of different species. Janis checks in with Instructor Riley to give her an update on her sore wing, which is her version of the truth. She's hoping to "face it till she aces it" for the whole migration.

"What shall we do today?" Beverly asks Lynn, Harold, and Markie as they paddle in place close to the shore.

"I've never felt better, and I can't wait to get back on the migration trail," Harold says as he flaps his wings and puffs up his chest to disguise the fact that he's sore all over and exhausted.

"How are you two lovely hens feeling this morning?" Harold asks.

"Pretty good. I was so worn out that I fell asleep instantly," Beverly says.

"Me too, until the noisy Canada geese woke me up," Lynn grumbles.

"Good," Harold says as he gives Markie a wink.

"You hens stay here. Markie and I will be right back."

Swimming like they're competing with the gentoo penguin—the world's fastest-swimming bird—Harold and Markie go to talk with Instructor Riley to discuss Plan B.

"Those two are up to something," Lynn tells Beverly.

"They are definitely mischievous Mallards. Nothing would surprise me," Beverly replies.

After just a few minutes, they hear, "We're back. Did you miss us?" Markie teases.

Jittery with excitement, Harold pumps his head up and down. "How do you hens feel about a side trip today to see something amazing?"

"What is it?" Beverly asks.

"What are you thinking?" Lynn asks as she aggressively leans into Harold, staring him in the eyes.

"It's a surprise," Harold says, leaning away from Lynn.

"Do you want adventure and fun, or do you want to be boring?" Markie asks.

"Who you calling boring?" Lynn asks as she circles around Markie.

"I don't think Markie means that we are boring," Beverly says, trying to relax Lynn.

"Sorry. I guess I'm a little on edge from not getting enough sleep," Lynn says as she stops circling Markie and calmly paddles in one place.

"Okay. Our next migration rest stop is Algar Lake. There's not much happening there, so we can make up rest time there. How about it? Are you up for an adventure?" Harold asks, rapidly flapping his wings, ignoring how sore they are.

Beverly and Lynn give each other a suspicious look before turning their backs on Harold and Markie to quietly discuss the offer.

Markie and Harold look at each other, shrug their shoulders, and patiently wait for their reply.

Lynn and Beverly turn back to face the drakes.

"Have you already been to where you're taking us?" Lynn asks Markie as she slowly stretches her neck towards him.

"No, but Jayson has. He gave us the directions, and Instructor Rilcy gave us permission to leave the flock for a short time," Markie explains.

Beverly and Lynn glance at each other, then nod in approval of the plan.

"Okay, but remember you promised that you'll look after us," Beverly reminds Harold.

"That's a promise."

"First things first. All adventures should start with a full stomach and a light preening," Lynn says.

With full bellies and feathers suitably maintained for a short trip, they prepare for takeoff.

With Markie in position as Lead Duck, Lynn, Beverly, and Harold space themselves in a single row behind him.

"Ready?" Markie asks.

"Ready!" he hears from each of them.

Following Markie's lead, they bolt out of the water, one by one. Flying over treetops, they head southwest.

"How long is this flight?" Lynn asks Markie.

"What? We just took off. Keep flapping."

After a bit of time, Harold asks, "How are you hens doing?"

"I'm feeling a little chilly, but I'm trying to take my mind off it by enjoying the scenery. I really like the forests and their bright colours. The wide-open grasslands look like a golden, shimmering carpet. Aren't they beautiful, Harold?" Beverly asks.

"Yes, Havenwood Cove has nothing like them," Harold says.

"Ugh. I can hardly wait to be south and get out of the cold," Lynn comments.

Markie, Beverly, and Harold each think the same thing: Lynn needs to go to bed early tonight.

"Okay, glad everyone's fine," says Harold.

"Look! Monsters!" Beverly shouts as she tips her left wing to point to

(907 kg) 2,000-pound beasts with dark brown coats and long shaggy hair on their shoulders, legs, and at the end of their narrow, swishing tails. Each has a large head, two small, curved horns that look like devil's horns, a beard, and a large hump on its back.

Markie looks down at the grasslands and sedge meadows. "They're not monsters. Those are grazing wood bison—also called buffalo! They're part of the world's largest free-roaming herd. Wood Buffalo National Park protects them and is helping bring them back from near extinction," Markie explains.

"Really? Lucky them that they are looked after. Is this what you wanted to show us today?" asks Beverly.

"No," Harold replies.

"Okay, you two. How about giving us a hint?" Lynn asks.

"It's a surprise. You're just going to have to wait," Markie replies.

"My bill is sealed," Harold teases.

Harold watches Lynn slow her flapping to position herself beside Beverly. He watches them chattering nonstop, trying to figure out what the big surprise might be. Plan B seems to be successful so far.

"Do you hear something?" Beverly asks.

"What's going on? What's that annoying noise? It's getting louder!" Lynn shouts.

Harold and Markie turn their heads to look back.

"Stay calm and keep following me! Lynn, get back in line in front of Beverly," Markie shouts.

"Harold! What's happening?" Beverly shouts over the hullabaloo while focusing on trying to fly normally.

"There's a plump of Canada geese coming up. Stay cool. They'll pass us," Markie tries to shout over the ruckus.

Honk, honk, honk, *hrink, hrink*, honk, honk, *hrink*, honk, *hrink*!

Hrink, honk, *hrink*, honk, *hrink*, honk, *hrink*!

CANADA GEESE IN FLIGHT

When in flight, a group of Canada geese is called a "skein," or sometimes a "team" or "wedge." When the geese are flying close together, they are called a "plump." On the ground, a group of geese is called a "gaggle." The term "goose" applies to the female, and "gander" applies to the male.

"Stay in your lane!" a goose says to Harold as she passes by.

"Flying by!" a gander honks at Beverly as his wing comes within inches of hers.

"Passing on your left!" another gander shouts, his wingtip brushing against Markie.

Harold tries to steady his nerves, stay focused on following Markie, and flap at a steady pace so he doesn't slam into Beverly. He's mortified seeing Beverly's trembling body and ruffled feathers caused by the powerful wind gusts from the flapping geese.

"You're doing great, Beverly! Just fly normally. They'll pass by us," Harold shouts over the deafening honking and *hrink*ing.

I hope she can hear me. Oh, this is not good. Plan B was going so well, Harold thinks.

"Hey there!" *hrink, hrink,* a goose says, slowing down to fly in rhythm beside Harold.

Fixated on flying straight, Harold gives a quick nod without turning his head.

"I'm Gwendolyn. You can call me Gwennie."

Harold swiftly replies, "Harold."

"Nice to meet you, Harold," Gwendolyn says, noticing Harold's a wee bit stressed and not interested in engaging in conversation. "Bye, Harold," she calls out, as she flies away to join her team.

"Bye," Harold mutters. The intense loud honking and *hrink*ing of the geese is drowning out his thoughts, and the beating sound of their powerful (1.8 m) six-foot wingspan is ringing in his ears.

The Mallards watch the plump of seventeen Canada geese fly ahead, and then with precision and little effort, they reposition themselves from the plump into their famous skein V formation. As they gain altitude and speed, the long, deep honking of the gander and the shorter, high-pitched *hrink*ing goose calls are fading.

Beverly, Harold, Lynn, and Markie take a minute to just breathe, chill, and fluff up their ruffled feathers while the churned-up air around them settles. Lynn stretches her neck to release some tension. Harold takes a deep breath, wondering how Beverly is feeling.

Markie asks, "How's everyone doing?"

"I'm feeling a little shaky," Beverly says.

Annoyed, Lynn says, "Seventeen is *not* my favourite number anymore."

"I didn't realize that geese fly in a V shape like we do with our flock," Lynn says to Markie.

"They sure do. They're pros at it. I'm surprised to see them flying so low today. During long flights, they usually fly much higher."

"I'm so mad! They had the whole sky, but they chose to fly right beside us. Why would they do that?" Beverly asks.

"I think they just like to say hi and meet some new friends en route," Markie explains.

"They scared Lynn and Beverly. If we meet up with them when we land, I'm going to give that gaggle of geese a piece of my mind!" Harold threatens.

"Don't worry about them, buddy. Think of it this way: the three of you just proved that you are adventurers that can handle challenging surprise situations. You should be proud of yourselves," Markie explains.

"I wouldn't say I'm quite ready to be happy with what they put us through," Beverly says.

The newbie feathered adventurers calm themselves down and get ready for whatever happens next.

CHAPTER 12

**"H**arold! Do you see what I think I see?" Markie asks.

"Sure do."

"We're almost to our surprise destination, hens!" Harold boasts.

Beverly and Lynn look around.

"Where? I don't see anything special," Beverly says, lowering her head and cranking her neck back and forth while looking at the ground.

"What are we supposed to see?" Lynn asks as she checks out the landscape.

"Look closer," Harold tells them.

"I see a lot of trees and a huge swampy area. It's cluttered with … with what?" Lynn asks.

"Looks like a mess of fallen trees with a lot of grassy mounds surrounded by water," Beverly says.

"Come on! We're going in for a closer look," Markie says as he pivots his body from being horizontal to being vertical. Tucking his wings in close to his body and pointing his head to face the ground, he rapidly descends into a deep dive.

"Really?" Lynn says before bravely following Markie's lead.

"Whoo-hoo! Come on, you two!" Lynn shouts to Beverly and Harold.

Beverly tucks her wings in and then calls out, "Here I go! Come on, Harold!"

Harold takes a deep breath, puts his fear aside, and follows her.

Keeping in mind possible newbie mishaps, Markie spreads his wings and lowers his tail feathers for drag, raises his body and head, then levels off at a safe distance from the ground. His entourage amazingly follows his lead and skillfully transitions from flying vertically to flying horizontally.

"That was a rush! Being horizontal for so long is boring," Lynn comments.

"That was kind of fun," Beverly says.

"Sure was," Harold says with some reservation.

"Now do you see what it is?" Markie asks as they slowly fly over the unique-looking terrain.

Harold's enjoying watching Beverly and Lynn look around, trying to figure it out.

"Was there a windstorm here?" Lynn asks.

Full of excitement, Harold says, "Okay, you lovely hens, give me some bill clacking for the unveiling of the surprise!"

Beverly and Lynn agree to play along even though they do not see anything to be excited about.

On cue, they clack their bills and quack loudly to support Harold's enthusiasm.

"It's the world's longest and largest beaver dam!" Markie and Harold shout.

"What? Really?" Beverly asks.

"Wow! It's nothing like Benjamin and Betty's dam; it's so massive and messy!" Lynn observes.

"Let's find out more," Markie says. "Follow me!"

In single-file, they fly to a raised dome constructed of sticks and branches, the gaps between are filled with mud, pebbles, and moss to make it watertight. One by one, they slowly and carefully land on top of the dome.

"My feet want to slip in between the branches," Beverly tells Harold.

"Lean on me."

Markie notices Lynn wobbling about and asks, "You okay?"

"I think so," she says, moving at a snail's pace, watching her every step. "I'm trying to find a comfortable place to sit." Lynn plops down next to

Beverly, shuffling and wiggling around until she's not being poked by sticks. "I'm good now, as long as I don't move," she laughs.

"Exactly! Don't move anything but your head," Beverly giggles.

Markie plants himself down on the top of the lodge next to a large, dish-shaped stash of interwoven branches.

"Is this little island a beaver lodge?" Lynn asks.

"It sure is," Harold says as he stands, trying to look dashing. His large, triangular webbed feet and toes are clutching onto whatever they can so he doesn't topple over.

The four feathered friends look around at the enormous area of fallen trees surrounded by pockets of water dotted with large mounds of over-grown grasses.

"This doesn't look anything like the dam that Benjamin beaver's family built. I like Havenwood Cove's better because we have lots of open water to play games like *Tag* and *Catch Me If You Can*," Beverly comments.

"True, but if you play *Hide and Seek* here, no one will find you for days," Lynn laughs.

"There's no place like home. I miss it," Lynn says.

"Me too. I wonder how Betty is?" Beverly says.

"Hey, don't be Duckie Downers. We're on an adventure!" Harold says, trying to keep Plan B upbeat.

"Let's find out more from the residents," Markie says.

"I don't see anyone around. HELLOOOOOOO!" Beverly calls out.

The ducks listen for a reply, but all they hear are the cheerful songs of a few songbirds and the rustling sound of dried-out leaves as a gentle breeze weaves through the nearby forest.

Markie and Harold carefully wander around on the top of the lodge.

Beverly twists her neck to see what they're up to. "What are you looking at?"

"I think it's their fresh air ventilation hole," Markie says.

Markie bends over, lowers his head into the opening, and shouts,

"Hello? Anyone home?"

He waits for a response, but there's only silence.

"Now what?" Lynn asks.

"Let's wait a few minutes and see if anyone comes," Harold says, feeling a twang of disappointment, worried that this adventure might not be as exciting and impressive to Beverly as he hoped it would be.

"Benjamin and Betty told me that they can stay underwater for a long time to escape predators, and they have a couple of underwater entrances to their lodge—so we might not see anyone today," Lynn comments.

"Harold, why did Jayson tell you about this place?" Beverly asks.

"He told Markie and me that this would be a great side trip to impress you. Are you impressed?" he asks nervously.

"It's an interesting place, and it's very thoughtful of you to arrange this for us," Beverly says, bobbing her head a couple of times.

"Agreed. You two are definitely full of surprises," Lynn adds.

Harold cautiously flaps his wings a couple of times, almost losing his balance.

"After the whole Canada geese fiasco, basking in the sunshine is just what I need," Lynn says, closing her eyes.

The sun's rays warm the ducks as they sit on top of the lodge. Patiently they wait for a beaver to show. The autumn colours of the surrounding forest, and the violet-blue sky dotted with fleecy clouds are mirrored in the pockets of still water in between the grassy-covered dams, and lodges.

Harold scans the water, anxious for something good to happen.

"Look! Over there!" Harold shouts, pointing his wing toward a ripple in the water.

Everyone looks in anticipation at a small ripple that's widening and coming closer.

"It's a beaver!" Beverly says, all giddy.

Harold's thrilled that this outing might not be a total bust. Then the ripple disappears—and his heart sinks into his stomach.

"Where did it go?" Beverly asks.

They eagerly search the surface of the water but don't see anything.

"There it is!" Lynn shouts.

The four friends watch the beaver swim towards the lodge, dragging a small aspen branch clenched in its mouth. It uses its hand-like front paws and its large, powerful, webbed back feet and claws to crawl up the side of the lodge, where it carefully lays the branch down.

"Hello, folks!" he says to his visitors.

"Hello!" the ducks reply.

"Whatcha doing sitting on my home? Are you friends of Maisie?"

"No. Who's Maisie?" Harold asks.

"She's a friendly Canada Goose, and we're a real team. She feels safer having her nest on the top of my lodge—high up and surrounded by water—and she lets my family know when there's danger around. She's gone south. Miss her already."

"We're migrating south, too," Beverly tells him.

"But we didn't want to fly by without coming to see your marvellous dam," Markie says.

Looking down, the beaver responds bashfully, "Oh, it isn't much."

"Looks impressive to us," Harold says.

"Just fooling with yah. Of course, it's dam impressive," he chuckles. "It can be seen from space. Did you know that? Call me Chopper."

"Hello, Chopper. This is Lynn, Beverly, and Markie. I'm Harold."

"Nice to meet you," Chopper says with a nod.

"Can you tell us a little bit about your work here?" Harold asks.

"I'd like to take all the credit, but my family has set up colonies and lodges here for generations. Together, we maintain the dam and keep adding to it. Clever relatives for choosing this wetland between the Birch Mountain highlands and the Peace Athabasca delta. We have it all; dense boreal forests, lots of fresh water, food, and wood to build our lodge to keep us safe from bears and wolves. We're also far enough away from humans. Happy to keep our pelts to ourselves, thank you very much."

"Sounds like you're living the beaver's dream," Markie comments.

"I think so, but it doesn't come easy. We work nonstop all day and into the night, right from when the ice thaws in the spring until the ice forms in the winter. Yup, we're surveyors, lumberjacks, stone masons, wood-cutters, builders, and engineers. It's nice to be remembered each year on April 7th—International Beaver Day—but I still don't think we're appreciated enough," Chopper says, revealing orange teeth just like Benjamin's.

"Thanks, Chopper, for telling us about your amazing dam and home," Beverly says.

"I wish you could meet my family, but beavers are always busy!" Chopper says, using his strong, nimble, finger-like nails on his front paws to fuss with the placement of the twig he'd laid down earlier. "Stop by anytime," he says as he slides into the cold water.

"He was super friendly," Beverly comments as she watches him disappear under the water.

"I really like him. I'm sure glad I wasn't born a beaver: work, work, work!" Lynn laughs.

"Harold, how about you lead us back to Lake Claire?" Markie suggests.

"Um, I guess I can."

"Of course you can! You know the way," Markie says with a wink.

Beverly and Lynn look at each other but don't say a word.

"Okay. Ready for takeoff?" Harold asks.

"I'll follow Harold," Beverly says, "And Lynn, you follow me. Markie can be at the end of the line to keep an eye on us. How does that sound?"

"Sounds like a plan," Lynn answers.

Beverly, Lynn, and Markie each stand up, face forward, and wait for Harold to spring into the air.

"Hurry up, Harold, or I'll topple over!" Beverly says.

Mustering up his most confident-sounding voice, Harold asks, "Ready?" while what he's really saying to himself is, *be a warrior, not a worrier.*

"Ready!" each of his fellow adventurers responds.

Right before Harold loses his footing, he bolts into the sky and lets out anxious *kreep*s to encourage the others to follow.

Beverly jumps up and flies safely behind Harold, and then Lynn and Markie join the line.

As they fly over the world's largest and longest beaver dam, Beverly sees Chopper come to the surface of the water, look up, nod, then give a goodbye slap of his tail on the water before disappearing.

"Harold, that was fabulous! You really did come up with a fun adventure," Beverly says.

Harold lets out an overzealous *kreep*. He couldn't be happier that Plan B is starting off so well. As he leads his friends to a higher altitude heading back north to Lake Claire, he thinks, *I've got this. I can be a great leader. No way Dylan the duckwad will ever win Beverly over me.*

The four happy adventurers call out and flap their wings as they enjoy the scenery and their peaceful flight. And Harold thinks that maybe, just maybe, his wish of impressing Beverly has come true.

CHAPTER 13

"Hey, buddy! You're a natural leader!" Markie shouts.

"Thanks!"

Harold boldly leads them through a low, dense cloud. With limited visibility, they continue flying straight ahead but find themselves confused by muffled bugling sounds that become louder with each beat of their wings. As they break through the cloud, they're all shocked to see a huge flock of oncoming Tundra Swans. Despite the fact that each duck has three sets of eyelids, they're each too nervous to blink.

"Yikes!" Harold shrieks.

Directly in front of him is a blockade of rapidly-approaching white-bodied Tundra Swans, with their powerful, massively large wings flapping furiously. Their mellow, high-pitched cooing of *woo-ho, woo-woo, woo-ho* calls are intensifying. Alarmed to see the line of Mallards, some swans instinctively try to put on the brakes and reduce their speed by lowering their black legs and webbed feet. Everyone realizes that in a few seconds, they'll collide if someone doesn't change their course. The black-eyed swans and the brown-eyed Mallards exchange piercing stares.

Harold's mind is ready to explode. With no time to waste, he regains perspective of this urgent situation and takes control.

"Stay with me!" Harold yells, beating his wings harder to lead his friends to a higher altitude. They follow, but there's no break in the oncoming wall of white. He darts to the right; they follow, but they're still in the path of the wedge of swans. Harold quickly rebounds and flies to the left. Beverly, Lynn, and Markie trail behind, but it's hopeless.

The massive barrier of long-necked, elegant-looking white swans with their enormous wingspan is almost upon them. Harold instantly reassesses the situation. Beverly, Lynn, and Markie's hearts feel like they're pounding out of their chests as they anxiously wait for Harold's strategy. There's no time for Markie to take the lead, and there's no time to dive below the swans.

"Stay with me! We're going right through the middle of them!" Harold shouts, knowing Lead Ducks have to lead.

Harold slows his speed to give the swans time to adjust their path. He stretches his neck forward, holds his head high, and gives penetrating glares of "move aside, coming through" as he lets out rapid-fire *kreep, kreep, kreep* calls in a combative tone. Even though they're terrified, Beverly, Lynn, and Markie follow Harold. To avoid a collision, the migrating swans have no option but to spread apart and open the centre of their wedge.

With their pointed black bills chattering, the Tundra Swans shout at the Mallards, "You're going the wrong way! Turn around! South is behind you!" Their smooth but high-pitched sounds are deafening. Hundreds of shocked and angry black eyes stare at the feathered friends as they fly past.

Feeling impressed with himself, Harold boldly leads his flock through the throng of angry swans. All is good until he hears a ruckus of hissing sounds. He looks behind and sees a few loose feathers twirling in the air.

"Where's Beverly?" he shouts, just as he hears a piercing shrill of, "HELLLLLPPP!!!"

Harold looks down and sees Beverly plummeting headfirst to the ground. Horrified, Harold yells, "I'm going after her!"

Combating their own struggles to stay safe, Lynn and Markie stay focused on flying straight through the centre of the menacing swan barricade.

Harold bolts downward, slicing through the air with his wings tucked in tight. Steering himself with his tail feathers, he darts between swans. With Beverly within touching distance, Harold stretches his neck as long as he can. He opens his bill wide and desperately tries to clamp onto her webbed foot—but misses. Beverly's wings are hanging limp, catching the air and spinning her out of control; she's picking up speed and dropping fast. Her eyes are closed, and her bill is clenched tight.

With his adrenaline pumping and with unwavering determination, Harold opens his wings and gives three powerful flaps trying to gain maximum speed to catch up to her. Ignoring his pain, he stretches his body and neck to their limit. Harold again opens his bill wide and prays he can get a hold of her this time. He quickly calculates the speed that Beverly's falling with the angle of his bill to her left foot. Having only a split second to get it right, Harold clamps his bill shut and instantly feels the drag of her body hanging from his bill—he has her in his grip.

Using all of his strength and determination, Harold violently flaps to stay airborne until Beverly knows she's safe. Slowly she opens one eye and then the other, finding herself upside down and looking at the ground.

With her wings hanging limp and her legs splayed far apart, she's terrified, confused, and mortified to be in such a vulnerable situation. Clenching her neck muscles, she raises her head to see Harold above her, frantically beating his wings as he holds her foot in his bill. As the blood rushes to her head, she takes a deep breath and starts flapping her wings. Harold reluctantly opens his bill to set her free. Harold, Lynn, and Markie gasp as Beverly plummets toward the ground before orienting herself to fly right-side-up and straight to them.

Beverly explodes in anger. "You said you would look after me!"

Harold's body trembles, his eyes fill with tears, and his voice quivers as he says, "I don't know what happened."

"Are you hurt?" Markie asks Beverly.

"I need a few minutes. I'm still shaky."

"You poor hen. What happened?" Lynn asks, concerned.

"Harold swerved, leaving me blindsided and crashing into a swan, which sent me into a tailspin," Beverly explains.

"That's horrible! You must have been so frightened. Thankfully you're okay," Lynn says.

In broken words, Beverly says, "It was dreadful. I'm sure I'll have bad dreams about this. I could have died."

"Great save, Harold! You were like a superhero!" Markie boasts.

Beverly doesn't say a word. Harold looks away.

The graceful Tundra Swans, nicknamed the "whistling swans," are now far, far away, but the ducks can still hear the sound of the air whistling through their wings.

"All right, gang. Let's get back in line and head back to Lake Claire. Harold, you lead the way," Markie says matter-of-factly.

Feeling emotionally broken and defeated, Harold says, "Really?"

"You've got this, buddy. We're all fine. Let's go."

"Follow me," Harold says in a hushed voice.

Everyone gets back into their original position.

"No more excitement today, I hope," Beverly says with a hint of hostility.

"It's smooth flying from here on," Harold says, trying to convince himself and everyone else.

"Didn't you tell me that once before?" Beverly says sarcastically.

Harold silently leads his friends to Lake Claire. His thoughts are stuck in a loop, going over and over Plan B and the swan situation. He wanted to impress Beverly with the beaver dam, which he did. Then he put her in danger, but he rescued her. Overall, he thinks Plan B backfired. Big time.

Markie realizes he's going to have to help build Harold's confidence back up.

The remainder of the flight is uneventful—an exceptionally good thing.

As the sun sets, the four feathered friends do perfect landings on Lake Claire. Excited to have their friends back, Taleena, Davor, Easton, Jayson, Anne, Janis, Instructor Riley, Michael, and Susie cluster around them.

"Where did you go?" Anne asks.

Everyone anxiously waits to hear.

"Harold and Markie took us on an adventure. We visited Chopper the beaver to see his home and wetland," Lynn replies.

"That sounds nice, but Havenwood Cove has dams, canals, and a lodge that Benjamin and his family have built, so what's so special about Chopper's place?" Anne asks.

"It's the largest and the longest beaver dam in the world! It's twice as long as the Hoover Dam in Nevada," Markie comments.

Oohs and ahhs fill the air.

"That sounds so exciting," Taleena comments.

"It was. Quite an adventure. How about we tell you all about it tomorrow, and then you can tell us what you did while we were away? I'm hungry!" Beverly says.

"Yes, let's eat," Harold says.

Janis notices that Harold and Beverly are bobbing side-by-side but not looking or talking to each other. Sensing something's wrong, Janis decides they need her voice of reason.

"Hey, you two! What's up?"

"Nothing," Beverly whispers.

"Nothing, my tail feathers," Janis quacks.

"We had an incident during our flight back, and it put Beverly in harm's way," Harold blurts.

"Was it an accident, or was it planned?"

"It was an accident. It just happened," Harold says.

Janis calls to Michael, "My love, can you come here, please?"

"What is it, my little feather duster?" Michael chuckles.

"Tell Beverly and Harold why I have a sore wing."

"Oh, I don't think they really care to know," Michael says sheepishly.

"Fine. I'll tell them. Despite all of his flying experience, Michael misjudged a landing one day and smashed into me, and that's why my wing is hurt. I know he didn't mean to do it. Accidents happen to all of us," Janis explains. "So, you two need to make up. Now!"

"You had better do it. She can be a little bossy feather duster sometimes," Michael says, draping his wing over her back and giving her a loving squeeze.

"Sorry. I would never do anything to hurt you on purpose," Harold whispers.

"I know, Harold. I was just so scared. Then I got really mad," Beverly says.

"I'll always do my best to look after you," he replies, his warm breath mingling with hers in the chilly air.

"I know," Beverly says softly.

"Today was an unexpected adventure. Thank you. Well, for most of it," Beverly says with a little giggle and a nudge.

"My work is done," Janis says as she and Michael swim away.

Bobbing side-by-side on the icy water, Beverly and Harold watch the sun disappear below the horizon.

Most of Lake Claire's migratory guests are settling in for a restful night as the local entertainment is about to begin. First, a soothing chorus of *whooo, whooo, whooo*, courtesy of a resident owl hiding in the surrounding forest. Soon after, the second performance will be the coyotes who go by their famed stage name, "The Singing Dogs." Their unique perfect pitch of a wide range of sharp and dramatic yips and howls are both haunting and wondrous. As their performance magnifies and carries across the airwaves to audiences many miles away, everyone wonders if the performer is a solo artist, duo artists, or a pack. Are they calling out to friends, family, a potential mate far away, or are they letting others know where their territory is and to stay away?

For safety and warmth, the flock huddles together on their waterbed.

The entertainment is playing to a captive audience, but everyone is too tired to listen.

As the stars and crescent moon play peek-a-boo between the drifting clouds, Beverly leans in and whispers, "Goodnight, Harold."

"Goodnight, Beverly," Harold replies. And as he drifts off to sleep, he's still trying to decide if his Plan B outing was a success.

CHAPTER 14

arold watches as Beverly slowly raises her head, stretches her neck, ruffles her feathers, and opens her eyes, one at a time.

"Oh, Harold. You startled me," she says as his big brown eyes stare back at her.

"Good morning, sleepy one," Harold whispers.

Beverly cranks her neck and looks around. In between glints of the early morning sun reflecting off of the water, she recognizes some of the tipped-up tails. "Am I the last to wake?"

Harold gives her a little nod.

"I must have been really tired from all the excitement yesterday."

Instructor Riley positions herself to address the flock. "Good morning, everyone! I feel that the weather is changing faster than expected. The bitter cold north winds are ramping up, and they'll be nipping at our tail feathers within days. The snow threatens to fall at any time. How does everyone feel about leaving Lake Claire later today and flying south during the night to Algar Lake? The flying time is similar to the flight we just did. Do you all have the energy for it? Discuss it and get back to me," she says as she swims a short distance away and tips up to eat.

The Mallards huddle together, bobbing on the chilly water to discuss a night flight.

"Isn't flying at night really cold?" Lynn asks.

Beverly, Lynn, Susie, Taleena, and Harold anxiously wait to hear what the experienced migrators say.

"Beating our wings in flight helps keep our circulation flowing, which helps warm us up. You might actually be a little warmer than sleeping in the cold nighttime air and bobbing on the frigid water," Jayson explains.

"That makes sense. I've been waking up feeling like a ducksicle," Susie says.

"You won't be missing out on exciting new scenery as it's pretty much the same as what you have flown over already. No matter what, every day of travel is exhausting. The sooner we can get to our final destination, the sooner we can enjoy warm weather and months of relaxation," Davor adds.

Heads nod in agreement.

Instructor Riley paddles back to the flock. "Have you come to a decision?"

"Tonight's flight is a GO!" Michael says.

"Great! Enjoy the day, eat up, preen, relax, and we'll meet back here just before the sun disappears below the horizon," Instructor Riley says.

"Everything looks ducky," Lynn comments as she gazes around at the hustle and bustle of fellow migrators.

Taleena tells the four adventurers, "I met lots of nice birds yesterday, and I can take you around and introduce you. I met some lovely Whooping Cranes. Do you know they call their babies 'colts' because they have long legs and look like they're galloping when they run?"

"I didn't know that. I've never met a Whooping Crane," Lynn answers.

"Me either," Beverly says as Harold nods in agreement.

"I'll introduce you. Hopefully, they are still here. Are you ready to start our tour?" Taleena asks, bubbling with excitement.

"Can we eat first?" Harold asks.

"Sure," says Taleena, tinged with disappointment; she's ready and eager to start.

"Good plan, buddy."

"Just a quick snack. We won't be long," Beverly tells Taleena.

Everyone scurries around, foraging for a nibble.

Doing her best impression of a professional guide, Taleena asks, "Are you ready for my premium tour to begin?"

"Ready! Let the socializing begin," Beverly tells her.

The four feathered friends happily follow Taleena as she darts around clusters of bobbing waterfowl. Passing by, they are privy to the gossip of the last six months and conversations about who is travelling where.

Taleena stops in front of a bevy of Tundra Swans.*

"Hey, Taleena! Who are your friends?" one of the cobs asks.

"Hi, Wyatt. This is Beverly, Lynn, Harold, and Markie."

"Hello! Any friend of my new friend Taleena is a friend of mine," Wyatt says as he looks around. "I see the pens are having a chatter session. Nina, darling, can you come here and bring little Cleo and Chloe with you?"

The Mallards watch as a vision of a pure-white feathered goddess elegantly glides toward them. In tow are two young ones who have traces of gray tones on their head, neck, and wings.

"Taleena, it's lovely to see you again," Nina says, gracefully curving her willowy, long neck downward to warmly greet her cheek to cheek.

---

*A male Tundra Swan is called a *cob*, and a female is called a *pen*.

"Nina, these are my friends that I told you about: Beverly, Lynn, Harold, and Markie."

"Hi, everyone! These are Wyatt's and my little ones, Cleo and Chloe. They're a little shy," Nina says as each of her cygnets nestles itself under one of her wings.

"Hi," Harold says as Lynn and Markie each give a friendly head bob.

"You're beautiful," Beverly gushes, looking down at her dull, mottled brown breast feathers.

"Thank you. And you three hens are adorable with your stylish orange feet," Nina says.

"We met some swans in flight yesterday," Markie comments without mentioning the chaos.

"Doesn't surprise me. Our friends and family travel the same route twice a year," Wyatt replies.

TUNDRA SWANS

Tundra Swans nest and molt in the coastal plains of Northern Alaska in the spring and summer and spend the winters in Chesapeake Bay and eastern North Carolina. They are in transit almost half of the year (153 days), flying over (11,900 km) 7,400 miles each year.

"Are you going to stage at the prairie potholes?" Wyatt asks Markie.

"Yes, we love the potholes! This is Harold, Beverly, Lynn and Taleena's first migration, so they haven't been there before," Markie explains.

"You're in for a real treat. We might see you there because we continue across the eastern Great Plains and the U.S. Great Lakes regions, then we curve downwards along the eastern coast. How about you?" Wyatt asks.

"We'll rest and eat at the prairie pothole region as we head south-south-east," Markie tells Wyatt.

"Sorry, but we have to go. Cleo and Chloe are getting restless," Nina says, as the cygnets nip at her feathers.

Wyatt calls, "Travel safely!" as he, Nina, and their little ones swim away.

"You too. Bye!" Taleena replies. "Okay, duckies. Let's carry on with the tour!"

Beverly whispers to Lynn, "Nina and Wyatt are nice. Amazing how colliding with their friends in flight gave me the wrong impression of Tundra Swans; I shouldn't have judged them so quickly."

The ducks happily follow Taleena, stopping along the way to make new friends and greeting others that pass by until they find their path blocked by a spirited gathering of three Gadwalls, six American Wigeons, and one very boisterous, animated drake.

"Is that noisy drake a Northern Pintail?" Lynn asks.

"Sure is," answers Taleena. "You can tell by his brown head, and the white stripes that drape down each side of his neck and extend to the white patch on his breast."

Interested to know what the commotion is all about, Taleena stops directly in front of the Pintail Duck and waits for a break between his short bursts of wheezy, train-like whistles to ask, "What's all the fuss about?"

"Do you see the congress of American Bald Eagles lined up on the shore?" he abruptly replies.

The Mallards turn around to look.

"What are they doing?" Harold asks.

The Pintail glares at Harold and snaps, "They're each waiting for their turn."

"Turn for what?" Harold asks, ignoring the Pintail's irritated body language.

Just then, Harold notices the next eagle in line spread his wings wide, strut like a warrior for a few feet, then boldly jump up. Instantly, the eagle is pulled up into the sky, seemingly taken over by a force more powerful than he is.

"He looks like a blur of white and brown," Beverly says as she watches the eagle spin in tight rotations and then slightly slower ones as it goes up, up, up.

As fast as a lightning strike, and before Harold can say, "That's crazy," the eagle reaches the top of the twister and casually rides the cooled-off thermal air current.

Still ignoring the Pintail's body language, Harold asks him, "What is that?"

"It's a mini twister," the Pintail spits out.

"I've heard about those," Markie says.

"You have?" Lynn shouts over the noise of the spectators and the high-pitched screeches of eagles calling out to their friends to join them.

"Small ones like this are less common," Markie comments.

WHAT'S A MINI TWISTER?

When the sun heats a small area on the ground, the air above it heats up and rises, leaving an empty air space. That space instantly fills with cooler air that comes in from all four directions. This rush of air causes a circular corkscrew motion. As the heated air rises, it cools off, and the twister slows down and becomes wider. The process repeats itself until the ground cools off.

Beverly asks Markie, "Some of us have hitched a lazy ride on a thermal current while we are flying but never starting in the twister. Is it safe? I thought we're trying to stay away from wild air so we don't damage our feathers."

"I think it's a ride for wingnuts," Lynn comments.

"I think they're crazy to do it," Harold says.

"I'll show you how it's done," comes a familiar voice from the crowd.

Harold, Lynn, Markie, Beverly, and Taleena turn around to see a familiar face.

"Dylan! What are you doing here?" Beverly asks.

"I told you that I know your route and that I'd try to see you again, little sweet feet," Dylan says, puffing up his armoured-looking chest and flaring his colourful plumage.

Harold's heart sinks as he turns to Markie with a look of shock.

"Hey, Dylan," Markie says, a little too loudly. "Thanks for offering to show us how it's done, but Harold was just about to do that."

With his feathers twitching, Harold whispers to Markie, "I was?"

"Are you going to let Dylan the duckwad try to impress Beverly? You've got this, buddy! You'll do great."

Harold sees Beverly's big brown eyes gazing into Dylan's fiery red ones.

Harold puffs up his chest and looks directly at Dylan. "Yes, I was just going to say that I will show my friends how this ride works," Harold says calmly but with a slight stammer.

Markie gives him a supportive head bob.

"Harold, you were just saying how crazy the whole thing is," Beverly comments.

"Crazy for some, but for others, it's a ride of a lifetime, is what I meant to say."

"Go for it, little duck," Dylan says, issuing a dare.

"I will!" Harold responds defiantly but feeling panicky at the same time.

"Here I go," he says, hoping someone will stop him. But nobody does.

Harold slowly swims to the shore and gets in the lineup. Standing behind three large bald eagles, he feels like a featherweight—insecure and panicked.

With each step, the front of the line gets closer. Harold looks at Markie for emotional support.

With wide eyes and chattering bill, the terror is evident on Harold's face. Markie gives his friend an encouraging nod.

"Markie, should he be doing this?" Beverly asks with great concern.

"He'll be fine! I'd never let my buddy be at risk. He's braver than you think. Heck, he's braver than *he* thinks," Markie assures her.

Beverly watches in fear as Dylan paddles back and forth next to her, waiting for Harold to fail.

"He's next!" Beverly shouts. "I can't watch."

Markie yells, "Hold your wings straight out!"

With all the shrieking and ruckus, no one knows if Harold heard him.

Harold sheepishly gives the crowd one last look before he holds his breath, counts to three, waddles forward, spreads his wings, and flies into the vacuum of centrifugal force. It sucks him in.

"WHOOOOOAAAA!" Harold screams as his stomach surges up to his throat, and the pressure pushes his legs straight back. He tries to catch his breath, feeling every feather on his body being squeezed by the pressure of the air.

Keep your wings out, keep your wings out, he repeats to himself.

As if a supernatural force had taken over his body, he twists like a corkscrew, rapidly spiralling up, up, up.

"Open your eyes, Beverly!" Lynn shouts. "Harold's doing great!"

The crowd cheers him on, but all Harold hears is the whooshing sound of the air in this invisible chamber of motion.

Before he knows it, he's at the top of the thermal twister. Feeling the calmness of the gentle current, he opens his eyes, collects his thoughts, and tries to relax his lightheaded dizziness.

In between random wing flaps, he does a quick check to see if he's missing any feathers, it's all good.

Harold looks down at the spectators trying to locate Beverly, but he can't find her. He decides it's best to watch where he's flying; after all, crashing into an eagle would not be impressive. He looks around and proudly thinks, *I'm flying with the eagles.*

"Having fun flying with us powerful raptors?" a big-headed eagle asks, gliding by with his broad, flat, straight-out wings, and giving Harold 'the eagle eye' with his intimidating yellow eyes and piercing black pupils.

Harold wonders if he's being considered as food or friend, trying not to focus on the eagle's long, yellow-hooked beak that he knows could easily shred him to pieces. A female eagle glides by, even larger in size and just as threatening. To distract himself, Harold wonders whether Oliver the Golden Eagle would dare to tell a bald eagle that it's not a 'true eagle' but rather a sea eagle—especially after getting a close-up view of how the American Bald Eagle dwarfs other raptors.

After enjoying a few unnerving glory laps, Harold decides it's time to return to his birds-of-a-feather flock.

He sees a juvenile eagle, recognizable by its brown body with brown and white mottled wings and mottled tail with a dark band at the end. Slightly less intimidating at this stage than the adults, that will change at around five or six years of age when they develop a white head and tail and yellow beak like their parents. "Excuse me. Where's the exit?" Harold asks.

"Power up your wings and head in a straight line. You'll break through."

"Thank you."

With nervous determination, Harold focuses all his willpower; he speeds up, flapping frantically and breaks through the orbit of circular motion. Breathing a little lighter and feeling like he's somewhat back in control, he anxiously flies to Beverly, Markie, Lynn, and Taleena. As he lands on the water, cheers from surrounding waterfowl greet him. It's a welcome fit for a hero returning from a dangerous assignment. *Maybe this will elevate my aviator status,* he thinks. *Maybe I can even become a member of the KHC!*

He's snapped back to reality by the sound of Beverly's voice. "Harold, WOW! You looked incredible. You were flying with the eagles!" she shouts.

"Great job, buddy! I knew you could do it!" Markie brags.

"You looked like a blur on your ride up," Taleena says.

"What was it like?" Lynn asks.

"Awesome! It's certainly not for the faint of heart," Harold says smugly, looking directly at Dylan.

"Duckling play," Dylan says loud enough for everyone to hear, especially Harold.

"I'll catch up with you later, little sweet feet," Dylan says to Beverly as he swims away.

After Harold enjoys a little celebrity status with the surrounding ducks, Taleena leads the four feathered friends back to their friends at the meetup area that Instructor Riley mentioned earlier.

On the way back, Harold whispers to Markie, "Don't tell the hens, but my knees were knocking when I was waiting in the line. And if that wasn't bad enough, I closed my eyes for most of the ride up because I felt dizzy and my stomach was in knots."

"No worries, buddy. No one could tell. You looked fierce! Beverly certainly is impressed."

Feeling a boost of confidence from successfully braving the unknown, Harold thinks, *Maybe I* am *a warrior after all!*

CHAPTER 15

Back with the flock, most everyone is actively focusing on getting enough to eat and last-minute feather touch-ups. Beverly, however, is visiting every flock member who missed Harold's act of bravery.

"You should have seen him. He twisted so fast that he looked like a blur. He flew with eagles!" she boasts to everyone with their head above water.

Harold realizes that the thermal twister is now an unexpected success of Plan B.

The last remaining streaks of crimson sunset spill onto the lake as the sun slides below the horizon. Nightfall settles in, chilling the air with a biting threat of snowfall. Harold drapes his wing over Beverly to warm her.

The flock huddles together, bobbing on the icy water while they wait for their final flight instructions.

"It's Captain Jayson here! Instructor Riley and I have been going over our flight plan to Algar Lake. We should be landing shortly before sunrise. We'll keep our speed around a comfortable (64 kph) 40 miles per hour, and we'll be flying slightly above the low-flying clouds that you see right now. We might encounter a bit of turbulence, but nothing serious. During migration, we will start every flight in the original V position that we flew on day one. Positions, please! Jayson Air likes to be on schedule."

Drawing from his newly found confidence from the triumphant twister ride, Harold helps Line B get into position. "Susie, you are behind Instructor Riley, then Beverly, me, Lynn, and Markie."

Instructor Riley assists Line A. "Easton, you're first, then Taleena, Davor, Anne, Michael, and Janis at the end. Remember to pace yourselves, count to five between liftoffs, and don't forget to tailgate to save energy."

"You've got this!" Instructor Riley shouts, trying to be heard above the clusters of loud waterfowl on the lake.

With everyone in position, Instructor Riley informs Captain Jayson that they're ready for departure.

Instructor Riley says to the anxious Mallards, "If this is your first night flight, don't worry; you are with good wings. Nothing to be nervous about. You know the drill for takeoff."

Captain Jayson surveys the sights and sounds in the air, on the shore, and on the lake. "Incoming! Standby," he reports.

Boisterous *kow-hoo* calls fill the air as a flock of Tundra Swans make their final approach for a night of rest and food.

Bobbing on the chilly water and enveloped in darkness, Lynn shouts out, "Markie! How will we find our way in the dark?"

"Don't worry, Lynn! You'll soon see that you have excellent night vision. Your instincts will help you read the stars, and you'll feel the magnetic force. Trust our experienced migrators; this isn't our first time."

"Well, it's mine!" Lynn snaps back. "Magnetic force? What's he talking about?" she scoffs.

Captain Jayson analyses the sights and sounds and calls out, "All clear! Ready for takeoff!"

With limited visibility and this being only their second V formation flight, Harold, Beverly, and Lynn anxiously concentrate on what they have learned about takeoffs. Following departure protocol, they each spring up on cue, flapping and calling out as they follow their flock in the darkness.

"After a few flaps in the dark, Markie shouts, "Hey, our flock finally looks like an impressive skein!"

"A what?" Harold shouts over the sound of wings flapping.

"A skein. Ducks in flight," Markie explains.

"If a skein means cold, nervous Mallards, then we are definitely a skein," Beverly jokes.

"We're in darkness, Markie. You can barely see us, so that's why you think we look like an impressive skein!" Taleena laughs.

As time goes on, the flock flaps along while gazing at the billions of stars sprinkled among the moonlit sky.

"Wow! Did you see that?" Beverly shouts out.

Head bobs and enthusiastic oohs confirm that many of the flock saw the shooting star.

"Well, that was a fleeting moment of excitement," Janis comments, "Back to flap, flap, flap, repeat."

"I thought that I would feel warmer," Beverly tells Harold.

"Just keep flapping. You'll warm up."

The ducks continue to flap, quack, and *kreep* their way through the night sky.

"I'm bored and cold," Lynn quacks.

As time goes by, Jayson and Davor both appreciate their resting periods after their turns as Lead Duck. Before takeoff, the senior ducks decided that on this night flight, they would put the fate of the flight in the wings of Easton, with supervision—and the time is now.

"I'm still feeling like a ducksicle," Susie tells Beverly.

"I was told to keep flapping, and eventually, you'll warm up. I'm starting to feel warmer. It's either my flapping or the excessive layers of preening oil I put on," Beverly giggles.

"Harold, my first night flight is not as scary as I thought it would be. Boring, yes; scary, not so much. How about you?" Beverly asks him.

"Easy-peasy. I figure nothing could be scarier than the twister ride, and I did that," Harold boldly explains. But in his mind, he'd been concerned about what a night flight would be like.

"I guess so. You were extremely brave."

The silhouettes of the thirteen ducks are showcased against the backdrop of the moon, but with low-hanging clouds and wilderness below, no one can appreciate this picture-perfect image.

Tonight, the flock are lone travellers on their migration flyway. Tired, bored, and cold, they fall into a rhythm of flapping, quacking, and *kreeping,* until a mysterious glow of neon green catches everyone's attention. Suddenly, the sky comes alive with mystical-looking yellowish-green blazes of colour that move to their own rhythm. Susie, Taleena, Beverly, Lynn, and Harold gasp.

"What's happening?" Susie shouts as her eyes glaze over and her body trembles.

"Nothing to panic over, you lucky ducks! You're experiencing one of nature's wonders, the northern lights!" Instructor Riley explains.

WHAT ARE THE NORTHERN LIGHTS?

The northern lights (aurora borealis) are a result of the collisions between gaseous particles in the Earth's atmosphere and charged particles released from the sun's atmosphere. Different gases give off different colours. The aurora borealis can happen anywhere from approximately (96 km-241 km) 60 to 150 miles above the ground. They mirror themselves in the northern and southern hemispheres, centred over each magnetic pole.

In Norse mythology, the northern lights were thought to be the spears, armour, and helmets of the warrior women known as the Valkyries. They rode on horseback, leading fallen soldiers to their final resting place at Valhalla. The Inuit of Hudson Bay dreaded the lights, believing they were the lanterns of demons pursuing lost souls. In Alaska, Inuit groups saw the lights as the spirits of the animals they had hunted, namely beluga whales, seals, salmon, and deer. The Māori in New Zealand thought the southern lights (aurora australis) were reflections from torches or campfires, and the Indigenous Greenlanders believed that the lights were dancing spirits of children who had died at birth.

"Are we safe?" Susie asks in a squeaky voice, with tears ready to flow.

"Yes, it's safe. It actually doesn't touch you, so relax, keep flapping and calling out, and enjoy the greatest show on Earth," Instructor Riley tells them.

"The sky looks like it's on fire, and we're in the middle of it!" Harold exclaims.

"Too bad it's not warm like fire! These lights are spectacular!" Beverly shouts.

Mesmerized by the fluorescent glow of the yellowish-green rays of light, everyone's eyes are fixated on watching the rippling veils, streamers, arcs, and shooting rays of light as they twist and turn. Oohs and ahhs replace their mundane quacking and *kreep*ing.

"Markie, what's really happening?" Harold asks while everyone listens for the answer.

"This is a solar storm," Markie tells them.

"Yikes! Is there lightning?" Harold says.

"No lightning, but rumour has it that some ducks have heard faint crackling, whizzing, and buzzing sounds. But I've never heard them. Nothing to worry about, buddy."

"Whatever it is, it's mesmerizing!" Beverly says.

"How long do they last?" Lynn asks.

"They can last for a few minutes or hours," Markie replies.

"How come I've never seen it before?" Susie asks.

"The northern lights are best seen during long hours of darkness, and this is your first autumn," Markie explains.

"Are there any other colours?" Lynn asks. "I love, love, love, purple."

"Yes. What we're seeing now is the most common. The blue and violet colours appear at higher altitudes, and the red is at an even higher altitude, which makes them most rare."

"I've seen the blue and violet lights before," Janis says.

"Oh, they would be so beautiful. I hope I get to see them sometime," Lynn comments.

The ducks have temporarily forgotten how cold, tired, and bored they are as they watch the light show in complete wonder.

"What's happening? Am I flying straight or crooked? Where are we going?" Beverly shouts to Harold.

"You're doing great!" Harold reassures her, even though he senses something's wrong.

"I'm feeling a little dizzy! Anyone else feeling dizzy?" Lynn shouts.

Harold notices that Jayson, Instructor Riley, Michael, and Davor are exchanging low-toned calls.

"Easton, what's up? We're flying a little wonky!" Jayson yells.

"What?"

"You're leading us off course! You're flying up, down, and sideways, and everyone's following you!" Davor comments.

"You're getting everyone dizzy!" Michael shouts.

"I am? I thought I was flying straight. I think the lights are playing with my mind," Easton explains as he continues dipping and diving.

"Michael, take the lead!" Instructor Riley directs.

"I'm on it!" Michael says, moving from the fourth position between Taleena and Janis to Lead Duck.

Easton, looking puzzled and confused, falls back to the back of Line A behind Jayson.

"Easton, you did a great job, but it's time for you to rest," Jayson tells him.

Michael concentrates, determined not to be tricked by the hypnotizing light show.

"Phew! I'm starting to feel better. Not so dizzy," Lynn says.

Michael expertly leads the flock back on course, and everyone goes back to enjoying the spectacular phenomenon.

"Prepare for landing!" Michael alerts the flock.

Circling once around Algar Lake, Michael picks a prime resting location. Two by two, the exhausted ducks land safely on the cold and slightly choppy water.

"Can we just have an uneventful flight for once?" Beverly asks Lynn, not really expecting an answer.

"Wouldn't that be boring?" Lynn replies.

"I guess so," Beverly reluctantly agrees.

Now in need of rest and food, the flock huddles together, tipping up and feasting on similar water plants and insects as they have in their marsh in Havenwood Cove. Relaxed, they swim around in the shallow water—close to the shore, but not close enough to be a predator's early bird special.

"Looking at the aurora's yellowish-green glow reflecting on the water, I can't decide if it looks magical or eerie. I'm just too hungry and exhausted to really give it serious thought," Beverly says to Harold.

"Just think of it as dinner and a show!" Harold says. And with that, they continue their feast with the northern lights acting as an enchanted backdrop.

With full stomachs, the flock decides to get some shuteye before sunrise. While settling in, everyone notices that Easton's quieter than usual, and he's drifting away from the flock.

"What's wrong, Easton?" Jayson asks with great concern. Curious to hear his answer, everyone leans in closer to eavesdrop.

"I feel like I did a bad job of leading. I thought I was flying right, but maybe I wasn't," Easton says softly, his head dropped against his chest.

"You did an admirable job, Easton! You're young, and in time you'll learn how to counteract the challenges of the northern lights and the influence it has on our instinctive magnetic forces,"* Jayson promises.

Easton looks up to find himself surrounded by his friends, who are clacking their bills and pumping their heads to show they support him. He gives them an appreciative little *kreep*.

Lined up and snuggling together, the tuckered-out ducks prepare for sleep. Davor and Michael are on predator watch, so they will be the only ones who won't be able to get a full night's rest. They'll each keep one eye open and half of their brain awake, listening for noises and paying attention to movements in the water, waking instantly and alerting the flock of possible danger. And tonight, they'll also benefit from nature's glowing, yellowish-green night light.

The flock wakes to a slightly chillier morning. Are these snowflakes?" Susie asks Harold.

"I think so. It's my first winter, too," Harold replies.

"They're much more delicate and pretty than the icy bits that cover us during the night. I thought we would be in warm weather already," Beverly comments to Harold.

"Markie... wakey, wakey!" Lynn says, giving him a light bump. "When

---

*The northern lights have been linked to disruptions in power lines, magnetic compasses, and radar equipment—even on planes!

are we going to be south—the *real* south? The place where you said we will spend our winter in warm weather, swimming in warm water, and with fine dining—where exactly is that?" Lynn asks, hoping for answers.

"And a good morning to you, too," Markie says, his eyes still half closed.

Instructor Riley can see that everything is right on schedule; the newbie migrators are restless and discouraged, so today is the day for "the talk."

Hungry and cold, the flock seeks out food on the shore and in the shallow, marshy area. After dining on a very familiar menu, most everyone spends time rearranging and waterproofing their dishevelled feathers.

Harold, Beverly, and Lynn watch Markie join Instructor Riley, Michael, and Jayson in a private chit-chat.

"What do you think they're up to?" Beverly asks Harold.

"Don't know."

Markie swims back to his three feathered friends.

"What's happening, Markie?" Harold asks.

With a blank look on his face, Markie replies, "Nothing, really. Instructor Riley is going to get all the newbies together for a short meeting. This happens every fall during our trip south. It's kind of like an extension of the migration meeting we had at Havenwood Cove."

"What more is there to talk about? We learned how to tailgate, follow the Lead Duck, make noise, preen regularly, eat and sleep," Lynn says.

"And we're not smashing into each other," Beverly adds.

"There's a little more to migration than that. There's…" Markie's explanation is interrupted by an announcement.

"Listen up, first-time migrators! Please join me for a brief meeting," Instructor Riley says loudly.

Harold, Beverly, and Lynn exchange a skeptical glance.

Harold comments, "Oh, I bet she just wants to tell us how impressive our flying skills are."

The three newbies, with Susie and Taleena in tow, swim towards Instructor Riley. "You coming, Markie?" Lynn asks.

"No, but just remember that everything will be fine. Keep in mind that I have already done a round-trip migration, and I'm okay."

"Oh, that doesn't sound good. What does he mean by that?" Beverly says, as her stomach starts flip-flopping. "I think this meeting is much more than Instructor Riley telling us we've done a good job."

All the first-time migrators paddle in place in front of Instructor Riley, anxiously waiting for her to start the meeting. From the corner of his eye, Harold sees Markie huddled together with all the experienced migrators and whispering, giving quick glances at the newbies, then going back to whispering. Harold's feathers start twitching.

"So, how is everyone feeling?" Instructor Riley asks.

"Good," Harold says. Taleena nods in agreement.

"Fine," Beverly replies.

"I'm tired and cold, but I'm good," Lynn comments.

"Okay, I guess," Susie says.

"Wonderful!" Instructor Riley replies, cheerfully upbeat. "We come to Algar Lake because the airways are less busy, it's on our route, and Sir Lloyd's brothers Bill and Bob live here. We give them updates on how Sir Lloyd is doing, and on our spring migration north, we'll stop here, catch up on their news, and then relay it back to Sir Lloyd when we return to Havenwood Cove. Algar Lake is the perfect quiet spot for us to recharge before our next stop, the prairie potholes," Instructor Riley explains.

The newbies think this all sounds fine and good; perhaps they over-reacted and stressed themselves for no reason. Beverly's stomach stops churning, Harold's feathers stop twitching, and Susie, Taleena, and Lynn happily tread water.

"Markie's mentioned the prairie potholes a few times. They sound exciting, whatever they are," Beverly comments.

"The prairie pothole region is a paradise destination for waterfowl like us. Natural grasslands and wetlands of shallow pools of water for as far as your eyes can see. It's nicknamed the 'duck factory,'" Instructor Riley chuckles, giving them a wink.

Amused, the newbies clack their bills and pump their heads up and down.

"Are you bored, eating from the same menu day after day?" Instructor Riley asks.

Mutters of "yes" and "sure" rise from the crowd as heads nod in agreement.

"Be prepared to excite your taste buds, because you're in for a real treat with a larger variety of eats! Many of the ponds are the perfect shallow depth for us dabbling ducks to tip up and reach delicious plant roots and juicy critters hiding in the mud." Instructor Riley tells the eager flock. "You'll have lots of tall grasses to hide in while you sleep, preen, feed, and socialize. Best of all, some areas have ginormous fields that offer a smorgasbord of tasty grains—a ready-to-eat buffet! One of our favourite first stops is the Lutz Farm."

"I can hardly wait!" Beverly says.

"Me too!" Susie says, giddy with excitement.

"And you were worried that we would lose half of our body weight on this migration. I don't think so!" Lynn jokes.

"Wow! This all sounds amazing," Taleena says.

"Now, there is one drawback to this paradise," Instructor Riley warns.

"I knew this was going too well," Lynn whispers to Beverly.

A feeling of uneasiness settles over the group as they wait for Instructor Riley to tell them the rest of the story.

CHAPTER 16

"What could be worse than coyotes?" Harold wonders out loud.

The other newbies look at him, wide-eyed, wondering the same thing.

"You need to be aware of the human predator. They are dangerous. They travel alone or in packs. They hide in tall grasses or in the water. We are their prey. We put ourselves in grave danger if we let ourselves be fooled by their devious tricks," Instructor Riley tells the newbies.

"What kind of tricks?" Susie asks.

"They put imitations of us called decoys on the water so we think it's safe to land, then they try to lure us closer by imitating our quack and *kreep* calls. When you hear deafening *BOOM, BOOM, BOOM* sounds, it's already too late. You are being attacked. You MUST get away immediately! Focus only on yourself and flap your wings as fast and as hard as you can to escape. The air will be alive with bursts of hard, lethal pebbles coming at you from all directions. They're out to hurt you or worse," Instructor Riley tells the frightened newbies.

"What could be worse than being hurt?" asks a glassy-eyed Susie.

"Death," Instructor Riley replies.

Her answer shocks the group. Harold, Beverly, Lynn, Susie, and Taleena stop paddling as they try to catch their breath.

"But why? Why do they want to do this to us?" Lynn asks, her voice quivering.

"For food or sport," Instructor Riley says.

"That's horrible. Don't they know we have feelings, friends, and family? Don't we deserve to have a nice life?" Lynn replies, feeling distressed.

"Migration is serious. Just follow the Lead Duck's instructions. Your leaders will always do their best to keep the flock safe. We have exceptional hearing, and most times, we can distinguish fake calls, but sometimes our predators have practiced those calls and they can fool us. And even though we have exceptional eyesight and can see two to three times farther than humans, that only works to our advantage if we stay focused on our surroundings. Remember that many of us have done multiple migrations, and we are still here. Stay positive! Warm weather and good times are still ahead," Instructor Riley says, as positively as she can, in an effort to console the traumatized newbies.

"Why has no one ever told us about this?" Harold blurts.

"We don't want to stress first-time migrators with too much information all at once. We'll always prepare you the best we can," Instructor Riley says, noticing Harold, Beverly, and Lynn are shooting daggers from their eyes, glaring at Markie.

"Don't be upset with your friends for not telling you; they are sworn to secrecy. They also attended a meeting like this when they were newbies," Instructor Riley says, trying to prevent anger and hurt feelings. "I suggest you go and think about these things and maybe grab a bite to eat. We'll continue this meeting a bit later."

"There's more?" Beverly shrieks, as she and the rest of the first-time migrators swim away.

Davor watches as Taleena swims toward him, knowing it won't be a pleasant conversation.

"Markie! We need to talk with you NOW, please," Harold calls out from a distance.

Jayson and the other experienced migrators each wish Markie good luck as he swims away to talk to his friends, knowing full well what he is in for.

Markie takes a deep breath and concentrates on sounding upbeat to defuse Harold's anger. "So, how did your meeting go? When I had mine, it was a bit rough."

"Why didn't you warn me? We're buddies!" Harold asks, outraged.

"We're the four feathered adventurers," Lynn reminds Markie.

"You told us everything will be okay. We trusted you, Markie," Beverly says, her body trembling.

Overwhelmed, Susie quietly paddles in place with a blank stare.

"No, no, no! I'm done with this whole migration thing. I'm going back home," Beverly says as she looks at Harold.

"You can't. There's no food for us there," Harold tells her.

"I don't care. I'll live with Benjamin and Betty in their lodge. They let Marty muskrat stay with them when his home was destroyed. I'm sure they'll have something I can eat. Or I can spend the winter with Wanda in her den. Don't worry about me; I'll find my way back to Havenwood Cove. I was paying attention as we flew, plus I think my instinct to read the stars and feel the magnetic field, whatever that is, is kicking in," Beverly tells Harold.

"I'll go with you," Lynn says.

"Wait a minute, you two. I know you're in shock, but remember that we live every day and every minute with possible threats towards us. Instructor Riley was just giving you a tough love speech to help prepare you for the worst-case scenario. Just keep thinking about how nice it will be to swim in warm water, bask in the sun, and enjoy fine dining," Markie reminds them.

"And when exactly does that happen?" Lynn asks impatiently.

"Soon," Markie replies as he and Harold share a look, knowing that soon is not really soon at all.

"It better be," Beverly threatens.

Markie swims over to Instructor Riley to let her know that it's best not to call the newbies back to finish the meeting just yet as Harold says, "Why don't we look around Algar Lake and get something to eat?"

"Good idea. I'm hungry!" Beverly says.

"Me too. You coming, Susie?" Lynn asks.

"Harold," Beverly whispers. "There's an owl circling above us."

Looking up, Harold sees enormous yellow eyes scanning the flock.

The newbies huddle together, nervously bobbing close to the shore in between clumps of dried grasses, when they hear Jayson call out, "Bob?"

"Jayson! I thought that was you," the Great Horned Owl says before silently gliding to a nearby leafless, trembling aspen tree and perching on a sturdy branch.

Multiple greetings of "Hi Bob" come from the experienced migrators.

"Where's Bill?" Instructor Riley asks.

Bob lets out an alarming screech that rattles the ducks' nerves. The next thing the flock sees is a second Great Horned Owl fly in and perch close to him.

"Welcome back, everyone! We didn't hear you fly in. We must have been out for dinner," Bill says before making weird facial movements, opening his curved beak, extra wide, and spitting out an owl pellet.

WHAT ARE OWL PELLETS?

An owl eats its prey (mice, rabbits, birds, and ducks) either whole or in chunks. An owl pellet is formed in the owl's gizzard by combining and compressing indigestible materials like the skull, teeth, bones, feathers, and fur of its prey. Within six to ten hours after the prey has been eaten, one or two pellets are regurgitated (vomited) and spit out. Many different birds, like eagles, hawks, kingfishers, crows, jays, shorebirds, and songbirds, also form pellets of various sizes. Regurgitation also benefits the bird by cleaning its digestive tract, including the gullet.

The flock watches as the pellet drops to the ground with a thud.

"Gross!" Lynn says.

"Wait for it. There might be one more, depending on how much he ate last night," Markie tells her.

"Double gross! I'm not looking," Susie says.

"So, how's Lloyd, our dear brother? Or should I say, *Sir* Lloyd?" Bill asks, with a lighthearted *hoo-hoo hooooo hoo-hoo*.

"He's doing great," Instructor Riley tells the brothers. "He told me to tell you that he misses you both and to come back home."

"No can do," Bob says. "We know it's not like a Great Horned Owl to move far away from where we were born, but Bill and I had enough of the cold weather up north; we decided to break tradition and head south."

"And how's that working out for you?" Jayson asks.

The owl brothers shrug and lock eyes, then Bill turns to face the flock and says, "Well, it's not exactly as we'd hoped. It's still cold here, so we're trying to decide if we should move farther south. Unlike you Mallards, we have food here all year so there's no panic, but it would be nice to be in a warmer climate. We'll keep you posted."

Instructor Riley nods and says, "We're here for a couple of days, and then we're off to the grain fields and the prairie pothole region. We'll be back here on our spring trip north; will you still be here?"

"Should be. Staying put this winter and next spring but don't know about after that," Bob answers.

"Okay, we'll see you then," Instructor Riley tells them.

"Beware of old Earl, our resident coyote. We heard that he dug a den under the nearby low-growing shrubs just past the white spruce over there," Bob warns the group, pointing with his wing toward the spruce. "He usually sleeps during the day, but he's been known to wander around day or night if he's really hungry. We warned him not to bother you, but sometimes he can't be trusted—he's a cranky old canine. Bob and I will fly over occasionally and check on you," Bill says.

"Much appreciated. We know all too well about coyotes," Jayson replies, thinking about Prudence.

"Okay, we're off to get some sleep. Daytime's not really our thing," Bob *hoo-hoo hooooo hoo-hoo*'s.

Bill and Bob spread their fluffy, feathered wings* and silently disappear among the balsam and aspen trees.

Harold whispers to Beverly, "It's nice hearing the same *hoo-hoo hooooo hoo-hoo*'s as Sir Lloyd. They make me feel at home. I miss everyone."

"I miss Havenwood Cove and our friends, too," Beverly says, snuggling close to him.

"How did everyone like the night flight?" Instructor Riley asks the flock.

A chorus of "amazing!" rises from the group.

"Just missing purple. One cannot get enough purple. Look, even my speculum feathers are violet, which is close to purple," Lynn says, flaring her wings to demonstrate.

"Will we see them again?" Beverly asks.

"We might," Instructor Riley answers. "But let's talk about our next flight. Jayson, Michael, Davor, and I have discussed our upcoming flight to the Lutz Farm grain fields and the prairie pothole region.

"Every migration is a little different, and we have to adjust on the fly. We have our favourite spots to rest and feed, but sometimes they're gone—destroyed by floods, drought, or humans. If things have changed when we get there, we have no choice but to keep travelling. It doesn't matter if we're hungry and tired. Jayson and I have a sense that winter is coming sooner than we expected, which means that the fields, wetlands, and prairie potholes could be covered in ice and snow, leaving us with little or no food."

"I'm back to thinking about living with Benjamin and Betty beaver," Beverly whispers to Harold.

---

*The broad, rounded wings of Great Horned Owls have a velvety texture, with a soft fringe on the edges to muffle the sound of the airflow around them.

"We'll be fine," Harold reassures her, although he's equally concerned about their fate.

"So far, our flights have been half the distance of what we are capable of, so we can make our rest stop here at Algar Lake a bit shorter. How does departing here tomorrow morning at dawn sound?" Instructor Riley asks the flock.

HOW FAR CAN THE FLOCK FLY?

During migration, waterfowl fly an average of (64-96 kph) 40–60 miles per hour. They usually stop for 3–7 days to feed and rest after an 8-hour flight. Some ducks have travelled (1287 km) 800 miles in one day with a (79 kph) 49 mph tailwind. They fly at an altitude of (61 m-1219 m) 200–4,000 feet above the ground. A Mallard was recorded travelling at an altitude of (6401 m) 21,000 feet, which is dangerously in the airplane zone.

The newbies huddle together to discuss this option while the experienced migrators calmly wait for their decision.

Acting as "spokesduck" for the first-time migrators, Harold says, "Yes, the sooner we get south, the better. Shorter flights with shorter rest times work the best for us."

"South can't come soon enough for me," Lynn adds.

"I can't imagine flying a longer distance in one go," Susie says.

"Janis, how's your wing?" Instructor Riley asks.

"Oh, it's fine. I think the shorter flights are better for me. But I do notice it's getting a little stronger with each flight," she says—trying to sound convincing.

"Good," Instructor Riley says, somewhat convinced.

"Go and enjoy your day, stay safe, and we'll take off tomorrow morning at dawn. Be back here just before sunset. It's safer to sleep as a flock so we can all watch out for old Earl," Instructor Riley advises, then swims to the shore to forage.

The ducks spend the day eating, grooming, and resting. As nighttime settles in and the temperature plummets, everyone huddles together and prepares for sleep; legs and feet tucked close to their bodies, feathers fluffed, heads resting on backs, and bills slipped under back feathers. Hiding among a cluster of withered bulrushes, they hope that they're far enough offshore and away from old Earl.

As the harsh north wind rustles the bulrushes and scrubs their bodies, they're comforted knowing that they are protected by their predator alert team of Markie and Harold, with backup assistance from Bob and Bill. With only a sliver of moonlight and no glowing, mystical nightlight, they fall asleep, to friendly, protective, deep, and booming *hoo-hoo, hooooo, hoo-hoo*'s.

Just before sunrise, the ducks wake to another chilly morning—and a nasty odour wafting in the air.

"Gross! It smells like Squire when he's upset," Beverly says as she opens her eyes and shakes the icy bits from her feathers.

"Ugh! I miss Squire, but not his 'special scent,'" Harold says, gagging.

"Did you get any sleep last night?" Beverly asks Harold, trying to hold her breath.

"Sort of. At least half of my brain got some sleep. Being on predator watch is a big responsibility. And then that smell arrived! Markie and I have been breathing that sickening odour for a while. We decided it wasn't a threat other than to our noses, so we let you sleep," he tells her in a serious tone, his head held high.

"Thank you for that. With you and Markie on duty, I fell asleep right away," she tells him.

"Mission accomplished!" Harold boasts.

"So Markie, what's up with the stinky air?" Lynn asks.

"I think Bill or Bob either upset or dined on a skunk during the night.

Great Horned Owls have great hearing and eyesight, but lucky for them, a poor sense of smell," Markie tells her.

"Eat up, everyone! We'll be departing, and none too soon with the stench," Instructor Riley says, her warm breath lingering in the foul, nippy air.

They all anxiously forage for food to rebuild their energy reserves for their flight. Many are concerned about when and where they will be able to eat again.

"Okay, time to get airborne. Positions, please!" Captain Jayson says.

The flock promptly works as a team to get into their V position.

With his wings extended and resting on the slightly choppy water, Harold watches Jayson begin his pre-flight check. *One day, I'll be Captain Harold, esteemed member of the KHC, and Beverly will be impressed,* he thinks.

"All good to the north. All good to the east," Captain Jayson says as he squints with the first rays of sunlight hindering his vision. "All clear south. All clear west. Ready for takeoff."

Instructor Riley does a quick last-minute check to be sure that everyone's in position. Pleased with what she sees, she gives the flock a head bob, then starts counting to five. On cue, Jayson springs out of the air, *kreep*ing loudly as he gains altitude. He gradually banks to the southeast, and two by two, the flock becomes airborne. *If Jayson could look back, he'd be impressed that we newbies are becoming skilled flyers—perfect pacing and drafting,* Harold thinks.

Bill and Bob are fast asleep, missing this flawless departure.

CHAPTER 17

"**H**ere we go again: quack, *kreep*, flap, repeat," Beverly says to Harold.

"It's all going to be worth it!"

"I hope so. Do you know how many more flights we have till we are south?" she asks.

"Oh, not many. Just keep flapping," he tells her, remembering that Markie told him that there are lots and he's doing his best to hide the disappointing truth.

Time goes by slowly. The sun's rays gradually warm the air from biting cold to just plain chilly. Davor is in position as Lead Duck as the brisk northerly wind bashes into the left side of the ducks on their southeasterly flight.

"I'm trying my best to follow, but the wind is so strong that it's trying to blow me off course," Beverly shouts to Harold.

"Yes, it's persistent. You're doing great, you little adventurer!"

"Janis, how are you managing with the wind and your sore wing?" Harold asks.

"I'm a tough old bird, Harold. I'll just fight the current like the rest of you," she tells him as she struggles to stay on course.

"I'm bored, cold, and getting tired," Lynn announces to anyone who can hear her.

"Me too. Same old views—trees, a few open patches, a little water here and there. Nothing new and exciting. So what's the big deal with this migration?" Beverly says.

"Yeah!" Taleena and Susie agree.

"Oh, just you wait. Thrilling new landscapes and eats are coming up. Just keep flapping," Anne tells them.

"Promises, promises," Beverly says.

Harold hears Beverly's frustration. *This is not good. Markie and I need to talk about Plan B and come up with something to wow Beverly right away,* Harold tells himself.

Just as Markie opens his mouth to make a joke to all the bored newbies, the sky suddenly darkens, the temperature plummets, and the wind blows in with a vengeance, bringing pounding snow with it.

"What happened to the sun?" Beverly yells, beating her wings as hard and as fast as she can to counteract the strong wind.

"The wind's slamming me. I'm trying my hardest to fly straight!" Beverly shouts.

"Me too!" Lynn bellows, but the wind carries her voice away.

Markie looks around. "Oh, this isn't good. Be prepared!" he shouts to Harold.

"For what?" Harold yells.

"What's happening?" Taleena shouts.

"Help me, Harold! I can't see anything," Beverly screams.

"Keep flapping and quacking. I'm here!" Harold shouts.

Instructor Riley hollers, "Stay calm! We're in a blizzard. We have to fly through it. Focus on the bird in front of you. Call out as loud as you can."

The air is filled with frightened, riotous quacks and *kreep*s, mostly from the first-time migrators. Their boisterous voices are quickly fading as the powerful, howling winds sweep them away.

Panicked, Beverly says to herself, *I'll never complain about being bored again. Never, never, never!* "Harold!" she shouts. "The wind is trying to twist my wings!"

"I'm right behind you. Keep flapping!" Harold yells, even though he can only faintly see her in the whiteout.

"My feathers hurt, the snow's stinging my eyes, and I can't see!" Beverly shrieks, but Harold only hears "feathers" and "eyes."

Harold feels powerless. He can't help her. He can't even help himself.

"I can't see anything! I don't know if I'm flying straight or in circles! What do I do?" Susie shouts as the snow pounds against her body.

"Stay with me, Susie! Can you see me?" Instructor Riley shouts.

"Barely!" Susie squeals.

"We'll get through it!" Instructor Riley yells to the flock, but her message is lost to the raging wind.

"You're doing great!" Markie shouts to Lynn.

"Keep calling out!" Instructor Riley shouts, her message once again broken by the howling wind.

On wings and a lot of prayers, twelve exhausted, frenzied ducks battled their way through the freak storm.

With wind-scorched feathers and a whirlwind of emotions, everyone eventually settles down and starts to relax, ultimately going back to calmly calling out and flapping.

Clear, calm, cold skies ahead.

"Look!" Beverly shouts, noticing the forested area opening up to an expanse of fields as far as she can see.

"What are we flying over?" Lynn asks.

"That's a road for humans to travel on in their cars and trucks. We never want to land on those. Splat." Markie tells her.

"What are those?" Beverly asks as the ducks fly over a farmhouse and barn.

"That's where humans live," Jayson answers.

"Humans?" Taleena asks.

"Humans are a different species than we are. Remember when I said some humans are nice and some are predators?" Instructor Riley reminds the flock.

"Right," Beverly whispers as she recalls the shocking conversation warning about ducks being viewed as "food or sport."

Beverly has a sickening feeling that's something wrong. Panicked, her head whiplashes as she frantically looks around. Her heart pounds, her stomach churns, and with terror in her voice, she screams, "WHERE'S SUSIE?"

The horrified flock looks around, realizes she's missing, and begins calling out for her.

"She's not with us!" Harold shouts.

Hysterical, Beverly screams, "We lost her in the blizzard!" Her body shivers and she starts to feel lightheaded. "I should have kept an eye on her, but I couldn't see anything. The wind muffled our calls. We need to go back and find her. She's all alone!"

Davor instantly leads the flock back around to retrace their path.

In total desperation, everyone calls out Susie's name over and over as they scour both the skies and the ground. They search for what feels like hours, but with no Susie in sight, Instructor Riley makes the difficult decision to turn back. In her most calming, steady voice, she tells the heartbroken flock, "I'm so sorry, but we'll have to turn around and get back on our course. Let's all pray that she will find her way to us."

Devastated, the flock quietly turns around, leaving Susie to fend for herself in the cold—and soon, in the dark of night.

"I should have looked after her," Beverly whimpers.

"It's not your fault. The blizzard blinded all of us. We had to fight the winds to stay on course the best we could, and it carried our voices away. We were all in survival mode," Harold reminds her.

"But it could have been me," Beverly says helplessly.

"I will never leave you," Harold tells her.

"It could have been any one of us; it's no one's fault. We are always a flap of a wing away from catastrophe. Let's have some faith that Susie is more competent than we have given her credit for," Instructor Riley says gently.

Everyone nods, hoping that she's right.

"How's everyone holding up physically?" Instructor Riley asks.

"How's your wing, my little feather duster?" Michael asks Janis.

"Still attached, but sore," she tells him.

With sore wings and broken spirits, the flock of twelve softly call out and flap their way to their destination.

Harold, Beverly, Lynn, and Taleena take in the wonder of the new landscape: wide-open fields full of rows of golden-yellow-coloured stubble and swaths of loosely mounded barley stems laid out to dry.

"You're going to love it here. I call it 'Marvellous Mallards' Migration Mealtime Medley and Meetup.' Catchy, right?" Anne chuckles.

"I've never seen anything like this before," Harold says, still a little unsure of what Anne is talking about.

Trying to help, Instructor Riley adds, "To you first-time migrators, welcome to Saskatchewan, Canada's breadbasket province. This is Mallard dining at its finest!"

"Sask…. what?" Lynn asks.

"Attention, please!" Instructor Riley directs. "We have left the wilderness, and now we are approaching new terrain with new challenges. Human predators often wait around here for us to arrive. Remember their trickery. All eyes on duty. Davor will lead us in. First, we will do a fly-by to make sure it's safe to land. If ambushed, always remember to protect yourself first. We'll meet up when safe. Good luck, everyone! Davor, please prepare us for arrival."

"This sounds serious," Beverly says to Harold, her voice trembling.

"Just follow Davor's lead. He'll make sure we're okay," Harold encourages her, although his feathers are starting to twitch.

Flying over the frosty field, the flock cautiously quacks and *kreep*s.

"I don't see any real or fake ducks, and I don't hear any real *or* strangely unique-sounding duck calls. That's a good sign. But our human predators still can be lurking about," Markie warns. "Keep watching for anything unusual!"

"How will I know what's out of place or strange when I've never seen terrain like this before?" Beverly asks Harold.

"I was just thinking the same thing. I have no idea."

The newbies nervously follow Davor as they scan the landscape.

After a once-around fly-by, Davor leads the flock on the final approach onto the grain field.

Two by two, the ducks call out as each line touches down on a narrow strip of soil between rows of stubble.

Harold thinks of Susie, missing her. He recalls her memorable, not-so-perfect ground landing that was the talk of the marsh for a month.

"You've got this, Beverly!" Harold shouts.

Watching Instructor Riley, Beverly carefully lines herself up to follow her lead.

"Ouch, ouch, ouch!" Beverly says as her right foot kicks a rock, toppling her off-kilter. Her right wing scrapes along the tops of the stiff, straw-like stubble before she comes to a complete stop. It's a comedy of errors that she doesn't feel is so funny.

Oh, that's gotta hurt, Harold thinks, cringing as he watches Beverly's landing.

With the flock safely grounded, Harold, Beverly, Lynn, and Taleena stand in awe, surrounded by rows of golden-brown-coloured stubble evenly cut to the height of the tops of their legs.

"There's not much room to move unless you want to get poked and prodded," Beverly comments.

"Don't spread your wings or you'll feel like you are being stung by a swarm of angry bees," Anne cautions.

"This is nothing like what we have at home," Beverly says to Harold.

"Ouch!" Taleena blurts. "The sticks are jabbing me."

"What are those?" Harold asks Markie, pointing to a long row of mounded stalks that are slightly taller than he is.

"I'll show you. Follow me. Keep your wings closed so they don't get scratched up," Markie forewarns.

Markie carefully waddles up, down, and over rows of dirt and stubble, bending and flattening each stiff plant with every stomp of his large orange webbed feet. "Follow my path. Your feathers won't get so roughed up," Markie suggests.

"I think it's too late. I have been jabbed every which way," Beverly laughs.

"We are definitely going to need a preening party and foot massage," Lynn suggests.

"I'll preen your feathers for you," Harold whispers to Beverly.

"Oh, you naughty drake!" Beverly teases.

Markie stops beside a swath, which is a loosely mounded row of grain, cut and stacked to dry and ripen before being harvested.

"Watch and learn."

Markie stretches his neck, opens his bill, nips off the end of the barley stem with the spike and seeds, tilts his head back, and gobbles it down.

Harold, Beverly, Lynn, and Taleena watch with skepticism.

"What are you waiting for?" Markie asks, picking up his next spike tip to devour its seeds.

Harold picks a spike end, nips it off, tilts his head back, and gobbles it down.

"Come on, hens! You're going to love it," Harold tells them.

Beverly, still unsure about this new food group, daintily picks a spike and tries to nibble at its seeds, but they come apart and drop. Markie watches her picking them up one by one off the ground.

Frustrated, Markie says, "No, no, no. That's not how you eat barley! Watch me and repeat: grab, gobble, gulp. Got it?"

"Got it," Beverly says before demonstrating her way of grab, gobble, gulp, gulp. "That was a long one, so it needed two gulps," Beverly giggles. "I added the fancy two-step and tail wiggle for effect. What do you think?"

"Congratulations! You've mastered it," Markie tells her.

Like a floorshow act, Harold, Beverly, Lynn, and Taleena dance around chanting, "Grab, gobble, gulp, cha, cha, cha! Grab, gobble, gulp, cha, cha, cha!" in between gorging on barley spikes.

Markie rolls his eyes at their performance and goes back to feasting.

The newbies quickly replace their fancy *cha, cha, cha* dance routine with an improved time management routine of squat and devour. After all, they don't want to hurt the farmer's feelings by not eating the beautiful buffet he has spread out for them.

Little do the ducks know that the farmers grow barley, wheat, canola, rye, oats, mustard, lentils, and field peas for human consumption in cereals, breads, flour, condiments, and beer—but that none of it is for them.

Anne plots her route as she boldly waddles over to the newbies. "So, was I right, or was I right, when I told you the grain fields are amazing?"

Harold, Beverly, and Lynn nod in agreement and continue wolfing down barley seeds.

"Barley is tasty, and it's easier to eat than wheat which has a protective sheath, but wait till you try field peas. They're my favourite! They tickle as they roll down your throat," Anne says, waddling away to find her perfect location to squat and dine.

Feeling full and happy but exhausted from the events of the day, everyone cuddles together in a row. Leaning up against a swath mound offers some protection from predators and chilly drafts. In the darkness, their thoughts go to Susie and how she's out there, alone in the cold, with dangers lurking.

"Goodnight, Beverly," Harold says softly, giving her a little peck on her cheek.

"Goodnight, Harold. And goodnight, Susie—wherever you are," she whispers.

CHAPTER 18

As the ducks close their eyes to sleep, Easton and Jayson begin their shift as predator patrol. With a danger alert time of only seconds, they keenly listen to all noises, including the rustling sounds on the stubble—the friendly and curious prairie dogs and the predatory red foxes and coyotes. In the near distance, they hear "Porter! Porter, come here!" from Farmer Lutz's young daughter, Brooklyn, calling to her barking dog. The crunching sound of tires on a frosty gravel road is the only background music for the ducks tonight. Occasionally, car lights sweep over the field, casting eerie shadows that frighten the grazing white-tailed deer.

The flock wakes just before sunrise in a field dusted with snow.

Feeling frustrated by the ongoing cold, Lynn nudges Markie and asks once again, "Exactly when will we be waking to warm weather?"

"Soon," Markie tells her as he shakes the icy bits off his crispy feathers.

"Like I haven't heard that before," Lynn says grumpily as she puffs up her feathers and begins preening.

"Good guarding job last night," Michael tells Easton and Jayson.

"Thanks," Easton replies.

Jayson nods.

"Let's eat!" Davor announces to the group.

As the sun rises, the Mallards waddle about, gorging on barley seeds.

"Even though this buffet is amazing, Havenwood Cove is still the best," Beverly says to Harold.

Harold nods. "It sure is. But I do like all this barley!"

In between grab, gobble, and gulps, Markie asks Lynn and others that are nearby, "Do you know why Saskatchewan is called 'Land of Living Skies?'"

"Hmmmmmm. No. Why?" Lynn asks.

"Because the weather is unpredictable. Faster than you can say 'get your ducks in a row,' a sunny day can turn to a black sky with cracking sounds of lighting and rumbling thunder. You can watch a dust storm sweep across the wide-open prairie or see a twister form as it comes your way. That's scary, but being thumped on by hailstones is the worst. They hurt. Expect the unexpected, I say!" Markie explains.

"One blizzard was enough drama for me," Beverly comments.

Thoughts of Susie are on everyone's mind.

"I thought we were a team. We can't leave Susie alone out there to fend for herself. I'll go and look for her," Harold says to Instructor Riley.

"I really appreciate your concern and wanting to help, Harold, but this is your first migration, and we don't need you getting lost."

"I'll go with him," Markie tells Instructor Riley.

"Can I have everyone's attention for a moment, especially the first-time migrators?" Instructor Riley asks. "We don't like to talk about this, but sometimes not everyone makes the full trip during migration."

The newbies look at each other, trying to comprehend what they just heard.

"What if it were me? Would you just leave me?" Taleena asks Davor.

"We do our best to look after one another, but sometimes…" Instructor Riley's voice trails off, unsure how to finish her thought.

All eyes turn to Jayson as Instructor Riley asks, "Jayson, how would you feel about venturing out to do one more search for Susie?"

"Be happy to; she needs us! Our flock isn't complete without her," Jayson says, primed and ready to go.

"Great! You know our schedule and route. The flock will carry on to our favourite pothole today, and you can meet up with us there," Instructor Riley tells him.

"Wish me luck! I'll join you later, hopefully with Susie," Jayson says, turning around and waddling to a perfect takeoff location. With a nod to the optimistic, cheering crowd, Jayson lets out an exuberant *kreep* as he spreads his wings, jumps up, and starts flapping. With his expertise as a skilled aviator, he quickly gains altitude and heads northwest.

"I know he'll find her. He just has to," Beverly whispers.

"He will. Don't worry," Lynn says.

"I feel better knowing that when one of us is in trouble, someone will try to help," Taleena tells Davor.

"And how is my little feather duster feeling today?" Michael says, nudging Janis.

"Good. My wing is sore, but I'm thinking more about my rumbling stomach right now."

"Me too! I'm dreaming about eating lots and lots of seeds," Michael teases.

"What is that horrible clanking sound?" Beverly asks, covering her ears with her wings.

Markie stretches his neck and sees Farmer Lutz starting up a monstrous green machine with bright yellow wheels. "Farm stuff," Markie reports.

"Good time to go. Everyone ready to carry on to the prairie potholes?" Instructor Riley asks.

WHAT ARE THE PRAIRIE POTHOLES?

The Prairie Pothole Region (wetlands) are millions of shallow, water-filled depressions created by the recession and melting of the last ice age 10,000 years ago. Located in Manitoba, Alberta, and Saskatchewan, Canada, and North Dakota, South Dakota, Montana, and Wyoming, United States, the potholes fill with water from rain and snowmelt in the spring, creating wetlands of rich plant and animal life. This waterfowl paradise is a destination for breeding, nesting, and fine dining, with nutritious, tasty plants and aquatic invertebrates on the menu. Once the world's largest expanse of grasslands, the prairie potholes are rapidly disappearing due to increased farmlands and development.

With bellies full of barley seeds, the flock agrees that a water retreat, some grooming time, and relaxation is just what they need.

"How long is our flight?" Lynn asks Instructor Riley.

"Up, down. The potholes are just past the grain fields over yonder," she tells everyone.

"Remember, we must keep our guard up for human predators. Not everyone is as nice to us as Farmer Lutz and his family. I'll say this once more: if we are ambushed, it's every duck for themself. Get up high and fly as fast as you can out of the area. When you are safe, head south, and we'll do our best to meet up with you. If you get hit, keep flying for as long as you can, and when it's safe, we will double back and try to find you."

Harold watches Beverly lower her head and shift her weight from one foot to the other. "We're going to be just fine. Just pretend that you're enjoying a lovely afternoon flight around the marsh back home," he tells her.

"I wish I were back home; I don't think I'm cut out for migration—or being one of the four adventurers," Beverly mumbles.

Lead Duck Michael tells the flock, "We need to get our timing and pacing right. It's too hard to see each line over the swath mounds so let's try a zipper approach for takeoff. Get into a single line behind me. In your line position: first A duck, then first B duck, second A duck, second B duck, and keep going from there until you're all in line. Once we're airborne, flare out into our V. Got it?"

"Got it," everyone bobs their head.

The ducks waddle on the straw-like stubble to line up behind Michael, who's patiently waiting for them on a narrow dirt path that's littered with barley cuttings, seeds, and a few small rocks. After some initial confusion (and with the help of Instructor Riley), the ducks are lined up in proper sequence.

Michael looks behind and gives Janis a playful wink. With everyone in position, he searches the sky for incoming birds.

"All clear for takeoff!"

On cue, the flock starts counting: one, two, three, four, five. Michael bolts into the air, and like a fine-tuned machine, the flock departs with impressive precision, enjoying a chilly but gentle tailwind as they fly in a southeasterly direction.

The first-time migrators are wowed by the patchwork of fields of food that they believe is just for them.

"Wait till we get to the field peas. There are yellow peas and green peas, and they're super tasty!" Anne tells everyone.

"It's like you can see forever," Harold tells Markie.

"Get used to it. We'll be flying over wide-open fields of some of our favourite foods for days," he replies.

"I'm starting to feel a little more relaxed. I get so wound up. So many dangers and things to think about," Beverly tells Harold.

"We're going to be fine. Let's just enjoy the view," Harold says.

"Janis, it's wing check time! How are you doing?" Harold asks.

"Sore, but I'm hanging in. The tailwind is helping push me along," she tells Harold.

"Good. Not too much longer till we land, and then you can rest it," Harold says.

"Look! Ponds. Lots of them," Beverly shouts.

"Welcome to the prairie potholes! A waterfowl paradise of shallow pools, natural grasses, and grain fields close by. What more could we ask for?" Instructor Riley says.

"It's an all-inclusive resort for dabbling ducks. Check me in!" Taleena jokes.

Instructor Riley informs the flock that Michael will take them once around on a safety check, then, if safe, he will lead them in for a landing. She reinforces the message to always have a watchful eye out for human predators.

"My stomach's starting to feel not so good," Beverly tells Harold.

"We'll be fine. Michael's an experienced migrator," he reassures her, even though Instructor Riley's message is ruffling a few of his feathers as well.

Michael calls out, "Keep on the lookout and follow me."

The ducks cautiously quack and *kreep* as they circle a pond bordered with tall grasses, staying focused on everything on the ground.

"Lucky us. No ducks here; phony or real. We'll have this pond all to ourselves," Harold tells Beverly.

"All clear!" Michael announces. In preparation for landing, he tilts his back to lower his tail, then stretches his neck and focuses ahead and down. As he brings his wings back, he lowers his webbed feet and spreads all six of his toes for maximum braking upon touchdown on the water.

Feeling a sense of relief that everything appears to be okay, the ducks slow their speed and prepare for landing.

Harold keeps a watchful eye on Beverly when a slight movement in a patch of grass catches his eye. Suddenly, Harold finds himself locking eyes with a lethal enemy: a human predator.

"AMBUSH! FLY!" Harold hollers as the sounds of *BOOM! BOOM! BOOM!* fill the air.

CHAPTER 19

The peaceful sky becomes a combat zone, bombarded with deafening explosions of gunfire and deadly sprays of lightning-fast bullets targeted to kill. Horrific sounds of ducks squawking and shrieks of terror add to the chaos. Feathers fly as the disoriented, panicked ducks ricochet off each other in desperation to fly to safety.

BOOM, BOOM, BOOM!

Harold frantically flaps his wings as bullets whiz by his ears. As he gains altitude, he hears a gruesome, bone-chilling *kreeeep* followed by a splash. Safely out of gunshot range, he looks back to see two human predators holding guns and a dripping wet, black dog with a limp Mallard body dangling from its jaws. Shaking, stunned, and dizzy, Harold looks to the sky, hoping to see Beverly and the flock. In the distance, he spies the flapping wings of ducks fanned out in all directions.

"Beverly!" he yells uncontrollably. But all he hears is his rapid heartbeat and the swishing sound of his wings.

The ambush is over.

Harold's mind swirls in confusion. *What did Instructor Riley say to do? Think, Harold! Calm down and think,* he tells himself. *I know she said to fly south, and I can do that. But which way is south?*

Using his natural-born ability to calculate the position of the setting sun and the axis of the polarized light as a compass, Harold quickly flies south, bypassing the ambush area. He anxiously calls out for his flock while his thoughts keep replaying, *Who was in the dog's mouth? Is Beverly okay? Are Markie and Lynn safe? Who will I never see again? Where is everyone?*

Harold feels increasingly more alone and worried. His calls are becoming weaker and less frequent as he flies over the natural grass-lands that are peppered with shallow ponds and lakes. *Maybe I'm not a brave adventurer,* he thinks to himself, just as he hears faint, familiar sounds in the distance.

Am I really hearing quacks, or am I just imagining them? he wonders. With each beat of his wings, the sounds become louder and more recognizable. Quack! Quack*! Quack! Kreep! Kreep! Kreep!* Quack!

Seeing his friends bobbing on a pond, Harold bellows, "*KREEP!*"

His eyes filter through the faces looking up at him, and when he finally locks eyes with Beverly, he shouts, "I see you!"

Harold splashes down in a flurry of excitement, creating a wake that bounces the flock around as he swims directly to Beverly.

"You're okay!" he says, wrapping his wings around her.

"Harold! I was so worried about you!"

"Oh, I'm just fine. After all, I'm an adventurer—I'm your hot wings!" he reminds her.

"Hey, buddy! What kept you?" Markie asks.

Harold gives Markie a nudge and says, "Missed you." But as he looks around, he notices yet another absence. "Where's Lynn?"

"Don't know," Markie says with a shrug. "She hasn't shown up yet."

"Where could she be?" Beverly asks in a screechy voice.

Harold joins Instructor Riley, Davor, Taleena, Easton, Anne, Beverly, Markie, and Janis in calling out as loud as they can to attract the last remaining members of their flock.

Beverly flaps her wings wildly and shouts, "Here she comes!" They all watch as Lynn lands with a splash.

The flock greets her with open wings, relieved that she's safe.

"We're just waiting for Michael," Janis says, never taking her eyes off the sky. "Keep calling out," she begs, as she and all the ducks quack and *kreep* as loud as they can for their missing flock companion.

Harold is the only one who's quiet. He leans close to Markie, trying to get his attention between *kreeps*. "Markie," he whispers. "Michael didn't make it. He was shot down, and a dog took him."

Markie looks at Harold, his eyes wide. He lowers his head and says softly, "Thanks for letting me know. I'll handle this."

Markie swims to Instructor Riley and shares the tragic news.

In a firm but calm voice, Instructor Riley says, "Everyone, please stop calling out and come here."

With a sense of dread, the ducks reluctantly gather around. The previous chorus of duck calls is now just one desperate voice crying, "QUACK, QUACK, QUACK!"

Instructor Riley glides close to Janis and puts a protective wing around her. "Janis..." she begins.

Janis tries to wriggle away, interrupting with, "No. We have to keep calling out, or Michael won't be able to find us. QUACK! QUAaaaack." Her head lowers slowly to her chest in fear of what she's going to hear next.

In her most compassionate voice, Instructor Riley says, "Janis, you can stop calling out."

Time seems to stand still; the only sound is of the grasses rustling in the chilly autumn breeze.

"Michael won't be joining us," Instructor Riley says, using her bent wing to draw Janis in close. "I'm so sorry."

"No, no, no. He promised he would never leave me," Janis says, burrowing her head into Instructor Riley's chest and sobbing. She looks up to find herself lovingly cocooned by ten trembling, feathery bodies with ten kind, giving hearts.

"We are more than a flock; we are family, and when one of us hurts, we all hurt," Easton mutters.

Everyone gently clicks their bills in agreement.

"Michael was an amazing drake, a true leader, and a good friend," Markie says.

"He was always kind to me," Harold adds.

"I always enjoyed his witty humour," Davor adds.

Taleena struggles to get the words out, pausing before she says, "We will miss him, and we will never, never, forget him."

With her teardrops creating rings of ripples on the water, Janis quietly says, "Thank you. I know Michael was proud to be a member of this flock. He would want us to carry on and live our best lives." With a tinge of anger, she adds, "'Land of Living Skies?' *Horsefeathers*," then lowers her head.

"But horses don't have feathers," Beverly whispers.

"My point exactly. These 'Living Skies' just took my Michael from me," Janis says as she quivers, and looks at Beverly through watery eyes.

"We are here for you," Davor tells her as he holds Taleena close.

Barely able to breathe, Janis says, "Thank you, everyone. I need to be alone." She slowly paddles to a secluded clump of grasses and disappears into the greenery.

As the day goes on, the sun brightens the sky but not the somber mood.

In between tipping up and dining on water plants and insects, they hear Janis's sad, sorrowful quacks coming from her hideaway.

Beverly, Taleena, Lynn, and Anne stay as close as they can to where Janis is. "How can we help her?" Beverly asks. "I feel so helpless."

"I know she wants to be alone, but I think we need to do something," Taleena says.

From above, sounds of *kreep, kreep, kreep* echo over the flock. "Do you hear that?" Harold cries.

"Yes! Incoming!" Markie shouts.

The inbound calls grow stronger and louder.

The ducks enthusiastically call out to welcome the new arrival.

Janis rushes out from the grasses, quacking as loud as she can. The flock watches as she looks up, her heart full of hope.

Jayson skillfully glides in for a landing, barely creating a ripple in the water. Realizing it's not Michael, Janis swims back to her little sanctuary.

"Jayson, it's good to see you," Instructor Riley says, in a sad voice.

"Where's Susie?" Harold asks as he and the flock search the sky.

"I don't know. I looked everywhere for her," Jayson says.

The flock looks at each other in disbelief.

"Another one of our flock is gone," Davor says quietly.

"What do you mean?" Jayson asks.

"Let's have a chat," Instructor Riley says, leading him to a quiet area on the pond.

The ducks watch the two of them chat before Jayson shakes his head and swims towards Janis's hideaway. After a few minutes, Jayson returns to join the others with Janis close by his side.

"I know what we need: a hens' pampering preening party," Anne suggests, being mindful of Janis's feelings.

"Oh, that's a wonderful idea," Beverly says.

"I'm in! My feathers definitely need some maintenance," Lynn announces.

"And I'm looking a little tattered," Taleena adds.

"Janis, you will be our guest of honour. We'll pamper you first, and then the rest of us will help preen each other," Beverly says.

"Brilliant idea. No drakes allowed," Anne teases.

"What? We could use some preening. Sounds luxurious and cozy," Markie comments.

"Sorry, drakes," Beverly giggles as she gives Harold a wink.

The hens swim around looking for the perfect spa location for their pampering preening party—somewhere private and protected, surrounded by tall grasses.

"Hens, please position yourself around Janis so that all of her feathers are easily assessable for preening," Anne instructs.

In a soothing voice, Anne says, "If you're ready, Janis, please give us a big shake and fluff to open up your feathers."

Janis takes a deep breath, shakes her head, ruffles her feathers, spreads her wings, and puffs up her chest while she treads water.

"Perfect," the hens tell her.

"Just relax and close your eyes, Janis. We'll have you feeling at peace and looking beautiful in no time," Taleena says.

"Please be gentle with my left wing; it's still sore. You know, Michael used to help me preen. He was so loving and helpful. I love that he called me his 'little feather duster,'" Janis says, fighting to hold back tears.

"Yes, he certainly was sweet on you. Our pampering probably won't be as good as Michael's, but we will spoil you the best we know how," Lynn tells her.

To help lighten the mood, Beverly says sweetly, "Right now, you look like a *scruffy* feather duster, but not for long."

"Just close your eyes, Janis, and relax. Listen to the wind rustle through the grasses," Anne says, speaking softly.

Anne whispers to the hens, "Work on Janis's feathers that are closest to you. Thoroughly nibble each feather, one by one, starting at its base up to its tip. Use lots of your preening oil to make her feathers supple. Give her all your extra tender, loving care. Let the therapeutic allopreening begin!

WHAT IS ALLOPREENING?

Allopreening is social grooming between members of the same species, which includes cleaning or maintaining one's body or appearance.

Each hen reaches back to the base of her own tail feathers and gets lots of the fatty, waxy, preening oil substance on her bill, then gently applies it to Janis's feathers.

Janis lets out quiet "ahhs" and a couple of "that tickles" as she enjoys her feather maintenance massage. "I think you missed a feather on my crown. Nice not having to use my foot," she mumbles, relaxed and half asleep.

Beverly tenderly nibbles each crown feather again. With each little tug, Janis's head flops about gently.

"I think she's sleeping," Beverly mouths.

Anne whispers, "After a little inspection, I found each feather is perfectly lined up with its barbs zipped back together. She's insulated and waterproofed. I think she's going to be happy. Great job, hens. Let's let her sleep; we'll continue our party in another part of the pond. I expect to look as good as Janis when you're done with me," she teases.

The hens quietly swim away to continue their fun, leaving Janis to float around to wherever the ripples take her.

After enjoying blissful bonding time together, the hens decide to flaunt their feather perfection by joining the drakes for fine dining and chit-chat.

"Well, don't you look beautifully glossy and coiffed?" Harold tells Beverly.

"Thank you, kind drake," she says, wiggling her tail feathers.

"Where's Janis?" Harold asks Beverly.

"Sleeping."

"Wow! You pampered her to sleep. Bravo!" Harold says.

"Well, she's emotionally drained; she needs time to mend her broken heart and wing," Beverly says, sweeping her head side to side across the surface of the water, hoping to catch some tasty morsels in her slightly open bill.

"Poor Janis. When she wakes, she's going to be so sad again," Easton whispers.

Instructor Riley begins addressing the flock, "While Janis is sleeping, we need to have a meeting. First, on behalf of all of us, thanks to Harold for spotting the human predators and immediately sounding the alarm. Every second counts, and your keen eye probably saved many of us. That's the act of a leader," she says with a nod of admiration.

With a few appreciative head pumps, the ducks quietly click their bills.

"You're a hero," Beverly whispers.

With a playful nudge to Harold, Lynn says, "I guess you are a star, after all."

"Stellar job, buddy," Markie praises.

Harold thinks what he did was a natural, spontaneous reaction—but maybe he does have some natural leadership abilities.

"So far, our migration has consisted of shorter flying time and frequent rest stops," Instructor Riley explains. "We thought this was the best way for the newbies to build up their stamina and to enjoy the journey."

Harold, Beverly, Lynn, and Taleena look at each other nervously, waiting for what is coming next.

Instructor Riley continues, "Every time we set down for a rest stop, we are putting ourselves in grave danger. Susie is missing, and we have no idea what peril she might be in. We've lost Michael to gunfire. How does everyone feel about flying longer distances between rest stops?"

"How much longer?" Taleena asks quietly.

"We've been flying on average from sunrise to noon. I'm proposing we fly from sunrise to midafternoon, or else fly for the same amount of time during the night," Instructor Riley says.

"I think I can do that," Taleena says.

"I know you can," Davor says convincingly.

"I guess I can do that if it keeps us safe," Beverly says.

"Me too," Lynn agrees.

"Me too. But what about Janis and her sore wing?" Harold asks.

"She's an experienced long-distance flyer, but with her sore wing, we'll adjust our speed and flight duration if she needs us to. Please know this: we are easily capable of flying longer distances, and at much higher altitudes," Jayson replies.

"We are? I feel tired on our so-called short flights," Beverly says, as Lynn and Taleena nod in agreement.

"Listen, we are amazing flying machines built for endurance. Our body mass has a lot of lightweight feathers. Our bones are hollow. Our skull bones are thin. We don't have teeth or a bladder to hold weight. We have powerful flight muscles. We have multiple air sacs attached to our lungs and a four-chambered heart. Four! Our spindle-shaped bodies and wings are designed for peak flying performance. Now, are you convinced?" Jayson asks.

"I guess so," Beverly says reluctantly.

"How will you ever know what you can do if you don't try?" Jayson asks. "You know what they say: it seems impossible until you've done it."

"You're right. I keep forgetting that I'm one of the *four adventurers*," Beverly says sheepishly.

"Okay then; we have a plan. I'll discuss this with Janis when she wakes. If she feels up to it, we'll leave tomorrow night. After sunset, because human predators can't see us in the dark. You'll be happy to know that we have three upcoming rest stops all close together, and one of them is a safe zone—no human predators allowed," Instructor Riley tells the flock.

"That sounds too good to be true," Beverly tells Harold.

"When Instructor Riley said to us that migration is serious, I thought she was doomsaying. I believe her now," he replies.

"Me too. I didn't expect migration to be so brutal. I feel like a yo-yo," she says.

As nighttime sets in and the barometer drops, Janis and Jayson join the rest of the flock.

"To all my lovely hen friends, thank you for pampering me. I really needed that," Janis says.

"We're here for you," Lynn tells her.

"Janis, it's so nice to see you. Please join us," Instructor Riley says before addressing the entire flock. "We will travel tomorrow night after sunset and try to arrive at our destination well before sunrise when the human predators arrive. During the day, there is absolutely no flying: we stay put on water or land. We all play by the same rules. No sneaking away for field peas. Understand?" Instructor Riley asks, looking directly at Anne.

"Yes," Anne smiles bashfully.

The flock clicks their bills in agreement.

"And for some good news," Jayson teases the flock, "Tomorrow night's flight is pretty much the same flying time that you are used to."

"Bonus!" Harold cheers.

Beverly, Lynn, and Taleena bob their heads in excitement.

"See? Things are looking up," Harold whispers to Beverly.

"It's been a difficult day, so let's get some sleep. Who would like to be on predator guard duty?" Instructor Riley asks.

"I will," Harold says, feeling confident now that he might possibly be a leader.

"I'll join you," Markie says.

The flock bobs together, hiding among a clump of grasses that seems far enough from the shore.

"Let's say a little prayer for Michael, Susie, and dear Janis," Beverly suggests.

Eleven pairs of eyes gaze in wonder at the beauty of the twinkling sky as they reflect.

"Did you see that? A shooting star! That's my Michael telling me I'm going to be okay," Janis says.

"Yes," Anne whispers, hugging Janis tight. "That's exactly what that was."

CHAPTER 20

Morning comes early, and it's another chilly one.

"Don't give me that look," Markie tells Lynn as he shakes to toss the icy bits off.

"I'm not even going to ask you how much longer because you'll just say, 'soon.' And you and I obviously have different ideas what 'soon' means," Lynn says as she flaps her wings, trying to get warm.

"How are you feeling, Janis?" Harold asks.

"One day at a time, Harold. One day at a time."

"You know we are all here for you," he reminds her.

"I know," Janis says, tapping his wing.

"Morning, hot wings. You and Markie did a fine job guarding us last night," Beverly tells Harold.

"We're the 'Bodyguard Buds,'" Harold jokes.

"That's us!" Markie concurs. "Now, let's eat."

"Good plan," Lynn says.

The ducks spend the day lounging around their private pothole, dining on water plants and insects. Mindful of coyotes and foxes, they carefully waddle on the muddy shore to look for tasty treats.

Harold turns to Markie and quietly says, "We need to work on Plan B, and fast. Beverly feels overwhelmed, and she's not alone. Any ideas?"

"Well, being grounded during the day makes it a bit more difficult," Markie replies.

"Right. So it has to be something on the pond," Harold says as he swims around and thinks about it, and then says, "Markie, I've got it! Follow my lead."

Harold quickly swims to Anne, stretches his right wing straight out, and touches her back. *"Tag, you're it!"* he brags.

"Oh, is that so? Not for long," Anne says jokingly, surveying where everyone is with a quick turn of her head and swimming towards Beverly.

"Oh no you don't," Beverly giggles as she paddles away as fast as she can.

From the corner of her eye, Anne sees Markie hiding behind a fallen waterlogged tree stump.

"I'm coming for you, Davor!" Anne shouts, her bright orange feet moving as fast as they can to get her to the tree stump. Stretching her wing around it, she touches Markie's tail feathers and shouts, *"Tag, you're it!"* and swims away, laughing.

"Clever hen, using Davor as a decoy," Markie says.

"Let me see. Who should I tag?" he says as he casually swims around the pond, eyeing everyone. Using Anne's trick he pretends that he doesn't see Jayson peeking out from behind a clump of grasses.

"Beverly, you might have escaped Anne, but you won't escape me," he teases, swimming to the right side of the clump of grasses, and then going behind it.

Jayson darts to the left and around to the front.

Around and around they go, until Markie stops and Jayson bumps into him.

"Tag, you're it!" Markie laughs.

"What? So much for my quick reaction skills," Jayson jokes.

The afternoon of play and laughter puts the flock in a better headspace.

"That was so much fun. Thanks, Harold," Beverly says, snuggling up to him.

"Glad you enjoyed it. I think we all needed a break from reality."

"Harold can be our social director," Taleena cheers.

"Yay!" everyone agrees. "Great idea, buddy. Lots of fun."

"Wow! This flock definitely has some high-spirited ducks. Thanks, Harold," Instructor Riley says.

Jayson proceeds to update everyone. "Now is the time for any last-minute feather touch-ups and dining. Remember, proper preparation makes your migration experience more successful. We'll be leaving after the sun sets. Tonight's weather forecast: clear sky, excellent visibility."

He pauses for a moment before continuing, "And just one more thing: our migration will consist of a cycle of rest stops at prairie potholes and then grain fields. This gives us a variety of healthy food choices and relaxation areas."

"I like the sound of that," Beverly tells Harold.

"Me too."

Jayson looks around at all the head bobbing and realizes that this plan is a good one.

The newly energized, less-stressed flock prepares for a successful flight. Jayson resumes the role of Lead Duck and instructs the flock to take their V positions.

Instructor Riley does a quick count of the duck outlines on the moonlit water. "Impressive," she comments. "All good, Captain," she calls to Jayson.

"Right-o," Captain Jayson says as he scans the sky for silhouettes and listens for calls.

Everyone quietly bobs in place, waiting for further instruction.

"All clear. We'll go on the count of five. Remember to pace yourselves and fly a little higher than the duck in front of you," Captain Jayson says.

The flock starts counting. On five, Captain Jayson jumps up out of the water and starts calling out with energetic *kreep*s. Two by two, the ducks liftoff, calling out that they're airborne.

The duck's humdrum quacks and *kreep*s carry a long distance in the crisp night air. Surrounded in darkness with millions of glittery stars above them, the ducks flap along. Below them are moon-kissed ponds, scattered among blackness.

"What are the lights over there?" Harold asks Markie.

"That's a town. Humans live there. See the lights scattered in the dark?

That's where the farmers live. Just wait till you see a city. They're monstrous, dangerous, scary places, full of humans rushing around."

"Are we going to a city?" Harold asks nervously.

"We certainly try not to. The noise is louder than Farmer Lutz's equipment, and there are bright lights everywhere. The flashing, coloured ones can really throw us off our beat. And cities are full of clear, shiny glass; it's like a maze to try to fly around all of it. Humans are taking over."

"Glass?" Harold asks, not knowing what to make of all this.

"It's human predator trickery. If we don't have our wits about us, we're fooled into not seeing the glass, or we think we see other ducks. Believe me; it's not the greatest time to admire your reflection. Best to admire yourself in a pond—much safer. I must say I am a devilishly handsome drake," Markie boldly claims.

"Glass, city, busy, dangerous," Harold repeats, his voice cracking.

"You're going to be just fine, buddy. You've got me as your trailblazer!"

"Hey, Harold!" Beverly shouts, "I'm not going to say that I'm bored because I don't want another blizzard."

"Yes, don't you dare jinx us."

"Good thing that I'm cold; it's keeping me alert," Lynn comments.

"How are you doing, Janis?"

"I'm fine. Thanks for asking, Harold," Janis says, without her usual feistiness.

The time and distance go by slowly.

"Perfect time for a little lesson to explain how we know our route when we are flying in darkness," Instructor Riley says. "As I mentioned before, we are born with the ability to read the stars, feel the magnetic field, and find the North Star.* Look around—what do you see?"

---

*The North Star (formally known as Polaris) sits almost directly above the Earth's north pole. It's lined up with the planet's rotational axis, which is an imaginary line that extends through the planet and out of the north and south poles. This means that the North Star (or Pole Star) holds nearly still in the sky. And unlike all other stars, it neither rises nor sets, so it is in the same location from dusk until dawn every night and stays extremely close to true north.

The newbies study the sky while the experienced migrators carry on calling out and flapping.

"One, two, three… twenty, twenty-one… too many stars to count," Taleena says.

"I see a very bright star, and for some reason, I know it's helping keep us on course," Harold tells Instructor Riley.

"Yes. That's the North Star; it helps us orientate our inner compass."

"Me too. I can't really explain it, but I know that we are flying south to warmer weather—which can't happen soon enough," Lynn mentions.

"And Beverly, what do you sense?" Instructor Riley asks.

"It's kind of strange because I just *feel* it. I guess it's like intuition; you just sort of *know*."

"You are absolutely right. We are born with *homing* ability, which means we can navigate or return to a place even if we've been away for a long time. If you pay attention and take the time to observe, it will come to you. We will train you to navigate using landmarks and terrain, so stay alert and learn our path—the rivers we follow, the hills, and the towns and cities we visit or fly over. We have our favourite parks and rest stops, and we know where the friendly farmers live and which ones grow our favourite foods for us," Instructor Riley explains to the first-time migrators.

"Let's hope that Susie picks up her genetic vibes," Beverly says to Harold.

Captain Jayson announces, "I'm flapping tired. Time for me to take a break. Need a skillful flyer to take over. I'm a tough act to follow," he teases. "Anne, you're up!"

"Happy to take the lead, Captain."

"Great! Do you need directions?" Jayson jokes as he drops back to the end of the A Line.

"Funny. Not this aviator! But if I do, I wouldn't hesitate to ask," Anne quips.

"Exactly."

"Hang in there. You're doing great!" Jayson tells Janis as he watches her try to beat her wings in sync with the others—but not quite doing it.

Anne quacks loudly as she examines the sky and beats her wings with purpose.

"You're an expert pilot, Anne!" Beverly comments.

"You're making us hens look good!" Taleena shouts.

Anne lets out a loud quack of, "Hen power!"

"She's amazing," Harold tells Beverly.

"Hot wings, that'll be me one day!" Beverly brags.

"No doubt."

Instructor Riley and Lead Duck Anne have a short conversation. Then Instructor Riley calls out, "Listen up, everyone! Anne is going to lead us down onto a farmer's field of field peas. Big surprise there," she snickers. "Since it's still dark and well before sunrise, we should be safe from humans—but keep a watch out for four-legged predators."

Embracing her Lead Duck status like a pro, Anne banks to the right, reduces her speed, and prepares for landing. The flock calls out as they trail behind her.

"You've got this, Beverly," Harold says.

"You too," she replies. Beverly leans back and flares her wings up and back behind her while she lowers and splays her webbed feet and toes in front.

With just a few skid marks and dust in their eyes, the flock successfully lands on the harvested field.

"Oh, this is a much softer place to land than the last field," Beverly says.

"Yay. No pokey sticks stabbing us," Lynn adds.

"Remember, we are in prime human predator territory. We'll stay on land until later tonight and then make a short night flight to a safe zone with water where no humans are allowed. STAY *GROUNDED*. Understand?" Instructor Riley asks.

The sound of clicking bills in the dark tells her that everyone understands.

"A safe zone sounds wonderful. It will be nice to just relax!" Janis tells Lynn.

"Raptors and animals are still a threat, but at least no human predators. That's comforting," Beverly tells Harold. She then turns to their newest leader and says, "Great flight, Anne!"

"Thanks, Beverly. One day you'll be Lead Duck, too!"

"I sure will!" Beverly replies enthusiastically.

"Outstanding flying skills, Anne," Jayson adds. "Now I know why you were happy to lead us in. Field peas, right?"

"Field peas? Whatever do you mean?" Anne laughs.

"Brrrr, it's cold," Beverly says, standing on one leg as she tucks the other one in tight to her body.*

"I'll keep you warm," Harold whispers.

"Yes, please. Put your hot wings to good use!" Beverly teases.

As the ducks tend to their roughed-up feathers before dining, Anne waddles over to Harold, Beverly, and Lynn.

"Hey, you three! I want to see your expressions when you taste field peas for the first time," Anne tells them.

"I'm so excited! Look down," Anne instructs the group. "The ground is scattered with shattered pods, whole pods, and little green peas. Look! Here's a whole pod!" She picks it up in her bill, shakes it like a rattle, and then gives it a light crunch that cracks the pod open. Everyone watches as she spits out the shell, and six little round green peas drop to the ground. "See the peas? That's what we eat. Now you try."

Harold picks up a pea off the ground, puts it in his bill, and promptly spits it out. "It's as hard as a pebble. "Are you sure I'm meant to eat this? Are you playing a trick on me?" he asks Anne.

"No trick, and yes, we eat them. They're yummy and healthy for us."

---

*For ducks to reduce loss of body heat and to be able to walk on cold ground and ice without getting frostbite, they regulate the temperature of their legs and feet. They use a countercurrent heat exchange system in their arteries and veins in their legs.

Using the nail at the tip of his upper bill, Harold picks up another pea, places it on his tongue, and swallows.

"Well, what do you think?" Anne asks, slightly annoyed that he's not volunteering any information.

"Well, the little hairs on my tongue pushed it back to my throat where it determined it was safe to eat, and my small amount of taste buds said it's tasty enough to swallow, so that's what I did. I guess it was okay," Harold says.

"It's not so much the taste as the dining experience. Did you like how it felt when it left your throat and rolled down your esophagus?" Anne asks.

"Sure. I just hope my gizzard doesn't think I'm eating lots of rocks. It already has enough little pebbles in it to help grind up my food," Harold says as he and Markie exchange mischievous looks.

Irritated with the drakes, Anne turns her attention to Beverly and Lynn. "Okay, your turn. You two try them and tell me what you think," she says enthusiastically.

Beverly waddles around, searching for the perfect unbroken green pod.

"Found one," she says as she picks it up with her bill and shakes it. With a little crunch, the green pod splits open, and six little green peas spill to the ground. After spitting out the shell, Beverly picks up a pea and gobbles it down.

"And? What do you think?" Anne asks.

"Yummy! It tickles as it rolls down."

Lynn eats a pea. Puzzled, she looks at Harold and says, "What are you talking about? It's tasty!"

Harold and Markie break out laughing.

Anne rolls her eyes in frustration. "Have fun feasting on the green peas. Maybe we'll visit a yellow pea field sometime," she says.

"Can hardly wait," Markie snickers.

Annoyed, Anne waddles away, gobbling up peas along the way.

Beverly looks at Harold and Markie. "You two and your silly games. Come on, Lynn. These tasty peas aren't going to devour themselves!"

As the sun rises, the ducks cautiously waddle around on the massive open field, searching through the short, soft plant cuttings for peas and pods that escaped harvesting. With another fabulous feast right at their feet, each of them overindulges, almost to the point where they sound like rattles when they waddle.

"Look at my chest. It looks lopsided. My stomach is full of peas," Beverly giggles.

"Mine too. I'll be pooping* more than usual," Lynn chuckles.

"Havenwood Cove doesn't have anything like this," Beverly comments.

"We were promised new dining experiences, and we've got them!" Lynn says.

"Well, Instructor Riley did tell us we need to eat lots to have the energy for our migration. I'm just doing as I was told," says a sassy Beverly.

"Me too," Lynn laughs.

"Don't you dare spit a pea at me!" Taleena threatens Davor as she tries to waddle out of range.

"Game on!" Jayson says as he picks up a pea and spits it at Davor. "Gotcha!"

With a couple of beats of their wings, Beverly and Lynn leave the pea-spitting combat zone.

"You drakes can be such ducklings at times," Anne shouts, then picks up a pea and spits it at Harold—but misses.

"Sorry, Instructor Riley," Anne says bashfully, looking at the ground.

"No worries, but next time maybe get a little closer to your victim before you spit," she says with a lighthearted chuckle.

The flock spends the remainder of the day preening, dining, napping,

---

*A duck's poop is liquid, and they have no control over when and where they go. On average, they poop every 15 minutes.

and watching for predators—especially the eagle that is surfing the thermal current above the field.

As the sun begins to set, Lynn looks out over the wide-open prairie and says, "Look, Beverly! See the rainbow colours on both sides of the sun? That's called a 'sundog.' They're special. *Very* special," Lynn whispers.

"It's beautiful," Beverly says as she watches both the sundog and the sun slip below the horizon.

SUNDOGS

Sundogs are patches of light or rainbow effects on either side of the sun, usually at a 22-degree angle. They are created by sunlight reflecting off ice crystals in the sky. Sometimes they are two very bright lights, making it look as if there are three suns in the sky.

Wrapped in darkness, Captain Jayson and Instructor Riley gather the flock for a pre-flight orientation.

"Listen up, everyone," Instructor Riley says. "Other than Lake Clair, we've had our rest stops all to ourselves, but that's about to change. We have a short flight to our next rest stop, which is extremely popular with many species of migrating birds. It has it all: a lake with little islands, marshes, grasslands, shallow bays, and uplands. But perhaps the best reason is that no human predators are allowed."

"For sure? You mean it?" Beverly asks.

"Absolutely," Instructor Riley reassures her.

"What about foxes, coyotes, and raptors?" Taleena asks.

"It's not a perfect world. Even though coyotes and red foxes are good swimmers, they probably won't want to mess with a lake full of protective birds with pecking beaks. Safety in numbers, you know. Weather permitting, we'll rest there for a couple of nights. So let's get into our famous V formation and fly to paradise!" Instructor Riley advises the flock.

"You are going to love our next rest stop. It's the Last Mountain Lake Bird Sanctuary," Markie tells Harold, Beverly, and Lynn.

"It sounds so fancy," Lynn comments.

"Oh, it is. We regulars call it 'Club Mig'; 'Club Migration' to the new-comers. I'll show you around," Markie boasts.

"It sounds like an exciting new adventure," Harold adds.

With the aid of moonlight, the energized ducks waddle around, scrambling to get into position.

Once in place, Captain Jayson and the flock check the dark sky for silhouettes and listen for airborne travellers.

"All clear. Ready for takeoff," Captain Jayson says.

On the count of five, he bolts up out of the water and heads east with his motivated flock trailing behind.

"What is all that noise? It's getting louder and louder," Lynn shouts.

The air is rich with the sounds of birds calling out to each other: short, loud bugles, rattling bugles, grunts, nasally one-syllable honks, quacks, and *kreep*s, each trying to be heard over the others.

"Let's call out and proudly let everyone know that the Havenwood Cove flock is arriving. There's heavy traffic, so be on the lookout!" Captain Jayson shouts as he prepares for their final approach.

Out of nowhere, a lone Sandhill Crane crosses Jayson's path. Jayson's split-second reaction of putting on the brakes prevents a collision. The flock quickly follows suit by bringing their feet forward, spreading their toes, and using their tail feathers as rudders to stabilize themselves.

In a blur of yellow eyes, a bright red crown, and gray feathers, the offender shouts, "Sorry!" as it flies by, desperately trying to catch up to its friends, who are headed for the prairie grasslands.

"Pay attention next time, you featherbrain!" Captain Jayson yells.

Shocked by Captain Jayson's reaction, the ducks immediately become quiet.

In the darkness, Jayson lets out agitated loud *kreep*s as he skillfully darts and dashes through the chaos of fellow flyers. Finally, he spots a small, uninhabited area of the marsh where he safely lands his flock, and the traumatized newbies breathe a sigh of relief.

"Whew. That was some jagged flight. I've never seen so many birds before!" Beverly comments.

"It's like we were ricocheting at lightning speed," Harold says.

"You're right. We're lucky to find a spot to land," Anne replies.

"Great flying, everyone!" says Davor.

The flock—and the newbies, who are still a little shaken up from all the twists and turns—clack their bills in agreement.

"Apologies, everyone. I shouldn't have lashed out like that; that wasn't very professional of me," Captain Jayson tells the ducks.

"I would have told that crane where to go," Easton says.

"Believe me, I wanted to, but that wouldn't have helped the situation. Besides, we all make mistakes. Just remember that flying is serious, and one mishap can be disastrous. Enough said; let's enjoy this amazing paradise!" Captain Jayson says with a party like vibe.

The flock quacks and *kreep*s in praise of their leader.

"Who's ready for sleep?" Instructor Riley asks.

"I am," Lynn says.

"Me too. I want to wake up early and see what this place is all about," Taleena says.

With Anne and Davor on predator watch, the exhausted ducks huddle close together. Bobbing on the chilly water and tucked in among the tall, dried-out, golden-coloured cattails, they are protected from the bitter cold air and whatever dangers might lurk on the shore. They quickly fall asleep to the thunderous, droning sounds of beating wings and calls from thousands of birds.

Harold listens to tonight's lullaby, a collection of annoying avian sounds, before eventually drifting into a deep sleep.

CHAPTER 21

The flock begins to stir at its now-regular time of just before sunrise. Still in their sleeping huddle, the ducks are nice and warm, and they really don't want to move—but their growling stomachs tell them otherwise.

"How'd you sleep?" Lynn asks Janis.

"Fine, I guess."

"Morning, Harold," Beverly whispers in his ear.

"Good morning, sunshine."

"Who wants to go exploring?" Markie asks.

Beverly and Lynn look at each. "Sure, but let's eat first," Beverly suggests.

"That's a given. My stomach always comes first," Markie chuckles.

"Whoa!" Instructor Riley blurts. "Good morning, everyone. Before you go off to explore, here are some guidelines. First, be back here before it gets dark. Second, under no circumstance are you to leave the safe zone. *NONE*."

"How will we know where that is?" Taleena asks.

"Oh, you'll know. It's like an invisible line across the south part of the lake. You'll see birds on one side and none on the other," she tells them.

"Let me say it again: you can fly around in the safe zone, but under no circumstance do you leave the lake, marsh, and grassland areas. Do you understand? This means no visiting nearby farmers' fields for peas," Instructor Riley says, giving Anne the eagle eye.

"Understood!" the flock shouts, sounding like a duck army responding to their commander.

"Great! Jayson and I will be close by if you need us," she says, looking at Janis. "Now go have fun! Explore and make new friends."

"This feels like bird camp. Is there even such a thing?" Beverly chuckles.

The flock swims around their secluded marsh area, enjoying some tip-up eats while large, noisy birds with long, dark-gray skinny legs that drag behind them fly overhead.

"I'm full. I had some tasty plant roots, and I ate a yummy little critter that I had never tried before. I feel it wiggling around; it's probably gobbling up peas," Beverly giggles to Harold.

With stomachs full of delicious treats, Markie, Harold, Beverly, and Lynn decide to leave the tranquility of their hideaway and explore the wild, open lake.

"Wow! It's flight central out there," Lynn says, peeking out from the cattails.

"Let me see," Beverly says. "This is going to be an adventure! At least there are no human predators."

"Follow me," Markie says, breaking through the cattails and leading them onto the open area of the lake.

As he skirts his way around birds of every size and colour, Markie's voice is a chorus of, "Sorry, sorry, coming through, passing by, hello."

"Did you just push me?" Markie hears, stops, and looks up to see a giant American White Pelican staring down at him.

Overshadowed by the pelican's size, Markie is eye-to-eye with a sea of white feathers: he's looking at the pelican's broad chest with huge wings that look like saddle bags strapped to its sides. Markie can't escape the sharply pointed tip of the yellow-orange coloured bill poking into his chest. Markie's eyes nervously make their way up its extra-long, massive bill until they connect with two icy-blue eyes set in patches of bright yellow. Glaring at him, the beast lets out two deep grunts that sound like a croaking male bullfrog. Markie trembles. Harold, Beverly, and Lynn gasp. The pelican starts to make its first move by slowly stretching its long neck, spreading its massive, broad, white wings, exposing its black flying feathers. The beast grabs Markie and lifts him out of the water.

In a deep, gruff voice, the beast asks, "Markie? Is that you?"

Quivering and trying to catch his breath, Markie replies, "Paco?"

"Sure is! How are you, Greenhead?"

"You can put me down now," Markie stutters as he gasps for air.

"Of all the lakes in all the provinces, you swim into mine. What's happening, Markie?" Paco asks, giving Markie a little tap with his wing.

"Same old, same old; fall migration. You?"

"Yup, heading south back to the Gulf States. Friends of yours?" Paco asks, motioning to the three adventurers, still paralyzed with shock and trying to figure out what they just saw.

"Paco, this is Harold, Beverly, and Lynn."

"Nice to meet you. Glad you didn't rough up Markie," Lynn teases.

"Aah, I'd never hurt my old pal," Paco says.

"It's really good to see you again. Same time next year," Paco jests.

"Sure thing, Paco. But before you leave, will you show my friends your pouch?" Markie asks.

"Kind of personal, isn't it?" Paco laughs. "Just kidding." Paco swims back just far enough to demonstrate properly.

"Wait until you see this! You're going to be so jealous," Markie tells them.

Paco puffs up the yellow-coloured, fibrous skin that's connected to his lower mandible (which is the bottom half of his bill). It gets bigger and bigger until it's a huge pouch.

Harold, Beverly, and Lynn are mesmerized at such a sight.

"Watch this," Paco says, then plunges his head under the water.

The ducks wait in anticipation of what is coming next.

Paco's head suddenly pops back up with his humungous gular pouch heavy with water—and something inside is thrashing around, trying to get out. Paco starts slowly contracting his pouch as water cascades out, but the thrashing continues from the inside. He jerks his head back, and in one gulp, problem solved.

"That was one feisty fish," Paco jokes.

"Wow!" Beverly says.

"That's amazing!" Harold comments. "I want one of those!"

"Who wouldn't? Can you imagine how much food we could scoop up?" Markie says, laughing.

"I'm a dabbler, just like you ducks. And no, I don't dive down into the water like Brown Pelicans; they're such show-offs. But white pelicans are super smart! Sometimes we work together in pods to trap fish in shallow waters, open our pouches, and dinner swims right to us. And in case you're curious, no, we never fly with food in our pouch," Paco tells the ducks.

"Oh, now I'm really jealous," Harold says.

"Well, I'm jealous of how you Mallards just spring out of the water into flight. Do you have any idea how hard I have to work, running and splashing like crazy along the water, trying to get my big, clunky body airborne? I occasionally have onlookers cheering me on with chants of, 'You can do it, Paco!' It's embarrassing."

"Just goes to prove that everyone has good things and not-so-good things about themselves," Harold says.

"True. Very true," Paco agrees, before continuing, "And now, my Mallard friends, I've got to get back to feeding my big pelican body. Safe travels!"

The Mallards tell Paco goodbye and swim away to explore the shallower marshy areas of the lake.

The calm of the moment is interrupted by a shout from Lynn. "Beverly! Help me! I'm stuck!"

Beverly calls back, "Lynn, look up!"

"What?"

"Look up!" Beverly yells.

Stuck between two black sticks, Lynn looks up to see a mass of white feathers.

What's happening? she asks herself.

"Excuse me," says a soft-spoken voice. "Do I know you?"

"Who said that?" Lynn asks, looking around.

"Up here, my dear."

Lynn slowly looks up, up, up to see a lovely Whooping Crane looking down at her. It gracefully curves its long white

neck, lowering its red-crowned head down to be up close and personal with her.

"Hello," Lynn mumbles, looking past the heavy yellow bill she gazes into the Whooping Crane's bright yellow eyes.

"Don't be alarmed, but you seem to have wedged yourself between my legs."

"I'm so sorry. I was swimming around, not looking where I was going," Lynn babbles.

"Yes, indeed. It wouldn't be the first time this sort of thing has happened to me. At least you didn't topple me over," the Whooping Crane says with a little chuckle.

"I'm Delilah."

"I'm Lynn. It's nice to meet you."

"I'll just pull up my left leg and move it away, and then you are free to swim by," Delilah says.

"Sounds good to me."

Beverly giggles as she watches Lynn try to untangle herself from the Whooping Crane's legs.

"You're free to go," Delilah says.

"Thanks! May I ask you something?"

"Certainly."

"What do you have attached to your legs?" Lynn asks.

"What? Oh, these. Humans put these tracking bands on me so they can see where I am; they're able to follow me wherever I go. I've had two different kinds of bands: some are the analog kind, which are coloured bands like these are," she says, gesturing to her leg, "and some are the digital models that can track us like GPS. It seems like an invasion of privacy, but I'm grateful for it! My species is endangered, and without help from the humans who care enough to help us, my family, friends, and I might be gone. Forever."

"Forever?"

"Forever. Extinction is a real possibility."

"Maybe *my* species is endangered," Lynn shrieks.

"Oh, I don't think you have any worries about that. I've seen lots of Mallards on my migrations from my nesting grounds at Wood Buffalo National Park in Alberta all the way down to my winter home in Aransas National Wildlife Refuge in Texas. Many of them are sporting silver leg bands. See? Mallards are special."

"Aaaahhh, yes. I met some of your friends in Wood Buffalo National Park.," Lynn says.

Lynn sees Beverly laughing and remembers that she's waiting for her. "I have to go, but I'm glad I swam into you. Bye, Delilah."

"Be safe, little hen."

Beverly greets Lynn with a smile. "So, was she nice, or was she mad at you?"

"Delilah was really nice to me! Do you see the coloured stripes on her legs? They're bands that humans put on her to try and keep her safe."

"So, why don't we have leg bands? Doesn't anyone care about us?" Beverly rants.

"Lots of us do. We have shorter legs, so Delilah says ours are silver metal. We just have to wait for our turn, I guess. Fancy, right?"

"Definitely!" Beverly says. "We haven't seen Harold and Markie for a while; I think we should catch up to them."

They swim around the maze of waterfowl, looking for the drakes.

"Hey, you two! Where'd you go?" Harold calls out.

"Oh, we were just chatting with a crane," Lynn snickers.

Energized and anxious for feedback, Markie asks, "So, what do you think of Club Mig?"

"It's a beautiful, long, skinny lake with super clean water that offers something for everyone. It's definitely a happening place, just like you said," Harold says.

"Yes, it's *the* hot spot for the migrating jet set. It's where all the cool birds come to meet up, rest, and eat. It's the see-and-be-seen kind of place—because you certainly can't carry on a conversation with all the noise. I feel like a bobblehead, nodding up and down and pretending I hear what they're saying. Who knows what I've agreed to?" Beverly shrugs.

"I love it here, Markie. I feel so young and alive!" Lynn says enthusiastically.

"You *are* young and alive, you silly hen," Beverly teases.

"It's exciting meeting new birds. Sometimes, you find yourself just bumping into them," Lynn says with a wink.

"Right now, I'm in hot pursuit of meeting a dashing drake. No luck so far, but I'm no quitter," Lynn tells them.

"What does everyone want to do?" Harold asks.

"I think I'd like to go back to our quiet spot," Beverly replies.

"I'll join you; quiet is exactly what I need right now," Harold says.

"I'm feeling kind of adventurous. Markie, do you want to join me in checking things out?" Lynn asks.

"Let's do it! We'll join the flock before dark—we don't want to be wild and crazy and break flock curfew," Markie teases.

"Sounds good. Have fun, you two, but stay out of trouble," Harold says as the two couples part ways.

After swimming through the mosh pit of waterfowl and ruffling a few feathers, Harold and Beverly join Instructor Riley and Janis among the cattails.

"How was the exploration?" Janis asks.

"Okay, but I think I'm more of a low-key and secluded resort kind of hen," Beverly replies.

"It was fun for a while, but then the noise gave me a headache," Harold says. "And you need to have your wits about you, ducking from low-flying arrivals and dodging flying poop."

"Janis! How are you feeling?" Beverly asks.

"I'm doing well, thank you. It was nice to have some alone time."

"Mark my words: most of the flock will party till curfew. Anne will be the last to arrive," Instructor Riley laughs. And just as she predicted, Easton, Jayson, Markie, Lynn, Davor, and Taleena arrive shortly before dark, and Anne rushes in behind them.

"Whew! Just made curfew," Anne says breathlessly.

Instructor Riley chuckles to herself as the flock beds down on the frigid water among the cattails.

"Move aside, Bodyguard Buds; the Sassy Sentinels are on predator duty," Beverly and Lynn boldly announce, as they pose like the feathered action sheroes that they think they are. As they patrol, an Arctic cold front blows into the Last Mountain Lake area, and they struggle to stay warm.

Chilled to the bone, the flock wakes just before sunrise, roused by the lively calls from the early departing birds. "Brrrr! It's freezing!" says Taleena, as she shakes the ice crystals off her feathers and pecks at the skim of icy water hugging her body.

"I can see my breath. See the little puffs of moisture?" Anne shows Janis as she exhales into the icy air.

The shivering ducks fluff themselves up and swim around, trying to warm up.

"My stomach is going to have to wait. I'm not ready to dunk my head in the icy water," Easton says.

Instructor Riley addresses the flock with, "I'm sure you're all feeling a bit colder this morning. An Arctic cold front blew through overnight, and the Sassy Sentinels did a great job keeping us safe despite the icy temperatures." The shivering flock clacks their bills in appreciation.

Beverly and Lynn nod in gratitude and then huddle to discuss their performance.

"We were soooooooo lucky we didn't have a predator attack during the night," Beverly whispers to Lynn.

"I know! With all the birds coming, going, feeding, and just having fun on the lake, I gave up trying to figure out if the ripples in the water were dangerous," Lynn tells Beverly.

"Me too. It would have been impossible to hear if there was a predator over all the commotion. And that scares the crud out of me," Beverly whispers to Lynn.

They make a pact to keep their secret to themselves—and to make sure that they're the best patrol team the flock has ever had.

CHAPTER 22

The ducks awaken under a crisp, clear blue sky, and as the sun begins to warm the air temperature from bitter to bearable cold, they feast in the shallow, marshy area to build up their energy reserves for the day's flight.

A shivering Lynn corners Markie in the cattails and stares him in the eyes. "Enough is enough. I wake up every morning colder than the day before. Please tell me how much longer it'll be until we get to the warm weather. And do NOT say 'soon.'"

Beverly bobs in place nearby, blocking Markie's only exit.

"The gig's up; you better spill it," Harold chimes in.

"You hens are going to love where we'll be wintering. Some noise, please!" Markie requests.

Instantly, all three clack their bills and flap their wings enthusiastically.

"Mighty adventurers! We will be snowbirding in the balmy weather of the Mississippi Alluvial Valley!" Markie announces as if he were a ring-leader at the circus.

All bill clacking and wing flapping stops. Puzzled, Beverly and Lynn ask, "Where?"

"Louisiana, United States of America! Our home away from home. The land of The Stars and Stripes," Markie patriotically replies as he stretches his neck, raises his head high, puffs up his chest, and points his right wing tip to his heart.

"Wait till you see the gorgeous wetlands!" Markie boasts.

"And just how long will it be until we get to see them?" Lynn asks.

"Soon," Markie says.

"Ugh!" Lynn grumbles.

"Well, I can't say exactly how long because there are variables like weather and stuff," Markie explains.

"Fine. I've heard of exotic places with royal palm trees that are so tall they touch the clouds. I'm picturing Beverly and I leaning against one, being cooled by the shade of its luxurious, long fronds and relaxing the day away. Is that close to what it will be like?" Lynn asks.

"Sure," Markie says, seizing the opportunity to break away from his confinement.

He motions to Harold and says, "Hey, buddy. Let's go for a little paddle."

As they swim away from the hens, Markie says quietly, "I don't have the heart to tell Lynn that we are only about halfway to our destination."

"I know. No need to upset her. Migration is much harder than I ever imagined. I still think about Susie and Michael," Harold admits.

"The philosophy of the experienced migrators regarding what first-time migrators need to know is 'less is more'; too much information will over-whelm and discourage them. But trust me, our destination will be worth it," Markie says, trying to put a positive spin on the situation.

"As soon as we can, we need to get back to Plan B. Hopefully, that will lift Beverly and Lynn's spirits. I know that *not* having that scoundrel Dylan around has picked up mine," Harold comments, sounding relieved.

Without human predators lurking around, the flock enjoys the next two days and three nights enjoying everything that Last Mountain Lake Wildlife Area* has to offer. They explore the lake, marsh, and natural grass-lands, birdwatch, and make new friends with species they've never seen before. It's not all play, though. They also rest to recharge for their next flight, eat regularly to regain their energy, and spend time preening their roughed-up feathers.

Once again in Captain mode, Jayson says, "Okay, gang. The sun has set, and it's time to leave. Follow me!"

---

*The internationally recognized Last Mountain Lake National Wildlife Area was designated in 1907 as Canada's first federal bird sanctuary under the Migratory Birds Convention Act, the first of this designation in all of North America.

"Here we go again," Beverly whispers to Harold.

"It's a good thing. The more flights we have, the sooner we get to warmer weather," Harold tells her.

Swimming in single file, Captain Jayson skillfully weaves the flock from their quiet cattail area through the massive gathering of birds to get to the international waterfowl departure area of the lake.

"Formation, please!" Captain Jayson shouts to be heard above the chaos.

The flock speedily gets into their A and B Line positions.

While they wait for a sedge of Whooping Cranes to become airborne, Captain Jayson shouts, "Get ready to power up your amazing wings!"

Once the whoopers are up, Captain Jayson yells, "Our turn! Visual check assistance appreciated."

The ducks scour the sky for silhouettes as they taxi into position.

Captain Jayson and the ducks spring out of the water, flying north for a short distance to get out of the congested air space before gently banking to the right and heading in a southeasterly direction.

"It was nice to feel special and safe for a while," Beverly tells Harold.

"I'm sure we'll stop at other places that appreciate us. The good news is we'll be back here in the spring," Harold says.

Guided by both their natural GPS of the stars and the experienced migrators reading the terrain, the ducks flap their way in the dark with only the glow of moonlight to help them.

Bored, cold, and tired, the flock gently move their heads from side to side as the light-sensitive protein molecules in their eyes detect, read, or see the Earth's magnetic field, which guides them to stay on course—another scientific marvel of migratory birds.

In the near distance, a cluster of lights illuminates the darkness.

"That's the town of Strasbourg," Instructor Riley informs the flock. "The human predators don't hunt for us in their towns since their hard pebbles can hurt other humans too—so we don't have to hide. Shall we give the town folk a big Havenwood Cove hello?" she asks.

THE BOOMERANG GANG

The flock replies with an excited "yes!"

"Okay, let's do it! Follow me," Jayson says, slowing his speed and leading the ducks safely above the street, mindful of traffic, lights, and wires.

Feeling like stars in a parade, the flock quacks and *kreep*s loudly as they slowly approach the centre main road of Strasbourg, Saskatchewan.

"Look! Humans are waving at us," Taleena shouts.

Honk! Honk! Honk!

"Even the cars are saying hello," Anne laughs.

With just a few flaps of their wings, the flock disappears again into blackness.

Their peaceful flight is suddenly interrupted by Captain Jayson yelling, "Whoa!" before he darts to the right and quickly gains altitude. "Grain elevator! They just seem to pop up out of the flat land," Jayson explains.

Thankfully, the ducks followed his lead, and there were no smash-ups into the tall, skinny, bright red wooden structure with its canary-yellow roof.

Markie tells Harold, "You don't want to fly into a grain elevator, but a visit inside would be nice. It's full of our favourite foods."

"That was a fun break from boredom!" Anne shouts.

"It feels nice making someone happy," Taleena says.

"The barking dogs didn't seem happy," Easton comments.

"Let's do it again in the spring," Beverly suggests.

"Good idea," Harold says.

The flock returns to the mundane routine of flying under the stars. Occasionally, they see bright lights of farmhouses scattered in the darkness, headlights of a vehicle on a country road, and potholes that shimmer in the moonlight.

Sensing the flock is bored again, Instructor Riley says, "See the cluster of lights ahead? That's the small prairie town called Balgonie. Would you all like to hear the true story about The Balgonie Birdman?"

Her question is met with silence. Everyone but Lead Duck Davor stops calling out.

"I'll take that as a yes," Instructor Riley says. "William Wallace Gibson, known as Billy, was born in 1876 in Scotland. At the age of seven, he moved to Canada with his family, who were settlers. Even as a young boy, Billy was obsessed with wanting to fly."

"He probably wished he was a bird," Beverly shouts.

The group laughs as Instructor Riley continues, "Billy had a wonderful imagination. He would ride his pony fast across the wide-open prairies and watch his tethered kites soar behind him. He studied how they flew, and he learned about aerodynamics. He designed and tested various styles of elaborate kites over the years—We won't talk about the nine unfortunate gophers he used as test pilots. Eventually, Billy was ready to design and build his dream flying machine."

"That's what we are!" Easton boasts.

More laughter from the flock as Instructor Riley agrees, then continues. "Bill, now a grown man, moves to Balgonie, Saskatchewan. He secretly hides from his community the fact that he is building a flying machine in a barn."

"Why doesn't he tell anyone?" Lynn asks.

"Because humans would have thought he was crazy and maybe even taken him away," Instructor Riley replies.

What's so crazy about wanting to be like a bird? Anne asks herself.

"Early one morning, while everyone is asleep, Bill tests his first flying machine. He winds up the spring-propelled glider and lets it go off the roof of a building in town; it flies (39.6 m) 130 feet across the road and then crashes into a boxcar."

"That's too bad," Beverly sighs.

"Oh, it's not over! Bill refuses to give up. He designs and begins building a 4-cylinder, 4-cycle engine that he brings with him when he moves to Victoria, B.C. For a few years, he has to put his flying ambitions aside and work to support his family and earn money for his dream machine. As soon as he can, he's back to building and designing his first, actual piloted—no gophers involved—flying machine, which he named 'The Gibson Twin-Plane.' On September 24, 1910, at Deans Farm near Victoria, William Wallace Gibson, age 34, with no flying experience, became the first Canadian pilot to fly in an all-Canadian designed and built plane."

"How far did it fly? How far did it fly?" Easton asks.

Instructor Riley continues, "A ground takeoff with an incline was not a challenge for the one-of-a-kind, powerful, and lightweight Gibson Twin-Plane. Its 40–60 horsepower gasoline engine roared, and its two propellers whirled at lightning speed as Bill and his plane soared between (9-15 m) 30–50 feet up in the air. In his (16 m) 54-foot-long and (6 m) 20-foot-wide machine, Bill was flying! He was realizing his lifelong dream of seeing the world from our perspective."

The ducks let out happy quacks and *kreep*s, in honour of a fellow flying enthusiast.

"Sitting in his open-air saddle seat with the breeze sweeping through his hair, Bill operated the wired-together functions of his sturdy flying machine, its double blue silk wings gleaming in the sunshine."

"Hey! You drakes have blue speculum feathers on your wings. He copied you!" Lynn shouts.

"Wait. There's more," Instructor Riley says. "Suddenly, a strong cross-wind hit his flying machine, causing it to bounce around. Bill realized he was making the situation worse by misusing the two rudders, so after flying (60.9 m) 200 feet, he cut the engine and safely landed the plane without damage. Bill and his beloved flying machine rolled along the bumpy ground for a long distance on its four skinny wheels until it came to an abrupt stop when it hit an oak tree. Bill was so concerned about flying that he hadn't designed a braking system."

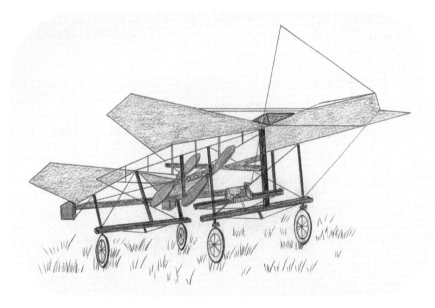

"We all know about not releasing our brakes in time," Jayson chuckles.

"Poor Bill. Well, at least he got to fly like us for a little while," Beverly says.

"Did he fly again?" Janis asks.

"Bill and his family moved to Alberta, where he designed and built a new model of a plane with more lift. He called it 'The Gibson Multi-Plane.' Bill promised his wife he wouldn't fly anymore, so he hired a pilot for test flights. The new and improved plane flew for a whole mile (1.6 km)."

"Wow!" Easton shouts.

"Right? But... the pilot crashed it on landing," Instructor Riley says. "And although Bill kept on inventing, designing, and building airplane parts, he never made another plane. He believed 'you have to hold onto a dream and see where it takes you.'"

"His dream took him flying like a bird," Harold comments.

"Jayson and I can tell you stories about other human wannabe-birds if you like." Instructor Riley tells the flock.

"That would be amazing!" Beverly says.

The flock clacks their bills in support of hearing more stories.

"We really *are* pretty fabulous. I mean, we can swim, walk, and fly! Who wouldn't want to be us?" Harold boasts.

"I guess I shouldn't be upset with having a sore wing when I hear about what Bill had to go through to fly," Janis adds.

"Bill accomplished so much, and he grew up in an itty-bitty town," Easton comments.

"Only your imagination and your efforts limit you," Jayson reminds the flock.

The story was the perfect way to help pass the time for the weary travellers. It seems like it had just been a few minutes—and not hours—when Davor announces, "We're almost in the United States!"

CHAPTER 23

A chorus of "seriously?" "wow!" "finally!" and "yay!" rise from the group, as their eyes eagerly scan the ground below.

"If you look down to your left, you'll see the International United States border crossing." Davor directs. "And newbies, please join the experienced migrators in giving our dear friend, Chuck, the U.S. Customs and Border Protection Agent, a big hello. Chuck loves us, and we love him!"

"What's he talking about?" Harold asks Markie.

"We come through the border twice a year, and Chuck likes teasing us. Just follow our lead," Markie tells Harold, Beverly, and Lynn.

Davor studies the sky and the flat landscape of farmland as they quickly approach a well-lit area with a large, one-story building.

"Okay, Mallards—let's let Chuck know the flock from Havenwood Cove has arrived!" Davor shouts. "Zipper formation, please!"

Everyone seamlessly merges to form a single line. Davor carefully slows the pace and lowers his flying height to safely fly through the carport. At just a few feet above the paved roadway, the flock is perfectly lined up to the building's side window. The red stoplights on the tall, bright yellow posts seem to welcome the ducks as they turn green.

"Let's go, team!" Davor shouts.

Straight ahead and leaning out of the window is Chuck, a tall, slender, older gentleman with kind eyes, a big smile, and a weathered-looking face, and he's enthusiastically waving for the ducks to approach.

"Welcome back, Boomerang Gang! Anything to declare?" Chuck asks with a belly laugh as he stretches forward as far as he can to greet them as they slowly fly by.

Davor gives Chuck a hello nod and a loud, friendly *kreep*, and each duck that follows greets him with the same affection.

"See you in the spring! Travel safely, quackers!" Chuck bellows.

The flock gives a festive goodbye call out and dips their wings as they leave the brightly-lit customs area.

Harold quickly looks back and sees Chuck in the distance, still waving.

Increasing their speed and gaining altitude, they return to their V formation, synchronize their flapping and pacing, and once again enjoy the benefits of drafting. Everyone is happy to conserve energy as they move through the darkness over farm fields and less-travelled roads.

"Well, that was Chuck. What did you newbies think?" Jayson asks.

"He's great!" Taleena says.

"Why did he call us the Boomerang Gang?" Harold asks.

"That's the nickname he gave us years ago because we're just like a boomerang; we fly away, and then we come back," Jayson explains.

"The Boomerang Gang—I like it!" Beverly says.

"Me too! It's catchy," Taleena comments.

"Chuck's the best," Instructor Riley agrees.

From the front of the V, they hear Davor's voice with an update: "Goodbye, Canada, and hello, United States of America! We are now flying high in the state of North Dakota!"

The first-time migrators become quiet.

"This is exciting, but I can't help but wonder what's happening back home," Beverly whispers to Harold.

"I was just thinking the same thing. I bet Sebastian's rushing around looking for food for his hoard. He's probably still getting into trouble with Miss Marie."

"Do you think they think about us?"

"I'm sure they do. After all, we think of them," Harold says, even though he feels he probably misses his friends more than they miss him.

"Adventurers don't get all sappy and homesick," Markie bluntly tells Harold, Beverly, and Lynn.

"I didn't say anything," Lynn quips.

"Yeah, yeah. But I know you were thinking it. First migrations are always tough, but after you've done one, you'll see that when you go back to Havenwood Cove that nothing has changed. Just more babies show up. Think of the stories you'll have to tell!" Markie explains.

"You're absolutely right. We are the four adventurers!" Harold says with conviction.

"Yes, real friends are always with us in our hearts and thoughts," Beverly says.

"And we are going to be spending the winter in warm weather. Right?" Lynn asks.

"Right!" Markie confirms.

Davor gently banks to the left. "Who's ready to set down for the night?" he asks, already knowing the answer.

"I'm ready!" Janis tells him.

"Me too!" Anne replies.

"Glad to hear that! We'll soon be landing in North Dakota's Des Lacs National Wildlife Refuge, which is another wildlife-safe zone," Davor tells his entourage.

DES LACS NATIONAL WILDLIFE REFUGE

In 1935, President Franklin D. Roosevelt established the Des Lacs National Wildlife Refuge in North Dakota in response to the dwindling migratory wildlife numbers. The 1930s dust bowl drought and established settlements along the river valley meant more hunting and fewer safe spaces for the birds, so he established a safe rest stop.

"Yay!" Beverly shrieks as sounds of excitement rise from the group.

"Listen up, everyone! This is a popular rest spot for migrating Mallards and shorebirds, but it's the hot destination for the Lesser Snow Goose and Tundra Swans," Davor says.

"Tundra Swans and I have a history. Me plummeting headfirst comes to mind," Beverly tells Harold.

"Well, now we know we have to watch out for them," Harold says with confidence.

"I don't think I've met a Lesser Snow Goose before. How will I recognize one?" Lynn asks.

"Bright white body, black wing tips, friendly little black eyes, and a smallish pink bill," Instructor Riley replies. "They're a cozy breed, with blended families. The blue ones have a white head and a blueish colour on the lower back and flank feathers. Their body colour can range from almost white to dark."

"They definitely look happy," Jayson adds. "The black serrated edge of their bill curves up to look like they're smiling, and the feathers on their face are stained a light orange from the iron in the Earth where they eat, which makes it look like they are blushing."

"Oh, now I really hope I get to meet one," Lynn says.

"Me too. The Lesser Snow Goose sound lovely!" Beverly adds.

"Oh, I guarantee you'll meet one," Instructor Riley snickers.

As they fly over farms and potholes, a high-pitched, howling sound becomes louder.

"What *is* that noise?" Lynn shouts.

"Be careful what you wish for," Instructor Riley laughs.

The rising noise sounds like a pack of baying hounds, and Davor struggles to shout above it. "Prepare for landing! All eyes on patrol, please!"

"This feels familiar!" Beverly shouts to Harold.

"I guess the best spots are always going to be busy," Harold replies.

"Focus, everyone! Prepare for landing!" Davor shouts.

With the help of moonlight, Davor and the flock inspect the sky and landscape for nearby air traffic. As they fly over the river embankment, the newbies are shocked to see a plethora of bobbing white birds—some mostly black with a bit of white—each chattering in a loud, single syllable, a nasally *whouk* or *houck*.

"Birds everywhere!" Taleena screams.

Davor knows the call-up announcing their arrival will be lost in all the noise, so he sets the flock down on the river near a marsh area, as far away as possible from the massive group of Lesser Snow Geese and their amplified barking sounds.

Bewildered, Beverly looks around, and yells to Harold, "I've got a feeling we're not in Havenwood Cove anymore!"

Stunned at seeing the blanket of white on the water and the blizzard of white in the sky, Harold shouts, "That's for sure!"

Lynn yells, "Wow! I can hardly believe my eyes and ears. They're everywhere!"

Safely landed, Instructor Riley teases, "Lynn, you mentioned you wanted to meet a Lesser Snow Goose. Well, here's your chance."

"I said ONE, not a river full."

"Just be thankful that they're roosting on the water and not flying in at the same time we are. They like to sleep during the night, so our timing is perfect," Jayson adds.

"How will we ever fly through the blizzard of them in the sky?" Beverly asks.

"Don't fret," Markie tells her. "We always manage, even though there are more birds here than I've ever seen here before."

"Oh, right! Remember the flight incident on the beaver dam trip?" Beverly says scornfully.

"That won't happen again. I promise you," Markie says.

"Sure, that's because the last one was with Whooping Cranes. You had better not be catching me on a wordplay," Beverly replies, unamused.

"Let's give thanks to Jayson and Davor for leading us here safely," Instructor Riley says.

The flock clacks their bills in appreciation.

"Okay, I'm ready for a little after-flight snack and then some rest," Jayson reveals.

"Who wants to be on predator patrol? Being away from the shore and with so many other birds around should make it an easy watch," Davor comments.

"I will," Easton says.

"Me too," Anne offers.

"Enjoy your evening. Stay close," Jayson tells everyone.

"We'll be okay," Harold whispers to Beverly.

"I guess so, but every time I get my courage up, something awful happens."

"I understand. I feel the same way, but that's what an adventure is: surprises. Some are good, and some are not, but every time we have a bad one and deal with it, we get stronger and braver. Look at Markie. He's pretty bold because he's had some adventures," Harold says, draping his wing over Beverly's back.

"Well, he didn't look so brave when Paco picked him up. He shook like a prairie rattler's tail," Beverly giggles.

"He sure did. Adventurers are a work in progress, I guess. It doesn't mean you're never afraid; it just means you try your best to confront difficult situations."

"You're right, Harold. I'm trying."

"Me too."

Bobbing on the marsh, Harold and Beverly snuggle close with Janis and the flock. Tonight's concert is neither restful nor enjoyable, thanks to the thousands of Lesser Snow Geese *houck*ing away.

Markie wakes with the poke of a wing. "Morning, Markie! How can you sleep with all this noise and cold?" He opens one eye and sees Lynn glaring at him.

"Hen, what do you want?"

"You keep telling me that we'll wake up in warmth one day. WHEN?" Lynn asks.

"One day. Just not this one."

"Ugh," Lynn groans, shaking the icy bits off her feathers.

"How did everyone sleep, knowing that Easton and I were protecting you?" Anne asks.

"Great!" Beverly replies.

The ducks clack in agreement.

Easton and Anne puff up their chests and do a wing tap.

"Gather close for a quick meeting," Instructor Riley asks.

"We will stay here for four days and leave the following night just after sunset. Remember, this is a zone that's safe from human predators. There are marshes, wetlands, and some grain fields close by for you to explore. Be careful and be back here before sunset each night. Jayson or I will be here if you need us. Any questions?"

"I'm going to stay close," Janis says.

"Wonderful. I look forward to your company," Instructor Riley tells her. "If that's all, go have fun and be safe," she tells everyone.

"First, I'm going to eat, tidy myself up, then explore," Lynn says.

"Sounds like a plan," Beverly, Harold, and Markie agree. Paddling around the marsh, they tip up in search of tasty eats.

Lynn nips at Beverly's tail just as she's about to tip up again.

"What's up?"

"Are you finding much to eat?"

"Not really; I only get a little morsel each time," Beverly tells her. "You?"

"Same. It's barely worth the effort," Lynn says.

"What are you hens talking about?" Harold asks.

"We aren't finding much to eat here," Beverly comments.

"Me too. It's going to be exhausting trying to find enough to fill my stomach," he says.

"How about we try another area?" Markie suggests.

"I have a craving for some grain," Lynn mentions.

"A grain field sounds good to me," Harold says.

"Me too," Beverly says.

"I know of a farmer's field that's close and safe—it'll have lots for us to eat. Follow me," Markie says.

The four adventures paddle out of their tucked-away marsh area to find themselves bumping their way through hundreds of Lesser Snow Geese to find an open space. Luckily, they spot a narrow strip of water perfect for departures and arrivals on the river.

"My ears are ringing from their annoying chatter. They just might be the noisiest birds ever! What could they possibly have to say all day and all night? Do they talk in their sleep?" Beverly groans.

"Have you ever seen so many birds? There must be hundreds of thousands of them. They're everywhere! The river is blanketed with them, and the sky looks like a shimmering curtain of black and white. The sun can barely find a spot to break through, so how are we going to?" Lynn asks, disillusioned.

"How do they keep from not smashing into each other?" Beverly asks.

"Haven't got a clue," Lynn replies.

"Get in a single line. Harold, you be at the end to keep an eye on the hens," Markie tells his three overwhelmed friends.

"I'll takeoff when I see an opening, and you follow!" Markie shouts.

As Markie watches for a breakout opportunity, Harold, Beverly, and Lynn stay focused on him while trying not to be pushed into a gaggle of geese that are coming closer and closer.

"How are we ever going to get airborne?" Beverly cries as the Lesser Snow Geese dominate the land and the sky.

"NOW!" Markie shouts as he springs out of the water and flies as fast as he can.

"GO, BEVERLY!" Lynn screams.

Panicked, Beverly bolts out of the water. She ignores everything around her and beats her wings as fast as possible, and safely catches up to Markie.

"I'm right behind you!" Lynn yells to Beverly.

Prisoners to the droning sound of flapping wings and the combination of high-pitched quacks, shrill cries, and hoarse-sounding honks of the Snow Geese, Lynn faintly hears Harold call out, "I'm coming!" He's desperately trying to catch up without smashing into a goose, or two, or hundreds.

Miraculously, the ducks break through the dense curtain of Lesser Snow Geese unscathed.

"Everyone safe?" Markie shouts while staying focused on the sky ahead.

"We're all here," Harold reports.

"Great. The field's coming up. Stay close," Markie shouts.

Markie feels his nervous entourage breathing down his neck as he leads them—with some sudden zigs and zags to safely avoid smash-ups.

"WHOA!" Beverly blurts as she zigs and breaks to let a Canada Goose fly by.

"Watch out!" Lynn yells as she zags around a goose who barely misses touching her wingtip.

Markie wastes no time, deciding to safely set the ducks down on the first open ground he sees. Surprisingly, all eight webbed feet touch down on the stubbly harvested wheat field without a major mishap.

"That was a survival challenge. Thankfully, we all passed," a shaky Harold says.

"I'm impressed by all of you," Markie tells the overwhelmed group.

"Thanks," Lynn says, still gasping.

"Ouch. I definitely prefer landing on the cushiony pea field. These stubbly fields scratch up my feathers," Beverly grumbles, stressed out from the flight, the birds, the noise, the cold, the migration—everything.

"I know; I'm going to need a pedicure after this," Lynn comments while checking out her feet.

Look! Lesser Snow Geese and Canada geese are everywhere. Why are they called 'Lesser Snow Geese'? They should be called 'Morer' Snow Geese," Beverly snaps.

"The last time I was here, there were only a few geese. I guess our timing is off on this migration," Markie explains.

"Really?" Beverly says sarcastically.

"Let's dine and dash," Harold proposes.

"Sounds good to me!" Lynn says, Beverly agrees.

"Great idea. But first, I'll tell you how to eat wheat," Markie says. "Wheat is not like barley. Barley spikes and seeds break apart in our mouth before we swallow them. Wheat doesn't. So, we only eat what's on the ground. These are the leftovers from the farmer's combine harvester or wind damage. We cannot eat a whole spike—which is the head with rows of kernels—at once because it's too big and tough to swallow. We don't want to risk choking. We only eat broken spikes and loose kernels. Bottom line, wheat is tasty but tedious. Any questions?" Markie asks.

"That's probably why Anne told us she prefers barley," Harold tells Lynn.

"What does a broken spike look like?" Beverly asks Markie.

"I'll show you." With his eyes studying debris on the bare ground between two rows of short stubble, Markie waddles a couple of steps and then stops. Using the nail at the tip of his bill, he draws a circle in the soil around a perfect example of a broken head. "Don't eat anything larger than this size."

Harold, Beverly, and Lynn move closer to inspect the sample.

"Right!" Lynn says, snapping it up. "No need to waste all those kernels."

"Okay, let's feast!" Markie says.

The four adventurers are on a mission to devour as much grain as they can, as fast as they can, and then leave as fast as they can.

Just as Beverly is about to pick up a broken spike, she hears a hissing sound. Startled, she looks up to see a large Canada Goose with its black head and white cheeks and chinstrap glaring at her with round, brown eyes.

Beverly quickly gobbles up the spike, then waddles away. *I saw it first— no bully is going to intimidate me.*

The field is full of birds acting like bumper cars, each waddling around with their heads down to the ground, gobbling grain like they're in a competition.

"I'm ready to leave," Harold tells Lynn.

"Me too. I'm full, and I'm tired of being shoved around. I'm probably black and blue under my feathers."

"I wonder where Beverly and Markie are," Harold says, looking around.

"Beverly!" Harold yells as he stretches his neck and rotates his head like a periscope.

"I see them! They're coming. I'm amazed that they heard you," Lynn comments.

"You ready to go?" Markie asks everyone.

"Ready!" he hears each of them respond.

"Follow me," Markie says as he weaves his way through the gaggle of geese to get to a perfect area for takeoff. "Line up, and let's leave this madness."

Markie surveys the ground and sky and plans his route in between two incoming flocks. On cue, Beverly, Lynn, and Harold follow Markie as he strategically leads them through throngs of geese to join their friends back at Des Lacs National Wildlife Refuge.

A bit shaky but safe, the four adventurers reunite with their flock and tuck in among the cattails.

"Where'd you go?" Anne asks them.

"To a nearby wheat field," Harold tells her.

"And... how was it?" Anne asks.

"It was bonkers! Sooooooo many geese!" Harold answers, speaking for the group. "But we tasted some new grains, and had a great—but somewhat frightening—adventure."

As the sun falls below the horizon, the air chills, the sky darkens, and the chorus of guttural calls and nasal *whouk, whouk, whouk* honks of the Lesser Snow Geese amplifies.

"What can they possibly talk about for so long?" Beverly asks Lynn.

"I don't know, but it's downright rude. It's not all about them; other birds share this space."

"They certainly live up to their reputation as the noisiest of all waterfowl," Markie says.

"Listen up, everyone," Instructor Riley says to the floating flock, as they nestle together for warmth. "We usually fly ahead of the masses of Lesser

Snow Geese, but this time we are trailing them, and we have a concern. They are eating most of the food before we arrive."

"That's why we left the water—there was hardly anything to eat," Markie comments.

"The wheat field was almost bare. A Canada Goose even hissed at me over a spike," Beverly says. "But FYI, *I* ate the spike," she giggles.

The flock clacks their bills, shakes their heads, and talks among themselves.

Instructor Riley continues, "The gossip around the marsh is that the Lesser Snow Geese are running out of food in their Arctic nesting area, and soon, they won't be able to feed everyone."

The ducks gasp.

"They're lovely birds, but they're voracious, aggressive foragers who are a threat to us because they eat the same plants as we do. They use their strong, serrated bills and powerful tongues to cut, tear, and rip a plant out by the roots. It doesn't matter if it's growing under the water or in the ground. They devour most or all of the plant. It will never grow back; it's gone forever. And now, they're ravishing the winter wheat that the farmers have planted."

Another gasp from the ducks.

"So much for their smiley-looking grin patch—they're really terminators in disguise," Easton says.

"Are we going to starve?" Janis asks.

"This is not good. It's bad. Really bad," Beverly nervously repeats.

Instructor Riley notices twitching feathers and distressed looks in the flock. "No need to panic. We just have to come up with a plan so that we get to the food source first."

"See? That's what adventurers do. We confront problems and come up with solutions," Harold whispers to Beverly.

"Do you have a solution?"

"Let me think."

Markie leans into Beverly. "Don't worry; we are survivors. We live with obstacles like toxins in water, dried-up ponds, and lead poisoning every day."

"Whaaaaat? Toxins and lead poisoning?" Beverly shrieks.

"Markie! You are *not* helping," Lynn scolds before she jabs her bill into his side.

"We'll be fine," Harold says to Beverly as he gives Markie a, "What were you thinking?" look.

"Sorry, buddy. I'm a realist. I'll try to think before I speak. Borrowing from the Greek philosopher Socrates, I should first ask myself, "Is it true, is it kind, or is it necessary?" I really have to work on the last one."

Instructor Riley rejoins the conversation with, "Jayson overheard some Lesser Snow Geese mentioning that the whole flock plans on leaving in three days because they will be well rested then. They prefer to fly during the daylight and roost on the water at night."

"What they really mean is rested and *well-fed*. They've probably planned their departure on how long it will take their flock of thousands to eat everything till there's not a blade of grass or a seed or a kernel left," Anne says.

"I agree," Easton says as his fellow ducks nod and clack in agreement.

Instructor Riley flaps her wings to gain control of the meeting. "How does everyone feel about departing earlier than we planned? We'll miss the chaos in the sky—although Lesser Snow Geese normally fly at a higher altitude than we do—and we'll have a better chance of getting to the food supply before the geese arrive if they stop where we are."

The flock discusses the matter while Jayson and Instructor Riley wait.

As the elected spokesduck, Markie asks, "Is there an option to fly during the day and stay safe from human predators? Some of the newbies are bored with flying in the dark; they're excited to see new landscapes and learn our route and visual markers."

Jayson replies, "Migration plans change according to the circumstances that arise. Instructor Riley and I are confident that since we are presently in a 'safe, no human predators allowed' zone, we can safely fly to our next rest stop during the day and land just after sunset—but only if you follow our plan."

The flock leans in to make sure they don't miss anything.

"You must be well rested, preened for top performance, and well-fed. We can leave mid-morning, but here's the twist: we must fly up to a high altitude almost immediately so we are safely out of reach of being ambushed once we leave the safe zone. Can you do that?" Jayson asks.

The flock discusses what is expected of them. Markie informs Jayson and Instructor Riley that the flock feels confident they can meet the criteria.

"Okay. We will depart in two days, around mid-morning. Make sure you are prepared. Until then, stay safe and stay close," Jayson tells the flock.

"I think I'll have a little bedtime snack before tucking in," Harold tells Beverly.

"Great idea; me too!" she responds.

Together, they paddle around the marsh, tipping up and skimming the surface of the water for tasty bugs and algae.

"I got a root, three grubs, and a few insects," Beverly reports.

"I got a slug, two small snails, and a bit of algae," Harold says.

"I hope we find more tomorrow, or we won't have the energy to fly," Beverly whispers to Harold.

As Taleena and Davor keep watch, the ducks huddle close, hidden among the withered bulrushes, and try to drown out the unruly nonstop chatter of their neighbours.

CHAPTER 24

Waking to the flapping sounds of wings overhead and the continuous loud, nasally *whouk*, *kowk*, and *kow-luk* sounds of the Lesser Snow Geese, Harold and the flock fluff their feathers to warm up.

The ducks complete their flight preparation to-do list, just as they promised they would.

Mid-morning on the day of departure, the ducks scrounge for food that the geese haven't devoured.

"Okay, follow me," Captain Jayson says as he leads the group on a path of twists and turns through the gathering of geese. Their deafening sounds reverberate in the duck's ears as they search for a small, open area for departures.

"Remember, we must reach high altitude almost immediately to be safe. Can we do it?"

A clamouring of "yes!" rises from the flock.

"No. I asked, 'CAN WE DO IT?'"

"YES, CAPTAIN!" the flock shouts.

With everyone in the V position, they start counting. On five, Jayson bolts out of the water like a rocket heading to the sun. Easton and Instructor Riley immediately follow, calling out loudly as they stay laser-focused on their target: Captain Jayson. As always, Instructor Riley's speed is excellent despite her wobbly-looking performance.

"You can do this!" Harold shouts to Beverly.

Nervously waiting her turn, she gives Harold a quick nod.

"We're up," Taleena says.

Beverly and Taleena nervously quack in sync as they zoom like projectiles to catch up to Instructor Riley and Easton.

"Look at her go!" Harold yells out proudly.

"Yikes! We're next," Harold tells Davor as he says to himself, *I am an adventurer.*

"You've got this, hot wings," Davor teases.

On cue, Harold blasts off the water like a missile targeting the cutest little tail feathers skyrocketing ahead of him.

"Whoo-hoo!" shouts the usually reserved Davor as he shoots up with his wing buddy Harold by his side.

"Wowzerrrr!" Harold hollers uncontrollably, as if a daredevil has invaded his body. A whizzing sound hisses in his ears as his wings slice through the air.

On cue, Lynn, Anne, Markie, and Janis rush to join the others.

"You're doing great!" Markie shouts to Janis, who grimaces with each beat of her wounded wing.

Once the ducks are out of ambush range, Captain Jayson levels off, surveys the sky, then banks to the right and leads the ducks southeast.

"We did what we had to do—but don't tell anyone I was scared," Beverly tells Harold.

"I saw you! You were amazing, my little rocket hen."

"I like that: rocket hen and hot wings," Beverly giggles.

"You were terrific as well," Markie tells Lynn.

"Thanks. I was trying to break the sound barrier to escape the gluttonous geese."

"Right? Goodbye and good riddance! They thought they owned the place," Beverly comments.

"I hope our next rest stop is quiet. Enough of these fancy, overcrowded, popular hot spots," Janis adds, quietly whimpering in pain.

"I agree. I tried to be friendly. I said hi to a few geese, but all I ever got was just a nod. No one stopped eating to see who was saying hi," Taleena says.

"Finally, the drumming sound in my ears has stopped," Anne broadcasts.

Flying high out of gunshot range, the flock starts to relax and calmly call out as the sun's rays warm them. It's a frigid autumn day with a slight northerly breeze, guiding the clouds along.

"What's not to love about a tailwind?" Harold says to Markie.

"I know. Legend has it that Maggie Mallard travelled (1287 km) 800 miles in one day with a nice tailwind."

"Even with a tailwind, I don't think I would be able to do that," Harold says.

"We're capable of doing it, but what's the rush? Unless I'm being chased by a flock of eagles, I'm happy to enjoy the journey and not be totally wasted when I arrive at my destination," Markie tells Harold.

"Maggie was determined, but the Black Brant Ducks are even *more* determined. We don't have to worry about them stopping and eating all the food supply. They're super focused on getting south as fast as they can," Davor comments.

BLACK BRANT DUCKS

Black Brant Ducks migrate nonstop from coastal Alaska all the way down to Baja California. They travel approximately (4,828 km) 3,000 miles in just 60–72 hours and lose almost half of their body weight.

"I guess I have to toughen up," Harold jokes.

"Pintail Pete told me that his Alaskan-born relatives migrate nonstop over water. He said they've been shooed away from top-deck buffets on cruise ships. Can't blame them for wanting a little rest and fine dining," Markie laughs.

ALASKAN-BORN PINTAIL DUCKS

Alaskan-born Pintail Ducks migrate nonstop (3,218 km) 2,000 miles over water to winter in Hawaii. In 1940, a banded Pintail Duck had travelled (128,747 km) 80,000 air miles (travelling from Athabasca, Alberta, Canada to Naucuspana, Mexico — (4,828 km) 3,000 miles each way, twice a year) over its lifetime when it was shot down by a hunter.

"Whoa. The flyway is busy today," Instructor Riley says, observing a flurry of activity of hundreds of birds.

"Well, at least they're keeping their distance. Are all those birds going to the same place we are?" Beverly asks, concerned.

"I hope not. I've had enough of the whole social scene and scrambling to find something to eat," Lynn says.

"Calm your feathers! You'll love where we are going next; it's quiet. And there are indeed humans, but not the predatory kind," Instructor Riley assures the hens.

The flock continues their flight south, enjoying the panoramic scenery of country roads, farmhouses, and ponds that dot the sprawling agricultural flatlands and rolling hills. Their birds'-eye view allows them to see the exquisite patchwork quilt of various-shaped fields of: pinto beans, dry beans, canola, flaxseed, oats, sunflower, field peas, and wheat.

Looking over their right wings, the ducks watch the last of the sun's rays cast a pinkish glow on the calm water and illuminate the golden grain fields as they fly parallel to the Missouri River.

"What's that?" Beverly asks.

"Markie, is this a city? With glass, flashing lights, and lots of humans?" Harold stammers.

"It sure is, but it's a smaller, friendly one. Don't worry; we're going to fly by it," Markie says.

"It's beautiful! I love all the little lights," Lynn says as a few more pop on.

"Look, there's a tall building, just like the grain elevators in Saskatchewan," Taleena says, excited.

"Well, not *quite*," Markie chuckles. "That's Bismarck, the capital city of North Dakota, and that stunning, 21-story Art Deco State Capital Building is known as the 'Skyscraper on the Prairie.' It's (74 m) 243 feet tall and in no way resembles the grain elevators of the Canadian prairies. But good eye, Taleena!"

Davor banks to the left, and Instructor Riley advises the flock that they'll be landing soon.

Harold, Beverly, Lynn, and Taleena miss that announcement, distracted by the sights below: cars, buildings, flashing lights, humans, and wide roads busy with vehicles going places.

"Oh, more lights just popped on!" Lynn says, intrigued by the illuminated buildings.

"Harold, could you have ever imaged anything like this?" Beverly asks him.

"No. Just think of the stories we can share with our friends back home."

"Prepare for landing," Instructor Riley says.

"I wonder where we're going," Beverly asks.

"Markie said it's a nice place and that we'll be safe there," Harold replies.

Davor and the flock lower their altitude, reduce their speed, and announce their arrival. Flying over a wide, one-level, tan-coloured building with a green roof, they approach a vast area of ultra-short grass—but not like the stubble in the farmers' fields. A narrow pathway weaves its way around a pond, with circular areas and evergreen trees scattered throughout.

"Why do we need a safety watch if there are no human predators?" Beverly asks.

"Coyotes," Markie answers.

"This doesn't look like a farmer's field," Taleena comments.

"It's not," Anne tells her.

"What is it then?" Lynn asks.

"I don't want to ruin the surprise. How about I take you on a tour tomorrow when we can see everything? You are going to love it here. Maybe, even more than visiting the field of peas," Anne jests.

"Sounds good to me," Lynn says.

"Me too!" Beverly agrees.

"Make like a zipper," Instructor Riley shouts.

Immediately, the ducks weave and merge together into a single line.

"We're getting good at this," Harold brags to Markie.

Following Davor's lead, the ducks prepare for their final landing as they follow a narrow, serene creek that is hidden by grasses, bushes, and leafy trees on both banks.

One by one, they gracefully splash down. Everyone releases tension by shaking out their wings, stretching their necks, and letting their legs and feet dangle as they float.

"Oh, that feels good. My wing muscles are a little tight," Harold says.

"Mine are sore," Beverly says.

"I can hardly wait to relax my neck muscles tonight," Lynn says.

"Good thing we zippered. With our (0.9 m) three-foot wingspans, I don't think there's enough room for two sets of wings side-by-side," Harold tells Markie.

"Listen!" Lynn tells everyone.

They all freeze, listening for a threat of some sort.

"I don't hear anything," Beverly whispers.

"I know! Isn't it wonderful?" Lynn says.

"You're right. It's just what we all need—peace and quiet," Janis says as she shakes out her left wing and leaves her right wing limp-resting on the water.

"I'm tired—but first, I'm going to eat," Easton says.

"Good plan," Jayson agrees.

Markie leans close to Harold, Beverly, and Lynn and whispers, "Follow me."

With the moonlight hiding behind a canopy of trees and bushes, the three newbies follow Markie in the darkness as he paddles along the calm water between two steep banks of dense vegetation before he stops and says, "This is a good spot to poke around for grubs and worms."

"First things first; I'm parched," Lynn says as she dips her bill under the water, fills it up, then slowly raises her head, tilts it back, and swallows.

"Aahhh. Three more dips should do it."

THE DUCK'S BILL

Its bony skeleton creates the shape and the fleshy covering gives the colour. The bill's sensitive touch receptors are similar to ours in our fingertips and palms.

With their webbed feet acting like snowshoes, the four friends shuffle around on the creek bank, poking their bills into the soft mud, searching for crustaceans, grubs, worms, and plant roots.

After dining and some preening, the flock settles in for the night on their chilly, private waterbed with millions of stars above peeking through tree branches. Tonight's soundtrack is the sound of silence, welcome after the previous night with the thousands of noisy, pushy birds.

The ducks wake feeling refreshed, calm, and thankful that they won't have to scrounge and fight for food.

Instructor Riley addresses the group as they all stretch and ready themselves for the day. "Before Anne gives you her famous guided tour, I want to let you know that we will stay here for two days, two nights, and then leave the following morning. If we can do what we did last time, reaching high altitude fast, we can leave mid-morning and be safe from nearby human predators. Is that doable?"

"We can do that!" the flock replies.

"Good! Stay close. First-time migrators, enjoy your tour, and we'll see everyone back here to sleep. Janis, please update me on your sore wing. That's all," Instructor Riley says.

"Harold! Beverly! Lynn! Are you ready?" Anne asks.

Lynn looks at Markie and says, "Aren't you coming?"

"I've been on Anne's tour before," he answers.

"Yeh, but not with us."

"Fine. I'll tag along," he says with a smile.

Like a proper tour guide, Anne turns to the small group and says, "Okay, let's begin. Follow me."

Anxious to show off the surroundings, she quickly paddles to a narrow, steep path hidden in a thicket. Slowly and carefully, they waddle up the embankment.

"Don't worry about your feathers getting ruffled—it will be worth it," she says.

Reaching the top of the path, the newbies look around in awe at the perfectly maintained field of green.

"It's so soft," Beverly comments as she shuffles her feet around.

"I've never stood on anything so comfy," Lynn says, prancing like a pony.

"Sure feels nicer than stubble," Harold adds.

"This is nothing like a farmer's field; this is a fancy place for fancy humans. They come here, walk around, or ride on little machines. They look up to the sky, they look around, sometimes they squat and feel the grass, then they stand and swing a stick at a little white ball," Anne explains.

"Hmmmm. Bizarre," Harold comments.

"What do they do after they hit the little ball?" Lynn asks.

"They go look for it, then they hit it again," Anne says.

"Definitely bizarre!" Beverly giggles.

"I know," Anne agrees. "Apparently, it's called 'golf.'"

"The humans here are really nice to us, and they leave us alone, unless..."

"Unless what?" Harold asks, intrigued.

"All I can say is that humans don't like to share, so don't ever take one of those little balls. They will yell at you and chase you around. The balls are too hard and big to eat, so there's really no point in taking one unless you want entertainment," Anne cautions.

"Sounds like fun," Markie winks at Harold.

"Don't even think of doing that—we don't want to be shooed away," Anne scolds.

"If you hear a human call out, 'fore!'—DUCK!" Markie says. "You don't want to be hit by a whizzing ball."

"Good to know," Harold says.

"Follow me," Anne directs, leading them to a pond lined with tall, natural grasses along its border.

"I just found my perfect place to unwind. Perhaps a little grooming and dining. Care to join me, Beverly?" Lynn asks.

"Absolutely. I'm feeling fancy—like I belong here."

"Drakes? How about you?" Lynn asks.

"Sounds good to me," Harold says.

Markie nods, "Sure."

"Is this place amazing, or is it amazing?" Anne asks.

"It's beautiful. Quiet and safe. What more could we ask for? We will highly recommend your tour to our friends," Beverly promises.

"Well, everyone, your VID tour is officially over," Anne tells the group.

"VID tour?" Harold asks.

"Very Important Duck!" Anne laughs. "It's the Very Important Duck tour! And now that it's over, I'll leave you here, and Markie will make sure you all get back before curfew. Right, Markie?"

"Right."

"Later!" Anne calls out as she waddles off, tilting side to side with each step.

Beverly and Lynn eagerly nibble the lush green grass on their way to the pond.

"This is luxury! I feel special," Lynn says, floating around without a care in the world.

"Me too. Even the grass tastes fancy! I'm going to see what else there is to eat. Bottoms up," Beverly says.

Almost immediately, she springs up with her bill wide open, clutching a little white ball then swims to the edge of the pond and drops it in the tall grass.

"That must be one of the human's golf balls that they hit and chase. The pond is full of them!" Beverly says excitedly.

Curious about what Beverly's doing, Harold and Markie waddle over to check things out.

Looking at the ball, Harold taps it with his bill. "Hmm, I wonder what's so special about it?"

Markie gives it a little kick. "Don't know."

"The pond is full of them!" Beverly boasts.

"Really? I want to see for myself," Harold says as he enters the water and tips up.

Within a minute, he pops up with one clenched in his bill but drops it.

"Easy come, easy go," Markie laughs.

"I bet we can find more than you can," Lynn challenges the drakes.

"You're on!" Markie says, slipping into the water.

"Drakes vs. hens. We'll put our stash here, and you can put yours over there," Markie says.

"Start!" Beverly shouts as four rumps rise into the air and bright orange legs and feet rapidly move back and forth.

Each duck surfaces with a ball and swims as fast as possible to add it to their stash.

From beyond the pond, they hear someone yell, "Fore!"

"DUCK!" Markie shouts as a little white ball drops from the sky and splashes into the water.

"It's mine," Markie shouts.

Tipping up, he retrieves it and adds it to the drake's pile.

The ducks look up to see humans with sticks yelling at them.

"Hey! Leave it alone," a man shouts as he runs over to the pond to see where Markie put it.

Nervous, the ducks swim to the middle of the pond and watch from a safe distance.

An angry man with a red face that matches his shirt looks down at the grass to see a large collection of balls—an assortment of many white, a few pink, two orange, one red, three blue, lots of yellow, and one with hearts on it.

"Gordon, you've got to see this!" the man yells.

"Wow! What a find," Gordon says as he and his friend zealously grab the golf balls, stuffing them into their pockets until they're full. Not wanting to leave any of the balls behind, the men tuck in their golf shirts and drop the balls into their makeshift pouches. With ear-to-ear grins and a tip of their caps, the men look at the ducks and say, "Thank you, little quackers." They turn and slowly walk away, trying not to drop their windfall of golf balls.

"Anybody else think they're kind of waddling like ducks?" Markie laughs.

"For sure!' Harold replies.

"Well, I think we did a good thing," Beverly comments.

"I think so, too," Markie says.

"They gathered up the balls faster than Sebastian gathers pinecones," Harold jokes.

"All I know is that our pile of balls had more than yours did," Lynn says.

"If you say so," Markie comments, giving Harold a wink.

"I say so because it's the truth," Lynn says.

"Hens are the winners!" Beverly cheers and bobs her head.

The four friends spend a lazy day enjoying themselves at the pond. Occasionally they hear a call of "fore!", then DUCK, and wait for the splash.

"I think it's time to go; it's starting to get dark, and I don't need a scolding from Anne," Markie says.

Waddling back to the creek, Harold stops and turns to see what's keeping Beverly.

CHAPTER 25

"FLY, BEVERLY, FLY!" Harold screams.

Seeing the panic in Harold's eyes, Beverly beats her wings as if her life depends on it. With scrambled thoughts and a pounding heart, she shrieks in pain as her tail feathers are ripped out. Delirious, she calls for Harold, but no sound comes out.

Harold bolts into the air with power that he didn't know he was capable of.

"You're okay, you're okay," he reassures her as they fly around, directionless.

Trembling and tearful, Beverly asks Harold, "What happened? I don't understand what happened," her voice quivering.

"A coyote was tracking you, but you're safe now."

"I felt him, Harold. He pulled out my tail feathers," she says through her sobs.

"You're safe now. You did great. I'm so proud of you. Let's just take our time and fly back to our flock. I'm right beside you," Harold tells her.

They leisurely fly back to their worried friends.

"What happened to you?" Markie asks Harold.

"Are you okay?" everyone asks Beverly, realizing something traumatic has happened.

Harold answers for the shocked Beverly, "A coyote attacked her and tore out some of her tail feathers. She escaped with her life because she acted fast. I'm so proud of her." Harold says as he drapes his wing over her shivering form.

"Let's take a look," Instructor Riley says as she swims around Beverly.

"Oh, that had to hurt! But don't worry, they'll grow back. At least you're still with us to share your tale of bravery," she says, followed by words of support from everyone.

"I think this makes you a true adventurer," Markie says.

"Absolutely! Markie's right," Jayson confirms.

"Really?" Beverly stutters.

"For sure. You're a survivor!"

Harold whispers to her, "Rocket hen, you still have the prettiest little tail feathers—just slightly fewer than before."

"Okay, it's been a long and eventful day, so let's settle in for the night," Instructor Riley suggests.

"I'll be on predator patrol tonight," Harold says.

"No breaking up the Bodyguard Buds; I'll be on watch with you," Markie says.

"With so much vegetation on the creek banks, I believe we're safe, but it's best to be extra diligent since we know there's a hungry coyote nearby," Jayson says.

What Jayson and Instructor Riley haven't shared with the flock is that there is also a raccoon wandering around—they don't want to add extra stress.

The ducks nervously line up, prepared for a quick escape.

Beverly whispers to Harold, "If you hadn't turned around, I wouldn't be here with you right now."

"Don't even think about that. You're safe, and I am here with you. Go to sleep."

The Bodyguard Buds take their role very seriously, especially tonight. Guard duty is not so much a chore anymore: it's an honour to sleep unihemispherically.* A coyote's high-pitched barks and yips in the near distance serve as tonight's soundtrack, making the tired flock nervous.

They wake to a bright, chilly morning and the sounds of people chattering and the pings of little balls being hit.

"How did you sleep?" Harold asks Beverly.

"It took me a while, but knowing that you and Markie were on watch, I eventually fell asleep."

"Glad to hear that. I had a good night knowing you were sleeping. Today will be a much better day," Harold promises.

"I think I'd like to stay on the creek today," Beverly tells Harold.

"I'll join you."

"Hey Markie, I'm not waking up covered in ice crystals anymore, but I'm still waking up super cold. When will I not wake up feeling like I'm in a deep freeze?" Lynn asks, annoyed as usual.

"Soon."

"Ugh," Lynn groans.

"Hey Lynn, would you mind staying on the creek with Beverly for a few minutes?" Harold asks.

"Happy to."

"Let's go for a little swim, Markie," Harold says, giving him a look that lets him know something's up.

"Be back soon," Harold tells Beverly.

"Markie, Beverly's stressed, so we need to put Plan B into action today. I'm going to ask Instructor Riley if the four of us can leave for a little while and be back before sunset."

"Sounds good, buddy. I think both hens need a little cheering up. If Lynn doesn't wake up soon to warm weather, I'm concerned she'll pluck my feathers out, one by one, and enjoy it. I'll end up balder than when I molt."

---

*Ducks (and other birds, dolphins, and whales) are capable of unihemispheric slow-wave sleep, where one-half of their brain is awake with one eye open while the other half of their brain shuts down so the animal can rest.

WHAT IS MOLTING?

Keeping their feathers in excellent condition is vital to a Mallard's survival. Although their feathers are durable, they can break and wear out. Molting is the process of shedding old plumage for new feathers. Mallards molt twice a year, in early spring and late summer.

Harold and Markie speak with Instructor Riley and get the go-ahead for Plan B.

"Hens, how do you feel about going on a special little adventure today?"

"I'll pass," Lynn says.

"Me too. I'm happy just to stay put. I'm just going to pamper what's left of my tail feathers; I'm pretty sore back there. Besides, I've had enough adventure with blizzards, coyotes, and human predators. We're not safe in the sky, and we're not safe on the ground. I'm exhausted from the stress of it all and from flying, but thanks," Beverly explains.

"How about we eat, relax, do some feather maintenance, and then see how you feel?" Harold suggests.

"Sure, but I don't think I'll change my mind," Beverly tells him.

"Me either," Lynn says.

As the four friends tend to their daily rituals, Markie pulls Beverly aside and says, "I know how difficult migrations are, and I know you had a dreadful day yesterday but Harold has put a lot of effort into making your migration extra special. How about it? Why not give this outing a try? It's close by, and I really think the four of us will have some fun. Please."

"Fine, but if I end up hanging upside down, I'm done. Don't ask me again for any more adventure trips. Deal?"

"Deal," Markie says.

Beverly and Lynn discuss the afternoon outing, and together, they approach Harold.

"Harold, is your offer still good?" Beverly asks.

"Yes!"

"Let's do it," Beverly says while Lynn nods in agreement.

Harold gives Markie a wing tap and says, "I was hoping they would come around."

"So Harold, what's the plan?" Beverly asks nervously.

"We're going to the Applefest!"

"What's an Applefest?" Beverly asks.

"It's a party—a kind of social," Harold explains.

"Like the Annual Migration Meeting?" Lynn asks.

"No. It sounds like it's more fun than that. At least I hope so. Davor told us that there'll be food, music, and games," Harold says.

"You had me at food. Let's go," Lynn tells Harold.

"Great! We'll have a good time. Markie has the directions, so he'll lead us. It's nearby, and lots of friendly humans will be there. We'll be safe," Harold explains.

"We better be," Beverly says as she sneers at Markie.

"You ready, hens?" Markie asks.

"Ready as we'll ever be," Beverly replies.

"Single line, please. We'll swim on the creek till we get to where we poked around in the mud for grubs, and then we'll take flight from there," Markie explains.

They successfully liftoff into the chilly blue sky, flapping and calling out as they fly over acreages, horse farms, and paved roads.

"Prepare for landing," Markie tells them.

"Already?" Lynn says.

"Told you it was close," Markie tells her.

"Yeah, but you also say 'soon,' and that hasn't happened yet, so..." Lynn teases.

As they approach Buckstop Junction, a replica village of antique buildings from pioneer days, they see dusty dirt roads, wooden board-walks, and thinly grassed areas. They watch people of all ages wandering about, playing games, and running around. They flap to lively bluegrass music, and Lynn's nose sniffs the air that's rich with the aroma of yummy fairground food.

"Markie, just pick a spot so we can land. We're missing the fun," Lynn urges.

"Harold, this looks like it's going to be a lot more fun than our Migration Meeting!" Beverly says.

Thinking that Plan B is off to a good start, Harold puffs up his chest—but he reminds himself that he's had the same thoughts before, and they didn't turn out as he'd planned.

"No faceplants, please," Markie jests as he leads them toward landing on a flat, dirt patch hidden behind a pale-yellow wooden church with a tall steeple.

"We're getting pretty good at ground landings. Look! Hardly any skid marks and no big puffs of dust," Beverly boasts.

"I'm going to follow that yummy smell," Lynn says.

"Let's stay together," Harold suggests.

"Just a little advice: there are lots of different human foods here; some are not good for us, so be careful what you eat. Ask me if you are in doubt. We don't want any belly aches," Markie warns.

Strutting like a western posse, the ducks waddle around, trying not to be trampled by the large number of people moving in all directions.

"Here's an opening. Follow me," Harold says.

Breaking away from the crowd, the ducks are surprised to find them-selves in the middle of the dirt road, face-to-face with a fast-approaching marching school band. The music becomes louder as the wall of youthful musicians in their freshly pressed navy-blue band uniforms comes closer, their highly polished brass instruments gleaming in the sun. The pounding beat of the drums bangs in the duck's ears, and the clanging of cymbals makes them dizzy.

"What do we do?" Beverly shouts.

"We join them! They're playing our song!" Harold shouts as he turns around and starts marching like he's leading the band.

The three friends join Harold and boldly march like soldiers. With straight legs, they forcefully kick their bright orange webbed feet up high like they're punching the air. Keeping rhythm with the band, they quack and *kreep* loudly to the only song they know:

O when the Saints...

Go marching in...

The crowd goes wild, cheering them on, taking pictures, and singing along.

Exhausted from marching and not knowing the next song, they quickly waddle off to the side of the dirt road as the band passes by.

Unexpectedly, a crowd of children gathers around them.

Nervous and feeling trapped, the newbies squat and gaze into the little faces that are looking back at them.

"Harold, you said we'd be safe," Beverly whispers.

"We're supposed to be."

Skeptical, the ducks stay still, twitch, and wait to see what happens next.

Beverly feels uneasy as a hand slowly extends toward her. But when she feels that same hand caressing her neck, she looks up to see kind, chocolate-brown eyes.

"Quack," she says. The child giggles.

Harold lets out a soft raspy *kreep* as someone gently strokes his back.

The ducks are enjoying the attention and feeling relaxed when the children begin to leave—but not before one gives Harold a big, loving hug.

"That was wonderful. I guess there are some really nice humans," Beverly tells Harold.

"I shouldn't have judged them before I got to know them. Now I know for sure that not all humans are predators—and maybe now they'll know that we are nice, too. It goes both ways," Harold says.

"Did you enjoy meeting them?" Beverly asks Lynn.

"Absolutely!" Lynn says, neglecting to mention that she was sneaking nibbles from one of the children's ice cream cone—a tasty new treat.

"They smell nice," Harold comments.

"Okay, diva ducks, let's carry on," Markie says.

Waddling like they are the stars of the event and getting attention wherever they go, they stop at a large, brightly-coloured inflatable obstacle course.

"That looks like fun," Beverly says.

Not knowing any better, Beverly and Lynn waddle to the front of the line.

"Hey, back of the line," a young boy tells them.

Beverly turns around and lets out a loud quack.

"Come on, Lynn. It's our turn," Beverly says, excited.

"I'll race you," Lynn says.

"Okay. Starting now!" Beverly says as she immediately waddles to the bouncy structure.

Trying to balance their footing on the flexible structure, they wobble through tunnels, fly to the top of the climbing wall, and slide down the other side.

"I win!" Lynn brags.

"Congratulations! You're the winner of the bouncy obstacle course," Beverly says, graciously accepting defeat.

"Well, since I fell off the top of the climbing wall and slid down the slide on my belly with my legs and wings flailing about, it certainly wasn't my best look. But you know me and balance," Lynn chuckles.

"You're right. It wasn't your most graceful movement from what I saw, but you did reach the finish line first," Beverly giggles.

"It looks like you hens had fun," Harold says.

"Oh, we did," Beverly tells him.

"Where to next?" Lynn asks.

"I see something fun. Follow me," Harold says.

Waddling past a prairie schoolhouse and post office, a ring toss game, bean bag throw, and a teenager singing and playing her acoustic guitar, Harold stops at an antique, weathered, big green tractor with a flatbed of hay.

"Jump up! This will be a fun way to check out everything," he says.

"Great idea!" Markie agrees as he pumps his wings to get himself up to the hay bales.

With all four of the ducks safely squatting on hay bales and with everyone else on board, the tractor engine rattles and roars as it starts up.

"Okay, folks; sit tight. We're on our way," says the stocky older man driving the tractor.

"What are you doing?" Markie asks Lynn.

"Poking around for seeds."

"I don't think the driver will appreciate you tearing apart the seats," Markie tells her.

As the tractor rumbles along, the ducks enjoy looking at the festivities.

"Look," Beverly giggles as she points to twin clowns with massive

amounts of green and blue tightly curled hair under a petite, yellow bowler hat that contrasts their decoratively painted faces, each sporting a bulbous red foam nose. They are colourfully dressed in orange polka dot oversized shirts with huge neon yellow bow ties, blue suspenders, and red baggy striped trousers that drape over their gigantic purple shoes. Excited, rambunctious children line up to have their faces painted like animals by these fun-loving clowns.

"Oh, there's a pond with little yellow duckies floating in it," Lynn says.

"I think it's a game," Harold tells her.

"There's a game we would win a prize for. Apple bobbing!" Beverly shouts excitedly as she bobs her head.

"Markie, promise me that we will stop there before we leave," Lynn says as she points to a booth that's selling roasted nuts, kettle corn, and her new favourite tasty treat, ice cream.

"Fine. As long as you don't eat too much," Markie says, knowing that there shouldn't be too much spillage on the ground. Little does he know that Lynn is planning on waddling around and begging for food.

"Beverly, look over there!" Lynn says, pointing to the booths of homemade pies, cookies, and an assortment of other baked goods, jams, jellies, and relishes.

"What *is* that clanging noise?" Harold says as the tractor stops.

"Anyone want to see a blacksmith demonstration? You can jump off here," the driver says above the loud, jarring sound of the pounding and hammering of iron.

The ducks cover their ears and patiently wait as a few people leave the ride.

"Good, we're leaving," Beverly says to Harold as the tractor starts up.

"How adorable is that?" Lynn comments, gesturing toward a riding lawn mower that's pulling a wheeled train made up of brightly-coloured, glossy-painted barrels. Each of its nine barrels is occupied by enthusiastic children who wave, laugh, and shout hello to the four feathered friends.

A few even imitate quacking sounds.

The ducks happily bob their heads, flap their wings, and quack and *kreep* to join in the fun.

The tractor driver interrupts with, "This brings us to the end of the tour, but I've left the best for last. Don't forget to visit Vivian, our lovely Pink Heals* truck."

The ducks spread their wings for a soft landing and jump off the hay bales. The humans climb down and walk over to the pink-coloured fire truck that's also covered with pink accessories.

"Let's see what Vivian's all about," Harold says.

Taking notice of how humans wait for their turn, the ducks wait in line to tour the shiny pink fire truck.

Blasts of HONK! HONK! HONK! fill the air.

"Where are those darn geese?" Lynn shouts.

Beverly chuckles when she realizes what's happened. "There are no geese, Lynn; that's the horn on the fire truck. It's Vivian honking," Beverly explains.

"Well, Vivian is loud, and I don't want to deal with that right now. I think it's my cue to leave," Lynn says as she waddles toward the food booth.

"I think Lynn's got the right idea—let's visit the food booth and then head back," Markie suggests.

After exploring the food booth, the four adventurers join their friends back on the creek.

Lynn moans, "My belly hurts."

"I warned you not to eat so much human food," Markie tells her.

"I can't help it if humans thought I was really cute and kept giving me treats."

"Riiiiiiiiight," Markie groans.

"Thanks for such a fun day! It was a great break from the stress of our

---

*Vivian is one of 200 pink fire trucks and police cars which are a part of the Pink Heals Tour, supporting women (and their families) in their fight against cancer. Proceeds from donations and merchandise sales stay in the individual communities served by the Tour.

migration," Beverly says to Harold and Markie.

"Bellyache and all, it was super fun. Thanks!" Lynn says.

"We're glad you enjoyed yourselves. And if you liked that, Jayson told us about some other fun outings," Markie says.

Feeling pumped up from the success of Plan B, Harold adds, "That's right. When we return here in the spring, how does a riverboat ride on the Missouri sound? Or the zoo? That's where they have lots and lots of animals."

"Sounds good, but first, let's get south to warm weather before thinking of our spring trip back," Beverly suggests.

Lynn gives Markie a skeptical look.

"I know, I know. Soon!" Markie tells her.

"Hello, everyone! I need your attention for a quick announcement. Please make sure that you're prepared for our next flight. We are leaving tomorrow morning for one of our favourite spots, Lake Andes National Wildlife Refuge," Instructor Riley tells the flock.

"I assume it's safe there, right?" Taleena asks.

"Yes, mostly."

"And there's a bonus—a grain field that we can sneak onto after dark," Jayson says.

The flock cheers, clicks their bills, and flaps their wings.

Excited for the adventure that awaits them tomorrow, the ducks settle in for sleep on their chilly waterbed as darkness sets in.

"How will we get any sleep listening to raccoons fighting?" Beverly asks Harold.

"Well, as long as they're snarling and growling at each other, they're not going to bother us."

"I hope Easton and Jayson can hear over that brawl if there's a predator close by," Beverly says with some concern.

"They'll look after us. Get some sleep," Harold tells her as he gives her a playful nip.

CHAPTER 26

"Yay! Another cold morning!" Lynn says, giving Markie a nudge.

"What did you do that for?"

"Do what?" Lynn teases.

"Good morning, everyone! Jayson and Easton, great job protecting us," Instructor Riley says.

The drowsy flock clicks their bills.

"Get yourself set up for a full day of flying. We'll be leaving shortly," Instructor Riley advises.

"Another day of flying," Janis says, uninspired.

"We're getting there. And you know how wonderful *there* is, right?" Anne says.

Janis responds flatly with, "Yeah, I do."

With everyone completing their pre-flight checklist, they make like a zipper and follow Jayson as he swims along the creek to spring up into flight at the same open area where Markie, Harold, Beverly, and Lynn left to go to the Applefest. Once airborne, they skillfully reposition themselves into their famous V.

"Hey, we did as good a job as the Canada geese!" Beverly shouts.

Flying at a comfortable speed of (72 kph) 45 mph and travelling southeast at (152 m) 500 feet above the ground, the ducks enjoy a (48 km) 30-mile panoramic view of the Great Plains: prairie flatland with grasslands and grazing cattle. Small towns are scattered among the abstract design of agricultural fields: round, rectangular, irregular, and square shapes planted with wheat, soybeans, corn, oats, and sunflowers.

"Hey, Markie! All the fields have perfectly organized lines, but check out the wacky lines on that one," Harold says.

"Maybe the farmer had a runaway tractor," Markie chuckles.

"At least it's not boring!" Anne laughs.

Listless, the ducks flap and call out as they look around. Just off the tips of their right wings, they see the Missouri River bending and curving like a snake.

MISSOURI RIVER

The Missouri River is the longest river in North America, stretching 3,767 km / 2,341 miles. It's nicknamed the "Big Muddy" because of the silt it carries. Weaving its way to the Mississippi, it widens and narrows, has silt banks, sandbars in some areas, and banks with rolling hills in places to cradle it.

After a few minutes, Beverly says, "The river has disappeared. Back to fields and more fields!"

"Don't forget the farmhouses and roads," Lynn adds.

"What about the towns? Don't forget those," Taleena says.

"Right! Those things make all the difference; now I'm not bored at all," Beverly laughs.

"It's nice it's overcast today—no sun in our eyes," Easton comments.

The Lead Duck lineup of Jayson, Davor, and Anne is ready for a shift change.

Anne shouts, "Hey, Markie! You ready to take over?"

"Sure! Easy-peasy," he replies—with a gulp.

As Markie flies by on his way to the front of the V, Harold whispers, "Is this your first time?"

"Yup."

Dropping back to the end of the A Line, Anne notices the nervous looks on Harold, Beverly, and Lynn's faces.

"Don't worry; he'll be fine. He'll remember the route, and if he goes off course, I'll be more than happy to tell him," Anne snickers.

Markie searches the sky, surveys the landmarks below, and bravely leads the flock knowing that all eyes are upon him. *At least they have a new diversion from boredom,* he thinks.

"You're doing great!" Lynn shouts.

Markie carries on like he didn't hear her.

Harold studies Markie, recognizing what a great job he's doing.

Beverly sees Harold watching Markie and says, "Hot wings, one day that will be you."

"Yes, after I learn the route and memorize the landmarks," he replies.

"Me too. I need to study the terrain. I know that we are born with knowing how to read the sky at night and the sun during the day, but we also have to learn the route and landmarks, right?" she asks him.

"That's right."

Beverly thinks about that, a look of concern on her face. Choosing her words carefully, she says, "So, since Susie had never migrated before, she really won't know how to get where we are going."

Harold realizes that his answer must give a feeling of hope. "Maybe she joined another flock and is travelling south with them. When they travel back up north in the spring, there's a good chance she'll find her way home. Or maybe we'll find her."

"That's a definite possibility! I think we will see her again," Beverly says, feeling hopeful.

"Look! There's the river again," Lynn shouts.

Instructor Riley announces, "We'll soon be arriving at our destination, Lake Andes. You're doing a great job, Markie!"

As the sun begins to set on their brisk, boring, nearly six-hour flight, the ducks are ready to rest when they hear a familiar sound.

"Do you hear that?" Taleena says.

"What?" Beverly asks.

"No. It can't be!" Lynn shouts.

"I think it is," Harold says.

"Lesser Snow Geese! I'd know their calls anywhere," Lynn shouts.

"I thought we were going to be ahead of them so we'd get to the food first," Beverly asks.

"There are thousands of them, but we're definitely ahead of the ones we met at Des Lacs," Instructor Riley says, hoping to calm the irritated ducks.

"This is terrible," Beverly says.

"Let's wait and see how many there are. It's a big lake," Jayson adds.

Surveying the sky and ground, Markie calls out with authority, "This is your Captain speaking. Prepare for landing!" He pays close attention to a small plane landing on the Lake Andes aerodrome's grass airstrip. Markie chuckles, thinking the pilot probably needs to land before sunset as he most likely doesn't have excellent night vision like birds do; birds are the ultimate flying machines.

"Look!" Lynn comments, fascinated by clusters of lights popping on.

Markie reduces his speed and lowers his altitude. The flock follows him. Eleven pairs of eyes keenly look for obstacles of any sort as they fly over the small city of Lake Andes in South Dakota, before doing a once-around of the lake itself. Surrounded by pasture, grassland, agricultural fields, wetlands, and mixed woodlands, Lake Andes is a popular migration stop-over for shorebirds, waterbirds, and songbirds. The cottonwoods and bountiful tall vegetation make the area an ideal home for Ring-necked Pheasants, eagles, white-tailed deer, coyotes, and raccoons as well.

"Look down and over your right wing," Jayson says. "That's the cornfield we're going to sneak to."

The Havenwood Cove flock proudly quack and *kreep* their arrival even though no one can hear them over the ambient noise.

"Drakes and hens, this is your Captain again, we are all clear! Prepare for landing!" Markie says as he lowers his landing gear and touches down on the calm water at the south end of the Lake Andes.

Two by two, the flock follows.

With everyone safely down the flock clacks their bills and bobs their heads to celebrate Captain Markie's inaugural Lead Duck flight.

Puffing up his chest, Markie lets out a loud *kreep* of appreciation.

"I never knew how much wind force slams into the Lead Duck. I'm exhausted," Markie whispers to Harold.

"You did an amazing job!" Harold tells him.

"You really did," Lynn and Beverly agree.

Markie leans close to Harold and says, "I'll tell you a secret; I've always wanted to say, 'This is your Captain speaking.'"

"You sounded like you've said it many times before," Harold tells him.

The two friends give each other a wing tap before heading off to find some food.

For the next two days and two nights, the flock rests on the water, enjoys the abundant aquatic menu, sneaks over to the corn field for late-night snacks, and waddles around the muddy shoreline to explore the overgrown bushes and grasses. They socialize with migrating Pintails and Mallards, and maintain their daily routines while keeping watch for the abundance of American Bald Eagles that circle above and perch on nearby trees.

"Lynn! Come here! Face this way and strike a pose," Beverly says, pointing to the humans standing on the nature path who are looking at her.

"I'll join you. Fluff up your feathers, chest out, and hold your head high. Look friendly," Taleena says.

Click, click, click.

"Relax; they're leaving," Lynn says as she stops holding her breath.

"We are hen supermodels with our fancy eye streaks. Did you notice that the Pintail hens are the common-looking version of us? They don't have eye streaks." Beverly states.

Janis spends the days relaxing and tending to her sore wing while she quietly grieves for Michael. Twice a day, Beverly has Harold check to see if her three missing tail feathers are starting to grow in. They are not, so her rudder control is going to be a little wonky for a little longer.

On the water, the flock is restless, trying to sleep with the loud, annoying sounds of wings flapping and geese honking. The soothing sounds of a Great Horned Owl's *hoo-hoo hooooo hoo-hoo*'s can barely be heard over all the noise.

The ducks are awakened on the morning of their departure by the thumps of beating wings, honks, and the high, shrill cries of the new arrivals and departures.

"Let's get ready for takeoff," Jayson instructs.

As they complete their pre-flight checklist in the chilly morning air, Markie says to Lynn, "Remember, the more flights we make, the sooner we get to warmer weather," as she shows off her puffs of icy breath.

"Formation, please!" Captain Jayson announces.

The flock neatly get themselves into their V formation—not only to comply with Jayson's instruction, but also to impress the early morning birdwatchers who are observing them from the nature trail.

Instructor Riley says, "Captain Jayson and I have great news!"

"We'll be at our final destination tonight?" Lynn shouts.

"Well, no. Hmm, maybe our news is good rather than great," she responds. "Jayson and I estimate that we have a small tailwind of around (27 kph) 17 miles per hour today. It's coming from the north, so it will help push us along. Certainly better than the last couple of flights with winds fighting us."

"I guess it all helps," Taleena says, feeling a little discouraged that this migration is not over.

"It's helpful, you Ducky Downers. You'll see," Anne says.

"Oh, sure. A tailwind, and I hardly have a tail," Beverly jokes.

On cue, they spring out of the water and call out with extra enthusiasm as they fly over the birdwatchers.

"I think they liked that," Lynn says.

Heading on the southeast, diagonal line of their pre-determined path, they flap vigorously trying to warm their bodies.

Flying at an altitude of (91 m) 300 feet above ground, at a relaxed speed of (64 kph) 40 miles per hour, the tailwind helps give them a gentle nudge as they leave South Dakota and say goodbye to the Big Muddy. As the Missouri River snakes around, it picks up tons of silt on its way to just north of St. Louis, Missouri, where it joins up with the mighty Mississippi River and then heads down to the Gulf of Mexico.

"Is the tailwind helping you and your fancy new tail?" Harold asks Beverly.

"It's a little drafty. I really have to concentrate on keeping myself level."

"Well, you're looking mighty fine," Harold tells her.

Resigned to the fact that migration is twice a year, the first-time migrators barely say a word as they fly over the state of Nebraska and into Kansas. Though they pass over the Tuttle Creek Dam in the Flint Hills prairies, dense cedar forests, and the Great Plains—with its tallgrass prairie, rivers, towns, cities, and agricultural fields with their windbreaks of lined trees—they realize that these views will be re-runs of the same trip, over and over and over.

"Trust me—you will love where we are stopping," Markie tells Harold, Beverly, and Lynn.

"If you say so," Beverly says, rolling her eyes.

"Prepare for landing," Davor says, as he leads the flock to an upland prairie city.

CHAPTER 27

There is a cautious excitement among the ducks; this is the first time they're landing within city limits, so they know they need to exercise extra watchfulness. There are a lot of dangerous factors for them to be aware of—five highways, trains, an airport, vehicles, buildings, people, and electrical lines.

"That's Emporia, Kansas down there, and there on the southern edge of the town is the Cottonwood River," Davor explains as he guides the ducks high above the main street before banking to the right and flying over the river.

"Are we going to land on this river? It's moving pretty fast," Harold nervously asks Markie.

"No way! We're going to deluxe resort accommodations," Markie tells him.

"Final approach!" Instructor Riley announces.

"Prepare to be wowed!" Anne shouts.

"That sounds good. I think we all need to be wowed about now," Beverly says.

As they fly through a cluster of beautiful green and autumn-coloured leafy trees, the view opens to a small private lake with a water spray in the middle, borders of luscious plants, and canopies of trees. "Focus!" Davor shouts.

Two by two, the ducks glide into luxury. Once settled, they stretch out the kinks from the long flight and then float on the peaceful oasis. The newbies look around in wonder.

"So, did I tell you it's nice, or did I tell you it's nice?" Anne asks Harold, Beverly, and Lynn.

"Oh, you said it is nice, but you are wrong," Beverly says.

"What?"

"It's better than nice—it's fabulous!" Beverly laughs.

"Welcome to Emporia's Peter Pan Park, or what I like to call the Marriduck Migration Resort," Markie chuckles. "It's first class all the way, with lots for us to enjoy. There's an obstacle course, a massive area of mani- cured grass for eating and waddling around on, high-quality water features, and various dining areas offering different tasty eats. And the humans are nice to us here. What more could we want?"

"Any Lesser Snow Geese?" Lynn asks.

"Nope, not a one. I think this resort isn't large enough to accommodate such large flocks—this is more of a boutique resort," Markie explains.

Instructor Riley says, "Gather around, everybody. Let's get checked into this fine resort," she laughs. "We will be staying here for two days and two nights. There's a lot for us here, and there is another pond area just over there in the David Traylor Zoo of Emporia," she says, pointing with her bent wing. "Please do not leave the resort without permission from Jayson or me. Be respectful of the other guests and enjoy yourselves. Be back here each night around sunset. Did you hear me, Anne?"

"Yes, Instructor Riley."

Satisfied that everyone is safe and secure, she signs off with, "Now rest up, eat up, and have fun."

Harold turns to his three best friends and asks, "So what's first?"

"I'm hungry and tired. I'd like to eat, organize my feathers, then sleep," Beverly says.

"I'm with you. Besides, it's getting dark, and I'd rather explore tomor- row in the daylight," Lynn comments.

"Great plan," Harold and Markie agree.

"You'll find it's pretty quiet around here. During the night—and even during the day—a few humans watch over us and make sure everything is tidy for us. Some human guests wander around, too. Follow me. I'll show you where I like to dine," Markie says.

The four adventurers swim to a secluded area of the pond where there are ornamental grasses and rock garden displays. "Hey, don't do that!" Beverly snaps.

"What's wrong?" Lynn asks.

"Something nipped at my foot. If it does it again, I'll eat it," Beverly threatens.

Nestled under a beautiful wooden footbridge, the ducks prepare for sleep.

"I love this place already," Taleena says to Davor.

"Told you we only travel first class," he replies.

"Markie, have you seen any predators here?" Harold asks.

"Saw a raccoon once, but no coyotes."

"Glad to hear that! It's so peaceful here," Beverly says to Harold.

"This should help us to unwind. Sweet dreams, rocket hen," Harold whispers.

"Good night, hot wings."

The ducks sleep a little longer than usual in the restful surroundings, without flocks of geese flapping overhead. They awaken to the soft sounds of chatty humans walking on the bridge.

After exchanging pleasantries with the group, the four friends start their day with some aquatic morsels, grooming, and then deciding where to explore.

"Let me show you another really cool area," Markie says. Paddling along and enjoying the tranquility, Markie leads them to a larger pond that feels more like being in the wilderness.

A Pintail hen paddles by and says hello.

"Hi!" Markie replies.

"Are you by yourself?" Beverly asks.

"No, my flock is over there," she says, drawing attention to a group of fifteen Pintails. "I just need a little time alone; migrations are long and stressful."

"They sure are," Lynn confirms.

"Well, enjoy your stay here!" the Pintail says, as she swims away.

"Bye," Beverly says.

"See, no eye streak," Beverly whispers to Lynn. Lynn nods.

"It's so beautiful here. Let's stay for a while," Lynn suggests.

"Sounds good to me," Beverly agrees.

The four friends enjoy the sunshine and the warmer weather. They tip up and enjoy a feast of aquatic critters, without having to scrounge for leftovers. A duck always has room for a few more tasty morsels.

"Could this day get any better? You were right, Markie; it's so peaceful here," Harold says.

Just as Harold finishes his thought, a familiar sound rips through the air. Anxiously, they all look up to the sky.

"I know that annoying wheezy whistling *jeeeb*! No! It can't be," Harold says to Markie.

"Do you think it's them? Beverly whispers to Lynn.

"No, but it sure sounds like them."

Harold's mind is running wild, and his heart is racing.

Dylan and Dirk suddenly come into view as they clear the treetops and prepare to land.

Harold's black, curled tail feathers tighten.

"My worst nightmare is coming in for a landing," Harold whispers to Markie.

"Don't get yourself worked up," Markie tells him.

Dirk and Dylan boldly swim up to the four feathered friends.

"Drakes! Funny to see you here," Harold says.

"Not really. I told you that I checked out your flight path," Dylan says, staring Harold down with his fiery red eyes. And then he looks at Beverly. "Hey there, little sweet feet. Told you I'd do my best to see you again."

"Yeahhhhhh. You did say that," Beverly says, annoyed at his insistence.

"Come swim with me," he says.

"No, thanks. I'm here with my friends, and we were just going back to our flock," Beverly says, as calmly as she can.

As Dirk swims away in search of food, Dylan looks at Harold and says, "I'll bring her right back."

Harold opens his bill, but no sound comes out before Beverly speaks up.

"Ummm, he's not my boss. You don't need to ask for his permission, but you do need to ask for mine," Beverly says, giving Harold a quick nod while maintaining eye contact with Dylan.

"I'm sorry; I guess that *was* rude," Dylan replies. "Beverly, would you like to come for a swim with me?"

"Not really," she answers, "but I'll give you two minutes." She turns toward Harold, who looks completely defeated. "Don't worry, hot wings. I've got this. I'll be right back."

As Beverly and Dylan paddle to a quiet spot not far away, Markie asks, "Are you going to let that duckwad steal her from you?"

"Yeah, do something, Harold," Lynn practically demands.

"I'm thinking, I'm thinking!" Harold says without taking his eyes off Beverly and Dylan.

"He's coming on strong. You've got to fight for her," Lynn says, getting all wound up.

"I love her. I have done everything I can to show her," Harold says, feeling like he has proved his love and devotion.

"Harold, you treat Beverly like she's the most special hen, but have you actually ever asked her to be *your* hen?" Lynn asks.

"Umm, not in so many words," Harold says as his stomach churns and his head spins. He's suddenly filled with self-doubt that he hasn't done enough, and now he might lose her.

Feeling his muscles tense up, an agitated Harold asks, "What's taking them so long? She said two minutes, and it's been longer than that."

"Here they come," Lynn says.

"Act cool, Harold. Don't let Dylan see how upset you are," Markie tells him.

As they approach the group, Dylan looks at Beverly and says, "See you later, little sweet feet," while giving Harold a defiant look before going to find Dirk.

As calmly as he can, Harold asks, "So, how'd it go?"

"He asked me to join him, Dirk, his sister Tammy, and his Uncle Larry for the rest of the migration at their family winter home."

"And what did you say?" Lynn asks, her voice screechier than she expected.

"Harold, can we speak in private?" Beverly says, seeming a bit frazzled.

Fearing the worst, Harold agrees, and together, they swim to a quiet area. Before Harold can say anything, Beverly blurts, "Is it true?"

"Is what true?" he asks, shocked and confused.

"Dylan said that Mallard drakes have lots of hen mates—that you don't commit to just one mate. That you wiggle your tail for many Mallard hens, American Black Ducks, and even Northern Pintails! No wonder the hens look like us but without the eye streak!"

Puzzled, Harold asks, "Eye streak? What eye streak?"

"Never mind. I'm not some yellow rubber ducky that you like, then let float away in a river," Beverly says, both heartbroken and enraged.

"I would never treat you like that!" Harold says.

"So, it's not true that Mallard drakes get cozy with many hens and then leave them?" Beverly asks, looking into his big, brown eyes.

"Yes, that's true; Mallards don't mate for life like Canada geese, swans, and bald eagles."

"What?" Beverly shouts.

"But that's not me. You are the only hen for me—the only one I want, forever and ever."

"Are you sure?"

"Beverly, I should have told you how I feel—"

"Yes, Harold, you should have," Beverly interrupts.

He pauses, "—and I will, but not right now. Not like this," he says, as he gives her a little love nip.

"Okay, Harold. Let's go back to Lynn and Markie. Lynn's voice sounded screechy, and I'm concerned about her," Beverly says.

"Markie! They're coming back!" Lynn says.

"Just relax. Let them tell us what's happening in their own time," Markie says.

"Good idea."

"Hey, you two," Beverly says calmly.

"What's up? What's happening? Are you going with Dylan?" Lynn squeals.

"Nice going," Markie tells Lynn.

"Sorry. So?" Lynn asks as calmly as she can.

"Dylan who?" Beverly chuckles.

"Whew! I was so worried," Lynn responds.

"Let's go back to the flock," Beverly suggests.

Beverly and Lynn swim ahead of the drakes so Lynn can get the details.

"Did you ask her?" Markie asks Harold.

"No, but I hinted that I will. I want it to be special," Harold says.

"Good idea, buddy. Next part of Plan B: romance."

After Peter Pan Park closes to the public for the day, the flock waddles over to the children's outdoor playground that's full of fun activities.

"Race you!" Beverly says to Harold.

"Let's make it the hens against the drakes!" Anne shouts.

"You're on! You're going down!" the drakes chant, then huddle to discuss their strategy.

"No flapping way!" Anne shouts. The overzealous hens huddle and quack out a winning game plan.

"Hey Anne, come here. Let's discuss the rules," Markie says.

"Be right back," Anne tells her teammates.

When she returns, Anne says, "Hens, I've checked out the course. It's all solid ground, no bouncy stuff. Plenty of things are easy to navigate: decks, ramps, tunnels, balance beams, and a slide. But the swings are a bit trickier—you'll need to fly up, perch, wrap your wing around the rope, and hold on. Just be aware of that so you're ready for it. The first hen or drake that reaches the top of the castle wins for their team," Anne explains. "Beverly, you lead, then me, Lynn, Taleena, and Janis.

"I'm not quite up to it, but I can be a cheerleader! I will quack so loud no one will hear the drakes' raspy *kreep*s," Janis says.

"Great! Every team needs cheerleaders!" Anne says.

"We're ready!" the hens shout to the drakes.

With both teams lined up, Janis lets out a boisterous QUACK that would make a starter pistol sound like a squeak toy.

And they're off! Both teams waddle as fast as they can.

Quacks and *kreep*s explode like firecrackers as the competitors waddle, trip, pick themselves up, and carry on like true athletes. Using unique movements to combat their webbed feet and plump bodies, the ducks show impressive dexterity: scaling ramps and performing stylish belly slides.

"Get out of my way, Markie," Taleena says as she bumps him and motors past.

"Move aside, hen," Davor tells Anne.

"Make me," Anne laughs as she picks up her speed and spreads her wings to block him.

The hens are in the lead.

Oh, noooo!" Lynn shouts as she topples off the balance beam.

Everyone knows this part of the course will be tough for her.

"Come on, Lynn! Try it again! You can do it! Take it slow!" The hens momentarily stop competing to offer support for their teammate.

Without a minute to waste and determined not to let her friends down, Lynn flies up, spreads her wings, and gingerly lands on the narrow wooden beam.

"She's on it!" the hens chant. "Yay, you!"

"Oh, noooo!" Lynn cries. She holds her breath as she wobbles and sways, trying to get her wings into the perfect angles for maximum stability and balance.

Beverly calls out, "You've got this, Lynn!"

The drakes slow down and observe what's happening with Lynn, offering a few *kreep*s to show they're rooting for her, too. Above all, they know that fun and friendly sportsmanship is what's most important.

Moving at a snail's pace and with her heart pounding, Lynn's bright orange webbed feet grip the edges of the beam as she inches her way along it.

"We knew you could do it! Great job, Lynn!" her hen friends cheer before returning their efforts to the competition.

"We need to get busy! The drakes are right behind us!" Anne says.

With her wings tucked in tight and using all her leg strength, Beverly powers up the wooden ramp to the castle's peak. She doesn't even blink for fear of missing a step. Davor is nipping at her heels.

Reaching the deck of the castle, Beverly shouts, "Hens win!" She immediately flies up to the railing and thinking no one heard her the first time, raises her voice to shout even louder, "HENS WIN!" She sees all of her friends gathered together—standing perfectly still and surprisingly quiet—with all eyes on her.

"We won!" she shouts, but no one says a word.

THE BOOMERANG GANG

"What's happening? What's wrong?" she asks.

Harold slowly waddles to the front of the group and bends down on one knee.

"Beverly, from the moment I first saw you swimming in the marsh at Havenwood Cove, I knew that I wanted to be your forever drake and you, my forever hen," he says, giving her a wink. "I want a lifetime with you, enjoying and supporting each other in good times and bad. I want to have a family with you. I promise to make you feel adored each and every day so you never doubt my commitment to you. I will always try to keep you and our brood safe. Beverly, will you be *my* forever hen?"

Everyone anxiously waits for her answer.

"Yes, hot wings, I will be your forever hen, and you will be my forever drake."

Love and celebration all around. Happy dances, flapping, and joyous quacks and *kreep*s fill the air. Harold flies to join *his* hen on the castle's railing. Beverly gives Harold a little love nip on his neck as he wraps her in his wings.

"Best Plan B, *EVER!*" Markie shouts to Harold.

After an exciting, fun-filled day and a romantic, moonlit night, the flock happily falls asleep under their favourite bridge, while Anne and Taleena stand guard.

After completing their daily routine in the chilly morning air, they break into groups and explore the grounds. Janis joins Lynn, Markie, Harold, and Beverly for a little while as they paddle around the lake and waddle around the large, grassed area. Along the way, they enjoy meeting other migrators—Canada geese, Pintails, Mallards, and Wood Ducks (thankfully, not a Dylan or Dirk in sight). Davor and Taleena visit the David Traylor Zoo while Easton, Jayson, Instructor Riley, and Anne watch young girls play softball.

"I don't know what is so fascinating to humans that they want to hit a ball and chase after it?" Anne observes.

"Hey, that looks like fun," Beverly says, waddling up to the splash pad and jumping from water spray to water spray.

Lynn and Janis join her while children frolic and giggle around them.

"Too bad the lazy river is closed. Next visit," Harold says.

"Next time, I'll have to visit the picnic area," Lynn chuckles.

"Of course you will!" Markie jests.

Later that night, the flock huddles together under their favourite bridge and shares stories of what they did during the day.

"Goodnight, rocket hen," Harold whispers as he gives her a little nudge.

"Night, hot wings," Beverly giggles.

With Davor and Jayson on predator watch, the flock sleeps soundly, exhausted from their fun time at the Marriduck Migration Resort.

CHAPTER 28

In the chilly morning air, the ducks complete their pre-flight checklist, and reluctantly check out of the Peter Pan Park in Emporia, Kansas.

"So much for a fun time. Back to reality," Taleena comments.

"Today's destination is DeGray Lake, Arkansas," Instructor Riley tells the flock.

Flapping and constantly calling out, they fly over the rolling hills, tallgrass lands, and crop fields of southeast Kansas. Zipping over the northeast corner of Oklahoma and into Arkansas, the flock sees new terrain.

"Are the rolling hills getting taller, or am I imagining it?" Taleena asks.

"What happened to the grasslands?" Beverly asks.

"You were bored with farmland and grasslands, right? So, now you can enjoy the mountain experience. Get your wings powered up; we are going to elevate our flying altitude and skirt around the peaks," Instructor Riley tells them. "Take us up, up, and away!" she directs Davor.

"I hope we're ready for this," Lynn says.

"You'll be fine. What are you, a duckling?" Markie teases.

"When we land, you'll pay for that," Lynn chuckles.

"Harold, aren't the trees beautiful?" Beverly asks.

"They're almost as beautiful as you are."

"Oh, now you're just being quackers," Beverly snickers.

The flock flies through valleys with lakes and rivers and towns. They fly over and around dense hardwood forests dressed in autumn reds, golds, and greens. Sometimes, their path hugs steep mountain slopes—some with dramatic hardscapes, others sparsely treed.

"I feel like a true aviator!" Beverly shouts, the draft of the mountain air sweeping her words away.

"This is incredible!" Harold shouts.

They fly over the Boston Mountains (also called the Black Mountains, part of the Ozark Mountains), the Arkansas Valley, and the Ouachita Mountains (including Mount Ida, known as The Quartz Crystal Capital of the World).

After a gruelling eight hours of travelling (644 km) 400 miles at (80 kph) 50 mph, the flock sets down in a cozy, well-protected area of a lake. The flock looks around as the rosy glow of sunset lingers on the water.

"We will rest here for two days and two nights, then leave the morning after," Instructor Riley informs everyone.

With the waning moon illuminating the surroundings, the ducks notice the silhouettes of tall shortleaf pine trees, bushes, gentle lake banks, and the nearby DeGray Lake Resort State Park.

"This is beautiful. More natural than the last fancy resort, but nice," Taleena says.

"Fancy is special once in a while, but this reminds me more of being home," Anne says.

"Me too. I miss my friends. Do you think they worry about us and wonder where we are?" Harold asks.

"Friends think of friends. I miss them, too," Beverly says.

"My home was wherever I was with Michael. I don't feel like I have a home anymore," Janis whispers.

"Wherever we are is your home," Lynn tells Janis, giving her a comforting squeeze.

"Let me remind you that many of our friends are tucked away for the winter. So unless we are in their dreams, no, they are not worried about us," Jayson tells the flock.

"By the time we return, many of them will just be waking up—they won't even remember that we were gone," Markie says.

Even though the sun has gone down and the temperature is dropping, the newbies are too excited to sleep. "Flying around the mountains was thrilling," Beverly says.

"All of you first-time migrators showed off your aviator talents today. I'm very proud of all of you," Jayson tells them.

"One day, I will be a famous aviator," Beverly boasts.

FAMOUS AVIATORS

Bessie Coleman, 1892-1926, first African American licensed female pilot (aviatrix). She excelled in stunt flying, aerial tricks, and parachuting.

Amelia Earhart, 1897 Kansas — disappeared July 2, 1937, Pacific Ocean. American aviator that set many flying records. She was the first woman to fly solo across the Atlantic Ocean and the first person to fly solo from Hawaii to the U.S. mainland.

Eileen Vollick became the first licensed Canadian female pilot in 1928. She was also the first Canadian woman to parachute into water.

Orville and Wilbur Wright, American aviator brothers credited with inventing, building, and flying the world's first successful motor-operated airplane. On December 17, 1903, near Kitty Hawk, North Carolina, they made the historic first successful flight of a self-propelled, heavier-than-air aircraft. Orville piloted the biplane that stayed aloft for 12 seconds and covered (36 m) 120 feet.

"Maybe like Bessie Coleman, Amelia Earhart, or Eileen Vollick," Instructor Riley says.

"Yes, just like them! Who are they?" Beverly asks.

"All famous aviators," Instructor Riley tells her.

"Yes, then that's who I want to be like," Beverly says with conviction. "Hot wings, who do you want to be?"

"I want to be like Jayson and be a member of the Kitty Hawk Club."

"Harold, one day you will be. All you need is years of flying experience. I know you will make Orville and Wilbur Wright—and yourself—proud," Jayson says.

Noticing that some of the flock have already shut their eyes and tuned out the conversation, Instructor Riley says, "I think that's enough talk about flying; it's time to settle in."

"Hey, Sassy Sentinels, are you up to being on duty tonight?" Jayson asks.

"Absolutely!" Beverly and Lynn reply.

"Lynn, have you noticed that the weather is comfortable and not so chilly?" Markie asks her before he settles in to rest.

"Yes. Does that mean that *soon* is almost here?"

"*Maybe.*"

"Let's see if I wake up chilly," Lynn says.

Nestled on the lake with the waning moon reflecting on the water like a night light, the flock's bedtime concert is the distant chatter of humans at the nearby resort and the *hoo-hoo hooooo hoo-hoo*'s of a Great Horned Owl.

Waking to another clear and coolish day, Lynn gives Markie a nudge, "*Soon* is almost here—I can feel it," she tells him.

"Great. Believe me; *soon* can't come soon enough for me," he jokes.

Lynn giggles. She loves giving Markie a hard time—all in good fun, of course.

The ducks spend the day eating, preening, relaxing, and entertaining themselves by watching brightly coloured kayaks floating by and eavesdropping on hikers on nearby nature trails.

After tipping up and enjoying the variety of aquatic treats, the ducks settle in for the night, bobbing on the calm water. Hearing the patter of footsteps and the rustling of bushes, they choose a spot to cluster together away from the shore, and nestle under a canopy of tree branches to help protect them from owls and other in-flight predators.

With the Bodyguard Buds on duty, feeling and analyzing every ripple in the water, keenly listening for every flap of wings that flies over, and interpreting rustling sounds, the flock sleeps well.

CHAPTER 29

After waking to another nippy morning, the ducks forage for food on the shore and in the water. "Hey, Markie! How about an update on '*soon*'?" Lynn teases. Even though she's no longer waking to see puffs of her breath, she's still not warm.

"Sure. Here's your update: *very* soon."

"Ugh! What does that mean?" Lynn grumbles.

"Listen up, everyone! Today is our final flight to our winter home destination," Instructor Riley tells the flock.

Lynn looks at Markie. "Really? No joke?" she gushes.

"No joke. I told you! Very soon."

"I can hardly believe it. Soon is almost here!" Lynn says as she flaps her wings and swims around Markie.

"Settle down, you zany hen. Your ripples are bouncing me around," Markie teases.

The unexpected, wonderful news is thrilling to everyone, but mostly to the first-time migrators and Janis.

"I never thought I would hear those words," Beverly says to Harold.

"Me either. I'm exhausted—I never thought migration would be such a long haul. It's a good thing nobody told us what it's really like before we started."

"Okay, here's the scoop," Instructor Riley says. "Our flight is a short and easy one. We'll leave here when the sun is right above us and should arrive at our destination around sunset. Enjoy the morning. Relax, eat up, and make sure your feathers are in tip-top condition. Any questions?"

"Are we going to a human predator-safe area?" Taleena asks.

"Yes, at times, but...."

"There's always a but," Taleena says, shaking her head.

"There are always wildlife predators, and we'll talk about them when we get there," Instructor Riley tells the flock.

"Sounds like there are some new ones," Harold says to Markie.

Markie gives Harold a long, serious look. "Don't stress about anything right now."

"Well, now I AM stressed," Harold responds.

"If that's everything, enjoy your pre-flight time. Carry on," Instructor Riley says.

"I'm almost too excited to eat—but I will, anyway," Lynn laughs, then tips up.

"You are going to love our winter home," Anne tells the newbies.

"She's right, for once," Markie jests.

"I'm so ready to check out new desirable drakes," Lynn jokes.

Janis mumbles, "I just want to rest my wing. I'm tired of being a lame duck."

"Wait till you try the creole cuisine! You are going to love it!" Anne says excitedly, failing to mention: duck a l'orange, roast duck, Peking duck, duck confit and foie gras (duck liver).

"I'm with you. Cravin' some crawfish," Instructor Riley says.

"Crawfish?" Harold asks.

"Buddy, trust me. You're in for a real treat."

"We'll soon be relaxing under a luscious tall palm tree," Lynn tells Beverly.

"Sounds amazing," Beverly replies.

"I never said there are palm trees," Markie tells Lynn.

"You never said there *aren't*. So I'm staying with my dream that there are."

"Okay. It's your dream. Are there alligators in your dream?" Markie asks her.

"Alli-*what*?"

"Nothing," Markie mutters.

Prepped and eager to go, the ducks get into their V positions behind Captain Jayson.

"Enjoy today's journey because soon, all you will be doing for months is just relaxing, eating, and socializing in temperate weather. You'll probably be bored," Captain Jayson laughs.

"I don't think so. I can hardly wait to do a whole lot of nothing!" Taleena shouts.

Instructor Riley adds, "It's a perfect day for our last flight. The air is warming, and we have bright blue skies with very few clouds. The gentle south breeze shouldn't give us much of a pushback. Remember, just keep flapping; we're almost there."

On five, Jayson bolts out of the water with his entourage perfectly paced behind him. Leaving DeGray Lake, Arkansas, he leads them southeast, heading for their final destination: Duck Lake, Louisiana.

Today's flight, the last one on their migration south, gives the ducks a whole new attitude. Amazingly, they no longer feel like flapping for hours is a chore. Their quacks and *kreep*s sound almost musical. They're no longer bored flying over mundane scenery like they have seen many times before: rolling hills, flat lands, forests, roads, towns, meandering rivers, ponds, and lakes. They blissfully fly over Camden, Arkansas (the Star of the River) on the bluffs overlooking the Ouachita River, then Magnolia, Arkansas, staying away from the little planes using the municipal airport.

"We're passing over Homer, Louisiana," Instructor Riley calls out.

"Louisiana! That means we're getting close. Right!" Taleena shouts.

"Absolutely! Not much farther. We'll pass over Ruston, then Tullos, and then with a few more flaps, we will be at Duck Lake. It's almost time to rest your wings for months!" Instructor Riley says.

The newbies suddenly have an uncontrollable burst of energy.

"Hey, hot wings! Try to keep up with me," Beverly teases as she powers up her wings.

"Rocket hen, I'm on your tail. Be sure of that," Harold jokes.

"Does the sky seem busier and noisier? I see a lot more birds," Taleena says as she looks around and sees flocks of Canvasbacks, Pintails, and geese.

"What are you doing, Harold?" Markie asks as he watches Harold use his 340 degree field of vision to investigate the flyway.

"Just checking for red-eyed duckwads. Don't see any so far."

Markie doesn't have the heart to tell him that Duck Lake is popular for migrating Wood Ducks and a full-time home for some. Wood Ducks love acorns, and there are lots of oak trees there.

Instructor Riley tries to keep the flock calm. "Don't worry. We're safe. Everyone's staying in their own lane. Our Central Flyway route is merging with the Mississippi Flyway. The lower Mississippi River Valley narrows here, and it's a popular route."

WHAT ARE THE FLYWAYS?

The North American Migration Flyways consist of four main routes: the Atlantic Flyway, the Mississippi Flyway, the Central Flyway, and the Pacific Flyway. Millions of birds of different species innately travel their route twice a year. In the autumn, they leave their northern nesting area and travel south to their wintering area. In the spring, they travel north back to their nesting area. All around the world, migrating birds travel the same routes their ancestors have used for thousands of years.

"That said, we have a slight change of plans," she continues.

Harold looks back and gives Markie a stern look. "I hope this isn't bad news."

"We'll be fine, buddy. Remember, we always have to have our wits about us."

Harold starts twitching, *I'm sure this is worse than I thought,* he tells himself.

Instructor Riley boasts, "Believe it or not, we're ahead of schedule. That's some impressive wing power, Team Havenwood Cove! Anybody hungry?"

Energetic bill clacking and spirited quacks and *kreep*s rise from the flock.

"Alrighty, then! First, we'll visit a rice paddy," Instructor Riley tells them.

"Oh, that sounds exciting! I've never tasted rice before," Lynn says.

"Another new dining experience!" Taleena squeals.

"I can't believe we were worried. See, Beverly? There's nothing to worry about," Harold says.

"For sure. I need to work on staying calm and try harder not to over-react," Beverly replies.

"I'll do whatever I can to help you with that," Harold says.

"I know you're all excited, but I need your attention for a moment," Instructor Riley begins. "Earlier, when I said that we have wildlife predators, I also mentioned that human predators might be around."

Beverly's heart starts pounding. Lynn's mind races.

"Here it comes," Taleena whispers.

As her wing flapping becomes disjointed, Beverly shrieks, "I can't breathe!"

"You're okay. Take deep long breaths," Harold says.

Instructor Riley continues, "Davor will lead us on a lovely tour of our winter home. We'll land once the sun sets."

"Ummm, why are we going on a sightseeing tour when we're all tired and hungry?" Harold asks Markie.

He doesn't get a chance to answer before Davor leads the ducks safely out of ambush range and over Louisiana's bayou country—with its rambling muddy rivers, flat land, bottomland hardwood forest wetlands, grasslands, agricultural fields, Catahoula Lake, and Duck Lake.

"This is our winter home," Markie tells Harold.

"It's amazing," Harold replies.

"See that down there? That's Duck Lake," Harold says to Beverly.

CATAHOULA LAKE AND DUCK LAKE

Duck Lake, Louisiana, is in the Catahoula National Wildlife Refuge, located in the western Mississippi Alluvial Valley. The Havenwood Cove flock has no idea how special they are. They just show up in late fall and enjoy a shallow lake safe zone (no human predators allowed to hunt them) that has some of their favourite foods: chufa tubers and wild millet. Little do they know that the United States Federal and State governments work together to drain the lake in the summer to encourage moist soil plants to grow. Then they flood the lake gradually to just the right dabbling/puddle duck depth so it's ready for the wintering/migrating waterfowl and other wildlife.

Catahoula Lake is a natural freshwater lake that is managed by three state departments to ensure it remains a haven (though hunting is allowed in areas) for thousands of migrating waterfowl.

"Wow! Look how crowded it is! Not sure what I was expecting, but... " she responds.

"Crowded means safety in numbers, and we'll get to make new friends. But you're right about it looking weird; we've never seen big trees growing in the middle of the water. There aren't any trees in Havenwood Cove's marsh," Harold recalls.

"Sure there are—they're just not standing upright. Benjamin beaver and his family gathered them and stacked them," Beverly giggles.

"Benjamin and Betty would love it here since the trees are already in the water—they wouldn't have to drag them from the woods," Lynn laughs.

"I wonder how everyone is at home?" Harold says.

Markie jumps in, "Everyone is just fine. They're either sleeping or suffering through the cold and snow."

"Oh, right," Harold mumbles.

"The best part about being here is that there's no snow and no cold, just rain. Like water off a duck's back! No problem; we're water repellent," Markie jokes.

"Hey, Markie! Where are the palm trees?" Lynn shouts.

"I never said there are palm trees here. But you can relax under exotic Spanish moss," he says, gesturing toward the long, wiry, blueish-gray streamers gracefully cascading from the tree branches toward the water.

Lynn smirks, "Fine, I suppose."

At sunset, the sky blazes with bright orange, deep reds, and canary yellow. The calm water acts as a mirror, reflecting the clouds, trees, and the brilliant colours as the sun dips below the horizon.

"This feels like Mother Nature's housewarming gift for us!" Taleena suggests.

"Duck Lake looks like it's on fire. I've never seen such a beautiful sight. Other than the northern lights, of course," Beverly tells Harold.

"This is a good sign," Harold tells her.

Instructor Riley shouts, "Time to dine. Davor, take us to our favourite rice paddy!"

"Happy to," Davor says as he banks and leads the flock east.

"First-time migrators, listen up," Instructor Riley says. "This rice paddy is a new landing surface for you, and it's in between a ground landing and a water landing. The ground is very muddy, and the water is extremely shallow; it won't even touch your belly. You'll do fine, but we don't want any pileups, so please allow a little extra time between landings just in case there are any problems."

"Harold, what if," Beverly says, her voice trailing off as her thoughts run wild, imagining all the things that could happen.

"You'll do great; you're my fearless rocket hen adventurer," Harold says confidently while visions of Susie's and his failed landings dance through his mind.

"We've got this," Lynn says, looking for support.

"You sure do," Markie promises. "Easy-breezy. Just take your time."

With the sun down and no other flocks close by, Davor leads his friends once around the field.

"All clear! Ready for landing!"

The newbies study Davor's landing technique.

"No problem!" Harold shouts.

Janis tells Beverly, "Take your time. The field can be a little mushy and grip you."

"Great," Beverly mumbles. She's no longer nervous—she's scared.

With her bent wing, Instructor Riley does her typical tilted touchdown. Easton, however, is surprisingly impressive.

Beverly and Taleena quickly glance at each other.

"Ready?" Taleena nervously asks Beverly.

"Ready as I'll ever be," Beverly answers.

Harold watches them as they try to imitate Davor's landing.

As their webbed feet are sucked into deep soggy mud, Beverly and Taleena yell, "Whoa!"

"I'm trapped. You?" Beverly asks.

"Yup. I guess we need more practice," Taleena giggles, trying to wiggle herself free. "What now?"

"I have an idea. We'll flap like crazy to lift ourselves off the water, and our feet will follow," Beverly suggests.

"Definitely worth a try! We have to do something—we can't stay like this," Taleena says as she catches Easton and Instructor Riley watching in anticipation to see how they are going to set themselves free.

"Let's give it a go," Beverly says.

Together, they power up their wings, and their bodies slowly lift out of the shallow water. With hen power, determination, and some grunting, they hear the sucking, slurpy, squishy sounds as their feet slowly break free from the mud.

"Whoo-hoo!" Beverly shouts.

"Hen power!" Taleena boasts as she and Beverly fly forward a short distance and gently lower themselves down onto the rice paddy, but this time with their feet flat so they're standing *on* rather than *in* the mud.

"We did it," Taleena whispers to Beverly.

"We're true adventurers! We had a problem, and we solved it," Beverly says proudly.

Everyone's focus is now on Harold and Anne.

"You're going to do great," Anne encourages Harold.

"Hope so."

Beverly yells out, "You've got this, hot wings!"

Side-by-side with Anne, Harold looks forward, then quickly at Anne's body position, then back again. Touchdown!

"You looked amazing!" Beverly tells him.

Harold's eyes gleam. Maybe his reputation for faceplants and disastrous landings will be forgotten.

Next up are Lynn and Janis.

Lynn's head is spinning. After all, she is well aware of her balance issues.

"Just remember, the ground can be a little gluey, so try to land flat-footed. It's all about balance and not putting too much weight straight down at once. Keep your wings up high and flap longer than you usually do so you don't sink into the mud," Janis tells Lynn, thinking she's being helpful.

"Okay," Lynn says anxiously, her heart pounding.

The flock watches and waits to see what's going to happen.

"Here they come, Janis with her wounded wing and Lynn with—you know," Taleena says.

With great determination, Janis focuses on tilting a little to the left to compensate for her injured right wing. With a couple of jerky twists, she successfully touches down.

Lynn concentrates on what Davor's landing looked like and what Janis told her. But just before touching down, she panics and powers up her wings. Flapping like crazy, she over-angles her webbed feet and skis across the water. Frazzled, she suddenly stops flapping, lowers her feet with a sharp, downward angle, and finds herself stuck in the mud.

Sheepishly grinning at her onlookers, she groans and tugs each foot out of the suction grip of the mud.

"All good!" Lynn shouts, and the flock cheers as she extends her wings by her sides to help keep her balance.

"Mushy bottom, right?" Janis asks Lynn.

"Very."

"You'll get the hang of getting your balance and angles of your feet so you can waddle around," Instructor Riley advises.

With all the drama of Lynn's landing, no one noticed Markie and Jayson's skillful touchdowns.

"Nice landings, everyone!" Instructor Riley says as she gives Lynn a wink. "I realize everyone's tired and hungry, but before we eat and rest, we need to have a brief but important meeting."

While Harold and his first-time migrator friends quietly wait for the news, he thinks about what Markie once said: expect the unexpected.

Instructor Riley continues, "First, what do you think of the area so far?"

"Looks good," Taleena says.

"It's very different than anywhere we've been to so far," Harold says.

"Too early to say," Beverly adds.

"Yeah. What Beverly said," Lynn comments.

Instructor Riley continues, "Like us, everyone migrates here because it's too cold and there's no food at our home during the winter. We don't have an option, but you do have a choice. Attitude is everything; you can either embrace our temporary home and make the most of your time here, or you can sulk, be miserable, and waste the possibility for some amazing opportunities. In life, there are things we can't control and others we can. As for our protection, we can help ourselves to stay safe by following a few simple rules."

Here it comes; expect the unexpected, Harold thinks.

Instructor Riley continues, "Human predators are plentiful in this area."

Yup, I knew it. Harold nods.

The newbies gasp.

"We know human predators don't value us or our feelings; we are just sport or food to them. They're sneaky, cunning, scheming, and devious in how they sit and wait for us, hidden in their pine branch-covered hideaways. They wear clothing to match the surroundings, and they try to imitate our calls. We need to outsmart them to survive."

Harold drapes his wing over Beverly to remind her she's not alone.

Davor cuddles up to Taleena.

"We'll be okay," Markie whispers to Lynn.

"I want to go home," Beverly whispers to Harold.

"We can't. Not for a while. Don't worry; we'll have fun. I'll help keep us safe," Harold says, trying to convince himself as well.

"I realize that you first-time migrators are stressed and scared. Just remember, Instructor Riley and I have spent many winters here, and your safety is most important to us," Jayson tells the flock.

Instructor Riley clears her throat, and in a firm, strong voice says, "These are the rules. WHEN WE POP UP, THEY POP UP! You will most likely always hear a loud *BOOM* immediately following that action, and I don't think I need to tell you how dangerous that is.

"We are NEVER in the air between just before sunrise and just after sunset. NEVER. We can dine on agricultural fields and in the shallow areas of Catahoula Lake and Duck Lake during the night. During the day, we can rest, preen, and socialize in the centre of Catahoula Lake, which I feel is a little dangerous as human predators surround us. Or, you can spend the day and night on Duck Lake, which is a human predator–free area."

"Why would ducks go to Catahoula Lake with human predators around it?" Beverly asks.

"Catahoula Lake is a much larger lake and has a larger grazing area than Duck Lake. Many ducks go there without worrying about the risk, but not me. Humans are everywhere, except in the small safe zone. The lake is noisy. Humans zip back and forth in their boats, and the constant ambush sounds don't make for a relaxing environment," Instructor Riley says.

Bombarded with jumbled thoughts, the first-time migrators feel dazed.

"That was the tough love—now comes the fun stuff. Our winter cuisine is delicious and plentiful, with a wide assortment of choices. You will make new friends and reunite with others, and the weather is comfortable. What do you say? Do you want to give this place a chance?" Instructor Riley asks.

"We don't really have a choice, do we?" Taleena asks.

Jayson jumps in, "That's right. We have to be here till spring, but you do have a choice to try to enjoy the experience."

Taleena looks down, speechless.

"I'm tired and stressed, but I'm also excited to find a mate—preferably, an intelligent drake who makes me laugh, so I choose to enjoy myself," Lynn tells Jayson.

"Good. How about you?" Jayson asks Beverly.

"Like Lynn, I'm exhausted and stressed, but I choose to enjoy myself with Harold and my friends."

Jayson nods in approval. "Perfect. Harold, what about you?"

"I'm happy to be wherever my rocket hen is."

"Glad to hear you're all choosing to stay positive. Now let's eat!" Jayson says enthusiastically.

"Hold on, hold on! Sorry everyone, but we forgot to mention one last thing—and it's a big one. About (3 m) ten feet long big," Instructor Riley says.

"Miss Alli is one old, grouchy gator. But don't worry; any day now, she'll be burrowing herself into her mud hole for warmth and shelter for the winter. Being a cold blooded reptile like little Ruby, our red-sided garter snake friend back home, Miss Alli will brumate until spring when the weather warms up. That said, don't panic if you see her occasionally. Sometimes on warm, sunny days, she likes to crawl out of her mud hole to sun herself and warm up. The best news is that during brumation season, she's nicer than usual and kind of dozy. Lucky for us, she doesn't eat during her brumation, but she will still drink to hydrate. And the same goes for her friends."

ALLIGATORS AND THE SUN

Alligators have prominent ridges called scutes which run along their backs. These skin-covered bone plates are filled with blood vessels that act like solar panels, distributing the heat throughout their bodies. If the alligator becomes overheated, it cools off by opening its mouth. Alligators are nocturnal, meaning they are active from dusk until dawn.

"Friends?" Taleena questions, feeling overwhelmed.
"Are there any more surprises?" Harold asks.

The experienced migrators exchange looks. "No, I don't think so," Jayson says.

"Great. Now, let's eat!" Davor shouts.

Like ducks to water, the newbies quickly learn how to waddle and slosh about in the shallow water without getting stuck in the muddy bottom of the rice paddy. Poking their bills deep into the mud, they dine on waste grains left over from the harvest, seeds of weeds, and yummy aquatic insects and mites known as invertebrates.

"It's a buffet here! Maybe I will give this place a chance," Taleena says.

As they graze around the paddy, Harold and his friends have no idea that their love of eating snails* (and the healthy protein those snails provide) is greatly helping the farmers and the environment.

"Harold, many of these snails are too humongous for me to swallow. Are you finding some smaller ones?" Beverly asks.

"Sure am. Some smell swampy, but I don't care. I'm a madcap Mallard for mollusks," Harold jokes, then pauses. "That sounds like something Michael would have said," Harold whispers. "I miss him and his sense of humour."

"Me too. Poor Janis," Beverly says quietly.

Blanketed in darkness, Harold and his friends don't let the chatter and flapping sounds of incoming flocks distract them from feasting on the rice paddy's scrumptious treats.

"Attention, Havenwood Cove flock! It's time to go. Positions, please!" Instructor Riley calls out.

With full stomachs, the ducks get into their V positions behind Captain Jayson.

---

*The apple snail has become highly invasive, destroying rice paddies and crawfish farm production. Their shells can be the size of a baseball.

Many mammals (including seals, crocodiles, and whales) and birds (including ducks) swallow their food whole. To help with their digestion, they swallow grit and small, jagged pebbles, which are stored in the muscular part of their stomach, called the gizzard. These stomach stones (called gastroliths) work with the stomach muscles to help grind and crush the bird's food. In a very short time, a snail's shell will be pulverized and the snail liquified. Even dinosaur fossils have been found containing stomach stones.

Instructor Riley continues, "There's a lot of flapping air traffic, so keep a watch out and keep calling out. Ready?"

"Ready!" everyone answers.

Captain Jayson completes his safety checklist of listening for calls and watching for silhouettes in the dark, inky sky. "All clear! On five!"

Without a hitch, the flock is up and heading west.

Guided by moonlight and Captain Jayson's expertise, the flock manoeuvres its way through a throng of birds to safely touch down on the calm, cool water of Duck Lake.

As the sun rises, the newbies are eager to explore their new home.

"We're kind of a big deal. I mean, we have a lake named after us. That's kind of exciting," Beverly whispers to Harold.

"How about I give you the 'Markie deluxe guided tour' after we have a sleep and do some feather maintenance? I'm exhausted and looking a little scruffy. Besides, what's the rush? We're here for a long time," Markie tells Harold, Beverly, and Lynn.

"Sounds great. We'll stay on the water, right?" Harold asks.

"Always safest to stay on the water during the day—even here. We're in a safe zone, but you're still best to fly within the shoreline and not too high. Don't trust human predators. If you don't play by the rules, chances are you won't have to worry about the boomerang trip back home. Understand?" Markie says as he looks sternly into Harold, Beverly, and Lynn's eyes.

Answers of "got it," "yes," and "uh-huh" come from the three adventurers.

"Everyone, follow me," Jayson says. "I'll show you my favourite safe spot to rest."

Like ducklings following their mother, the flock swims behind Jayson as he leads them to an area that has dense, sparsely-leafed buttonbushes on the shore and in the water. "Look, we even have our very own bald cypress tree—Louisiana's state tree—here in our new home," Jayson brags, while the newbies inspect the oddity of a tree growing in a lake.

Instructor Riley adds, "It's cozy here, and we're not in the middle of all the traffic. We can hide among the buttonbushes and feast on their nutlets. For those of you who haven't had them before, you're in for a treat; nutlets are pollinated flowers that, come autumn, turn into reddish-brown hard balls of seeds that fall onto the ground or water. But don't get too distracted; you must be aware of foxes and coyotes. With that said, how does everyone feel about having this as our home base?"

"I like it, but the creepy-looking stuff dangling off the tree is making my feathers twitch," Taleena says as the other newbies eye it suspiciously.

"It does look a little spooky—like it could grab us," Beverly comments.

"Look around. Most of the trees have it," Harold says.

"Agreed, it's eerie looking, but it's nothing to worry about," Instructor Riley says. "It's called Spanish moss, and it just hangs, grows, and blows in the wind. The good thing is, it protects us from the rain—and believe me, there will be rain. It also protects us from the sun and hides us from raptors like the Red-shouldered Hawks—unless they perch on it. Can't do anything about that."

Knowing that the moss helps to protect them helps set the ducks' minds at ease as they settle in.

SPANISH MOSS

Spanish moss is actually not a moss, but an air plant that is a swampy cousin of the pineapple. Its long, silvery-gray, dried-out-looking tendrils mostly drape from live oaks and bald cypress trees. It causes no harm to the tree and gets its nutrients from the moist air and dust particles. The ghostly look of Spanish moss adds to the southern charm, especially on a foggy morning. One tale is that the French named it after their Spanish enemies' gnarly-looking beards. Spanish moss has a long Louisiana history of being used as medicine in the form of tea, as filling for bedding, as stuffing for voodoo dolls, as feed for cattle and horses, and as binding for plaster. Even automobile manufacturer Henry Ford used it to fill the seats of the Model T in the early 1900s.

Exhausted from a long flight the day before and a night of gorging at the rice paddy, the flock clusters together on the water, as far away as possible from the shallow shore and the chatter of nearby flocks. Predator guards Anne and Easton keenly listen for foxes, raccoons, and coyotes.

"I can't believe we finally made it here! I wanted to give up so many times," Beverly whispers to Harold.

"I know! Me too. But you did great, and we're here now. We're a team. We'll have a wonderful time here. You'll see. Get some rest. We're starting a new routine. We'll be like Sir Lloyd—sleeping in the day and mostly eating at night," Harold whispers.

Beverly closes her eyes and listens to the different sounds of her new home.

Boom, boom, boom shocks the airwaves. *Boom, boom, BOOM!*

Beverly bolts awake and shrieks, "What's happening?"

"You're okay," Harold tells her as he drapes his trembling wing over her quivering body.

"Are we safe?" Taleena cries out as Davor tries to calm her.

"Where do we hide?" Lynn yells, frantically swimming in a circle.

"I've got you," Markie tells her as he nips her wing to stop her.

"We're safe," Jayson says firmly to help calm the flock. "One day, the noise of distant ambushes will just become background noise. If we live by our set rules and look out for each other, we'll make it back to Havenwood Cove in the spring. Try to get some sleep. Anne and Easton will protect us. Tonight, after sunset, we'll visit a wonderful cornfield," he adds.

"Wait till you try the chufa tubers, wild millet, and buttonbush seeds. You're going to love it here!" Anne tells the newbies, and then gets back into predator guard mode.

After a much-needed rest for their body and mind and some necessary general clean-up, Markie begins giving his tour of Duck Lake.

"I really like the warm weather," Lynn tells Markie.

"No more seeing puffs of your breath in the mornings," Markie jokes.

"So, what will I have to bug you about now?" Lynn asks.

"Oh, I'm sure you'll think of something."

"True," Lynn giggles.

Markie leads Harold, Beverly, and Lynn around the lake, introducing them to some friends and meeting new ones.

"Sorry, didn't mean to bump into you," Harold hears as he feels feathers poke into his side.

"No worries," Harold says as he turns around toward the apologetic bird—and finds himself looking into two fiery red eyes. Harold's heart skips a few beats.

"Busy place. I'm Larry, and this is Tammy."

"Did you say 'Tammy'?" Harold stammers, remembering Dylan asked Beverly to winter with his sister, Tammy, and his Uncle Larry.

"Sure did. You know each other?"

"Nope. Gotta go," Harold blurts.

Markie observes Harold's fearful eyes and twitching feathers.

"Buddy, let's find the hens and duck out of here."

"Where are we going in such a hurry?" Beverly asks Markie.

"It's crowded here. I'll show you another area."

As they turn to follow, Lynn says, "Hey, Markie! If I don't find a dashing drake, you can be my backup plan. You *are* kind of cute and smart."

Markie abruptly comes to a full stop, and Beverly, Lynn, and Harold pile into each other.

"Say *what*?" Markie says as he turns to look at Lynn. "What are you talking about, hen?"

"I knew I'd find something to tease you about," Lynn laughs as she wiggles her tail feathers.

Harold and Beverly share glances of "something's up" as they notice Lynn and Markie gaze longingly into each others big brown eyes.

"Harold, wherever the four adventurers are, is home. We are going to be just fine," Beverly giggles.

QUACK!

(THE END)

THANK YOU

for joining the Boomerang Gang
on their migration journey.

They travelled from the Great Slave Lake area in the Northwest Territories of Canada all the way south to Duck Lake in Louisiana, United States. They flew approximately (3,260 km) 2,026 miles with nine rest stops.

Perhaps the next time you see ducks in flight, it'll be
Harold and his friends. Give them a friendly wave!

Partial proceeds from this book will be donated to Ducks Unlimited to support its efforts to conserve, restore, and manage wetlands and associated habitats to benefit North American waterfowl, wildlife, and people. Wetlands and other wildlife habitats are being degraded and destroyed, but together, we can help prevent this from happening. Search for "wetland conservation" in your area and find out how you can get involved and make a difference.

APPENDIX

THE BOOMERANG GANG
AND FRIENDS

THE BOOMERANG GANG

Harold—a young Mallard drake on his first migration.

Markie—Harold's best friend.

Beverly—the hen of Harold's dreams, both kind and spunky.

Lynn—Beverly's best friend, who likes to tease.

Instructor Riley—a respected Mallard hen with a lot of migrations behind her. She was born with a bent wing, but has adapted
and is one of the strongest flyers.

Jayson—the oldest and most experienced drake in the flock.

Janis—a hen with an old injury that slows her down.

Davor, Easton, and Michael—other drakes in the flock.

Anne, Taleena, and Susie—other hens in the flock.

FRIENDS BACK HOME
AT HAVENWOOD COVE

Ginger and Rusty III—native red foxes.

Sir Lloyd—a well-respected Great Horned Owl.

Benjamin and Betty—hardworking beavers.

Wanda and Winston—laid-back grizzly bears.

Miss Marie—a lonely (and cranky) porcupine.

Squire—a tough-guy striped skunk.

Baxter—a wolverine.

Sebastian—a busy red squirrel.

Murphy and Madleine—moose.

Ella—white-tailed deer.

Oliver—a strutting Golden Eagle.

Poppy, Prudence—snowshoe hares.

Harlow—Canada Lynx.

FRIENDS ON THE ADVENTURE

Wyatt, Nina, Cleo, and Chloe—family of Tundra Swans, Taleena's friends at Lake Claire.

Chopper—a friendly beaver who continues to enlarge the world's largest beaver dam.

Bill and Bob—Great Horned Owls, Sir Lloyd's brothers who moved south. The Boomerang Gang met them at Algar Lake, but they're considering moving farther south.

Paco—American White Pelican, a friend of Markie's they bump into at the Last Mountain Lake Migratory Bird Sanctuary.

Delilah—a Whooping Crane Lynn bumps into at Last Mountain Lake.

Dylan and Dirk—Wood Ducks. Not quite "friends"; Dylan has eyes on Beverly, and he keeps showing up.

ACKNOWLEDGEMENTS

CYNTHIA HAYNES

Editor extraordinaire. Thank you for believing in my vision and making my lifelong goal/purpose come true.

FELiCiTY PERRYMAN — DESIGNER

Your creativity and attention to detail far exceeded my expectations. Your whimsical embellishments are perfect for young readers. Thank you for making my book look amazing!

TAMMY WYATT

Your honest critiques and unwavering encouragement motivated me to keep writing and sketching. Thank you!

WILLiAM (BILL) D. BERRY

Thank you for the inspiration for my Madleine moose sketch.

A heartfelt 'thank you' to everyone who supported my writing aspirations.

ABOUT THE AUTHOR

Diane Bedford's endless curiosity, artistic creativity and her love of animals have come together to fulfill her lifelong ambition to write and illustrate this heartfelt, delightful debut novel.

Whether she's in the Amazon, swimming with sea lions in Galapagos, or on safari in Africa, her passion is connecting with nature and wildlife — especially with what is right outside her door.

Diane is a "Feather Society" member of Ducks Unlimited Canada and a contributor to many animal welfare and conservation organizations.

Diane lives in sunny Okanagan, BC, but you can find her at:

theboomeranggang.com

Printed in the USA
CPSIA information can be obtained
at www.ICGtesting.com
LVHW082129271124
797849LV00038B/1333